Druid's Go

By

Griff Hosker

Book 6 in the Sword of Cartimandua Series

Published in 2014 Copyright © Sword Books Ltd.

A CIP catalogue record for this title is available from the
British Library.

Part One
The Gold
Chapter 1

Decius Lucullus Sallustius, the nephew of the Governor of Britannia who was executed following a plot to overthrow the Emperor, cursed silently as he peered across the marshy estuary northwards. He looked over his shoulder at the string of heavily laden pack horses and his ten mercenary guards. He had a fortune in his grasp, the result of a profitable time stripping out gold from the Welsh mines, gold that had been mined for the Emperor but which Decius had stolen from under his dead uncle's nose. Yet for all his deceit, guile and treachery he was no better off than he had been for the new governor had posted his description and soldiers were searching for him on every boat leaving the shores of Britannia. He was trapped and, whilst the Brigante revolt had faltered, Northern Britannia was a dangerous place to be. Centurion, his lieutenant had urged him to head south. "Head South? Head back through the patrols which have our description with this line of gold laden pack mules? And how long do you think we would last? How far would we get? At least we know there are fewer Romans north of us."

"We could bury the gold and come back for it when things have quietened down."

Decius had gestured scornfully at the unshaven thugs who followed some distance behind. "And of course the gold would be safe from our associates eh?" Although Centurion was a brutal man given to plain speaking even he had recognised the sarcasm in his leader's tone. Centurion had been a centurion in the Second Adiutrix but when he had beaten to death a soldier who had fallen asleep on duty he had decided that desertion was a better option than facing the punishment and demotion.

Decius now scanned the far shore of the shallow estuary. They had been hitherto lucky. Since skirting Deva they had seen no signs of life and, more importantly, no signs of Rome and its soldiers. That of course meant no roads and no bridges, just the woods, rocks and fields of a largely uninhabited part of the province. They had headed east until Decius had found somewhere he thought they could cross the sluggish, murky waters of this un-named river. Had he planned his escape he would have secured some of the maps from his uncle's former home at Eboracum but this flight was on the spur of the moment. He knew that once across this river the land was empty as far north as the land of the lakes and, more importantly, there were places on the west coast where he could buy or steal a boat for his escape back to Gaul and, ultimately, Rome.

Centurion nudged his mount next to Decius. "Will we be able to get across? It could have deep parts in it? The bottom might be muddy."

"Yes and there may be a river monster just waiting to gobble us up. The answer is obvious, we will have to find out." He turned in his saddle and shouted to the man they called Tiny. He was of course the biggest of the mercenaries but he had two qualities which Decius needed, he was loyal and he was obedient. "Tiny. Bring up a mule." The huge man untied one of the mules from the string of ten he was leading and, giving the rest to the next man, trotted up to Decius. "I want you to take your mule across the water. Go steadily and wait for us on the other bank. Understand?"

"Yes." The ex- auxiliary took his mule gently down the bank and Decius watched as they entered the water.

"Why him?"

"He can be trusted. Would you let one of the others take a fortune in gold across a river? Most of the others would disappear over the horizon and the other reason is he is the heaviest. If he can make it then any of us can. I only wish we had brought more rope we could have made the crossing much easier." Decius held his breath as he saw the mule caught by the current; its feet were not touching the bottom. Tiny looked over his shoulder and tugged the struggling beast closer to his own mount. "So far he has not had to swim his horse."

"Yes but he only has one mule, we have sixty to cross."

Decius shrugged his shoulders. "It doesn't matter how many journeys it takes with you on one side and me on the other we can make sure that none of our companions takes it into his head to become suddenly richer. Once we are on the far shore we will be safe from the Romans and I think we can handle any of the locals."

Tiny was now three quarters of the way across the river and, although the mule was still struggling, the huge warrior had no problem controlling the powerful animal. Even Centurion allowed a smile to crack his scarred face as Tiny raised his arm in salute.

"Right. You take one across and then tether the two mules together. Send Tiny back and you make sure that all the animals are secured on the far side." He looked meaningfully at Centurion.

"Can you deal with the rest? There are some devious bastards there. A few of them have been eyeing the gold and your back."

"That's why I want Tiny over here." He gave a rueful smile; Centurion and Tiny were the only two who would not slit his throat in the night and he was touched by the ex-legionary's affection. Had he not caught his subordinate asleep on duty he would have made a fine officer but the threatened punishment had made him desert for which Decius was eternally grateful. "Now go on. Don't worry I will be safe." He slid his spatha from its scabbard and let it hang loosely and hidden next to his leg.

Centurion nodded and led his mule into the water. He had watched Tiny carefully and identified the route he had to take. He

3

still worried about Decius and, as he waded across the muddy water he kept glancing back over his shoulder. Decius had been good to him and the loyalty he had given the Second Adiutrix he now gave whole heartedly to the young man who had used his brains not for good but for selfish gain; he too was in the same boat and, as long as their fates were tied together he would be faithful unto death.

Turning to the remaining eight men Decius gestured for them to come closer. "We are going to cross this river. Tiny managed it and that big bastard is twice as heavy as any of you ladies so we should be safe." One or two gave a half smile at the humour but the rest looked doubtfully at the forbidding water before them. "You go over in pairs with eight mules between you. The one at the rear makes sure that the line goes straight. Clear."

Scarface, so named for the scar which ran through one whitened dead eye down to his jaw rubbed his scar and spoke up. "Why risk crossing this river at all? It looks dangerous."

Edging his horse towards the man Decius growled, "Because I want us to get across the river and unless you have suddenly become master here that is what we will do."

"Look, sir," the 'sir' was almost spat at Decius, "we have more than enough gold here for all of us. Let's split it now and go our separate ways."

Decius was aware of two things happening simultaneously; he saw the nods of agreement and he heard the splash of hooves in the shallower waters behind him. His horse was now nose to nose with Scarface's white blazed mount. "I'll ask one more time Scarface. Are you the leader or am I?"

Decius saw the almost imperceptible nod Scarface gave to his brother off to Decius' right as the would be killer started to draw his gladius from its scabbard. While most of his men, ex-soldiers, preferred the shorter stabbing gladius, Decius, like his brother Livius, had been taught to use the longer cavalry spatha, that

4

training now saved the life of Decius Lucullus Sallustius. He brought the blade in a huge arc slicing down on the unprotected neck of the unfortunate Scarface. The razor sharp blade sliced through flesh to rip into the artery and end the usurper's life. The blow threw the man man's corpse from the saddle and freed the sword. Hearing the roar of rage from the dead man's brother Decius slashed the blade backhand at the man he knew was approaching from his right. The blade caught him just below the helmet and it cut easily through the top of the surprised warrior's skull. There was a sudden silence and Decius looked anxiously around wondering why none of the remaining six had attempted to kill him. He saw that they were not looking at him but behind him; turning he saw Tiny with a childlike grin on his face and a mighty war hammer in his hand. Nodding his silent thanks Decius turned to the others. "Now then ladies. Would anyone like to join the brothers with the brains of a flea?" They shook their heads. "Then split yourselves into pairs and get these beasts across the river."

As they sullenly went to their task Decius gestured Tiny over. "Collect their weapons and search them. I suspect they have some of our gold about them. Tether their horses together ,"and Tiny," he leaned over to pat the big man on the back, "thanks."

Tiny grinned happily at Decius. It was a disconcerting sight as the man had lost his front four teeth in a fight and the gaping maw looked terrifying.

Decius was pleased, as they pulled the last mule from the river, that they had only lost one mule and its golden load. It had been a total accident, the rope holding it giving way and it had been swept towards the sea, its braying call mournfully mixing with the screech of the seagulls. The loss was annoying but would not hurt Decius as they had two less men to pay and they had discovered money hidden in their clothes and saddle bags, obviously the

5

brothers had decided to go into business for themselves and rob the mules.

The exhausted mercenaries slumped on the ground looking furtively at each other. Decius nodded to Centurion and Tiny who stood behind the men on the ground. "Now it appears that Scarface and his thieving brother stole some gold from us." He emphasised the word 'us'. "Now I say us because we will all have a share of the money when we divide it. The reason none of us keeps the gold is because we might die and that would mean less for all of us to share." He lowered his voice to add more weight and threat to it. "You have one chance to hand back any gold you may have borrowed and that chance is now. When Centurion and I search you tomorrow morning any gold you have about you will be your death warrant."

Panic spread upon their faces. Scarface had been the leader. They had planned on murdering Decius and Centurion in their sleep; now that the leaders of the plot were gone they did not know what to do. They started in shock as Centurion roared out, "I will personally crucify any bastard who does not hand over his gold now."

Decius hid the smile behind a hand as they raced for their saddle bags. The amount of gold was immaterial; he was making a point that he was leader and that any form of dissent would be severely dealt with. Even so he was surprised by how much they had stolen. The recovered gold was split between the dead men's horses.

Later as they finished off their frugal meal Decius addressed them all again. "Now that we are all of the same mind I will tell you what we intend to do. We will head north west towards the land of the lakes. Once we find a place with boats big enough to take us and the gold we will either buy or steal such a boat and then head down to Gaul or Hispana. When we are there you will all receive your share of the treasure we have accumulated." He was a very persuasive and articulate speaker. He made it sound like the gold they had was just the start.

One of them looked up as though about to speak and then thought better of it. Decius saw the gesture and said, "Come on man spit it out. Now is the time for conversation and not a knife in the back."

The shock that his leader had known what he intended made the warrior speak out. "But what if we want to settle in Britannia? It is the land and people we all know."

"Then you would be more stupid than even dead Scarface for they will be looking for ex-soldiers who are suddenly rich. But if that is what you wish then when in Gaul buy a boat and return." The man looked satisfied and Decius scanned the other faces. "Any more questions? This is your one and only chance to ask them."

Looking at one of his companions another mercenary ventured. "Aren't there Brigante north of us and haven't they just revolted? I fought them once and they are seriously nasty bastards. I would like to keep my wedding tackle intact."

"Yes and yes but we will just have to be careful. I have travelled these lands before and they are empty. You will all take it in turns to scout far ahead so that we avoid any such encounters but remember we are all going to be rich men; isn't that worth a little danger? For remember the alternative is to face a Roman force and believe me they would have your heads on their forts before you could draw swords." He saw that their faces were downcast and he realised that he needed these men; the mules would not drive themselves and the six mercenaries might mean the difference between success and failure. Failure would not only mean the loss of the gold but either crucifixion at the hands of the Romans or a much worse fate at the hands of barbarians. His voice softened, "I believe that the hardest part of this journey is behind us. Three or four days travel will bring us safely to the coast and I doubt not that we will find a boat once we reach there.

As the men settled down for the night Decius walked the mule line with Centurion. "Do you believe all that you just said?" Centurion waved a dismissive hand towards the already sleeping soldiers.

Weighing his words carefully, for Centurion and Tiny were his only allies in the inhospitable land which surrounded them, he nodded, "I believe it is our only hope." He paused before he continued. "I do have a worry, well two if truth be told. My brother is serving with an ala of cavalry, Marcus' Horse." Centurion face showed his surprise. "So you have heard of them? They are a formidable force and they patrol the land of the lakes. Were they to stumble upon us then our venture would be at an end."

"And the other thing?"

"There are rumours that the Brigante are now led by a powerful witch and she too is known to have her base in the land of the lakes. It would not do to fall foul of a fell witch especially as this gold we bear was taken from the sacred mountain of Wyddfa and witches take a dim view of theft from their holy places."

"Which leads me to ask, respectfully, why are we heading there, when it would seem to be the most dangerous place for us to be?"

"The alternative is to cross the spine of this rocky little island and then cross all the major Roman roads which run north to south chancing Roman patrols, informers , bandits and ,once we reached the east coast, we could have to avoid the fleet which protects the shipping which travels to and from this rich little island." He spread his hands to make his point. "When I worked for my uncle I saw just how prosperous and efficient the Romans were. There are a couple of villages on this coast and we will try

8

those. It may be that we do not come close to the Brigante or the ala."

Centurion shook his head, "It seems to me it is a gamble but you have been right up to now so let us roll the dice. I will sleep first, wake me when you are sleepy."

"Do you not think my words had the desired effect?"

"I think they will behave but I would not like to bet either your life, or mine on it, would you?"

Half of Decius' worries were needless if he did but know it. Even as they headed north the remnants of Marcus' Horse were gathered for the last time at the legionary fortress of Eboracum. They were pitifully few in numbers; there were only three officers still remaining from the seventeen they had had when at full strength, Julius, Livius and Sergeant Cato. They could barely muster two turmae of troopers and many of those who still mustered showed the signs of the ravages of battles over the past year.

Julius had spent the morning with the Governor and Legate discussing the fate of this famous force. Julius had not had time to talk to either Livius or Cato and he knew that they would be surprised, not to say shocked with his words. The faces before him were only a tiny portion of the ones Julius remembered; the lucky ones had retired or left with minor injuries. The far greater numbers were those who had died in battle, amongst them his brother and the greatest warrior amongst the troopers Decurion Macro. He shook his head absent mindedly to clear away the sentiment.

"Men, today is a sad day. Today is a day I did not foresee coming, certainly not as long as I was prefect of this ala. Marcus' Horse is now a fraction of the force it was and it has been decided to disband it as an ala." With the exception of Sergeant Cato every man looked aghast, Livius in particular, he opened his mouth to ask a question and then thought better of it. He was too well trained an officer to be insubordinate and interrupt his commanding officer. "Some of you are due a pension either now or soon and any man who has served eighteen years will be granted his pension and a plot of land on the border. For those younger men," he glanced at Livius, "there is the chance to transfer either to the Gallic Horse based at Coriosopitum or the cavalry unit attached to the Ninth." He paused to let his words sink in. "You will need to tell me of your decision within the next two days." Some of the men began to talk to the trooper next to them. Julius held his hand up and there was absolute silence once more.

The attention of the guards on the walls was totally focussed on the drama unfolding before them. They were witnessing the end of an ala which had been famous since they had rescued Queen Cartimandua almost forty years earlier. The inns and taverns or Eboracum would have but one topic of conversation at the end of this working day and that would be the disbanding of Marcus' Horse and the retirement of its swallow tail standard.

Julius rode to the end of the line. "I would like to thank you men, you brothers in arms, for all that you have done in my time with this glorious ala. You have always done more than even I could have expected, you have never retreated and never shown dishonour. Our brothers who are no longer with us but with the Allfather are looking down now proudly on the last of their comrades and I would like to clasp the arm of every one of the finest warriors not only in Britannia but the Empire."

As he rode down the line speaking a few words to each man and clasping forearms in a soldier's salute there were many silent tears shed. It was, as the Governor himself had said, 'the end of an era'. Finally he embraced Sergeant Cato and then Livius, both of whom were fighting to remain stone faced. As he turned to face the ala for the last time every troop pulled his spatha from its scabbard and raised it in a last salute roaring, as a man, "Marcus' Horse!"

The silence echoed strangely around the fortress as every eye in the fort, sentries, clerks, farriers was fixed on the dramatic tableau. Time seemed to stand still until every man slid his sword back into his scabbard and led their mounts back to the stables and barracks. Only then did a murmur of comment rise like the buzz from a swarm of bees. Livius and Cato dismounted to face the Prefect. "Bit of a surprise eh Livius?"

"That is putting it mildly." He glanced over at the Sergeant. "What about you? Did you expect it? Are you happy about the decision?"

Cato shrugged, "I was going to take my pension this year anyway, the prefect, er sorry sir, Marcus has asked me to help him with the stud." He paused. "I am sorry to see the ala go but remember all my comrades are either dead or retired... a long time ago. I have buried enough comrades, now I just want to raise foals."

Livius nodded, "And you sir? The Gallic cavalry or the Ninth?"

Julius' face darkened and he became sad. "Neither, I am to return to Rome. My father is not well and I am to take his place in the Senate. I am going home."

"But surely this is your home Julius!"

"It is my adopted home but I was always destined to return to Rome and take up my family obligations, we have always served in the military and then in the Senate," he shrugged, "a tradition. Now that I am the only son... well let us just say that I feel obliged to continue to serve my family and Rome at the same time."

Cato took the reins of their mounts. "Right then sirs I will see to these horses now."

"A last dinner tonight eh Sergeant?"

11

"Wouldn't miss it for the world sir."

"And you Livius? Any thoughts?"

"It has all been so sudden I…"

As Cato led the horses away, talking to them all the time, Julius put a paternal arm around the last officer's shoulders. "I would like to offer you some advice and give you some information. The role in the Ninth is a new one. They are to be called the Exploratores."

"I've heard that term but I never knew what they were."

"Well they are the eyes and ears of the legion. In the old republican days the Cavalry of the legions fought like the legions in blocks of men." He looked pointedly at the soldiers on the wall. "Unlike the legionaries they were not very successful. Gradually they became glorified messengers and the men who would have formed the cavalry joined with either auxiliary units as I did or the legions as foot soldiers. Finally someone realised what a good job the auxilia did and decided to use them that way. The legions which did that showed how successful they could be, giving better warning of an enemy and not charging off to death and glory."

"How are they different from the ala then?"

"Much smaller units not thirty men but little pockets of ten or so and they operate less openly."

"Less openly?"

"Less battles and charges more information gathering, pretending to be locals, working behind enemy lines things like that."

"Spies?"

Julius considered for a moment. "I suppose you could say that. Gaelwyn would have been perfect for an Explorate; able to track, hide, able to speak many languages. Which is why, young Livius I recommended to the Prefect of the Ninth that you would be perfect as a decurion in his Explorates."

"You flatter me I…"

"I never flatter, you of all people should know that. I have watched you since your uncle placed you with me to gain experience. You speak the important languages. You are a good tracker."

"Not in Gaelwyn's league."

"Who is? Most importantly you are a good cavalry officer who has intelligence. Your men worship you. If you take this post I guarantee that the Gallic cavalry will have no recruits from the last of Marcus' Horse." Julius paused to let his words take effect. "The other factor is to do with the posting. The Gallic cavalry will be sent to Wales to fight the Silures and Ordovices but the Ninth is staying on the border, here in the land you know."

"Close to Morwenna." Livius had a personal score to settle with the witch who had deceived so many in the ala and killed friends who were dearer to Livius than his own family.

Julius shrugged, "She could have gone back to Mona."

"The new Queen of the Brigante? I don't think so." He looked up at the blue sky dotted with fluffy clouds appearing over the Praetorium. "I do like this part of Britannia. It is not my home, not the place where I was born but it is the place I love. I will take the posting with the Ninth." His eyes became harder, "If only to rid this land of the witch Morwenna and make it safe for Ailis and her children."

Chapter 2

Optio Septimus Aurelius was pleased to be out in the wild again and away from the camp. Although he had been with the Ninth legion for over twenty years he preferred the detachment duties better. He was old for his rank but he was an engineer. The six men with him were almost young enough to be his grandchildren but they were a good team. They were all eager to learn from the most experienced engineer in the Ninth. They had spent the night in the deserted fort of Glanibanta. It would soon be repopulated with Tungrian auxiliaries but it had been a pleasant way to spend the night, safe and secure in the work of others. He had been lucky to secure the services of a mule for it saved the backs of his legionaries and increased their speed. This would be his last engineering job before he took his pension and the little piece of land west of Lindum; he was to survey a route from Glanibanta to the coast with a view to building a fort somewhere on a high pass. He felt proud that he had been given the task, perhaps the engineering tribune had heard of his endeavours over the years, whatever the reason it was a fitting laurel to a successful, if uninspired career. He knew the younger optios teased him about his increasing waistline and receding hairline but, as he had trained most of them, he took it in good part.

As he looked around at the beautiful scenery he reflected that it was good to be walking in such fine country. He constantly scanned the valleys through which they passed seeking out the rocks and materials which would be useful to the legions when they came west to build the road and the fort. It was one of the skills he liked to demonstrate, the ability to do two jobs at once and do them very successfully.

"How far do we go today Optio?"

"Well Julius that depends."

"Depends on what?"

"It depends on the country. We have to make sure that the road is as straight as it can be and that there are enough raw materials to make the task easier. If the valley is straight or the ridge straight then we will have an easy time but Mother Nature has a habit of making rivers and valleys curve, just to annoy engineers."

The young legionaries smiled. They had all been pleased to be working with the old engineer. In the legion he was a legend and they knew they would learn much from him. Unlike some of the younger optios he never felt the need to impress them with his knowledge or humiliate them with their lack of it. He was almost like a teacher or a kindly uncle demonstrating a skill. It would be a nice little holiday from the rigours of the legion.

He smiled paternally at them as they grinned and joked along the path. He liked to think that if he had had sons then they would have turned out like these young soldiers before him. Perhaps when he retired he would find a Brigante woman who would find an older, overweight and slightly balding Roman an attractive proposition and bear him some children; he would like that. "Come on you wasters we have twenty miles to go today and we have much to do. Drusus take the lead and find an easy path for my old tired bones."

Tadgh examined the trail to check for footprints and breathed a sigh of relief when he found none. Aodh had given him the responsibility of looking after Morwenna, the Queen of the Brigante and her two acolytes and fellow witches, Maban and Anchorat. The handful of men at his disposal was far too small and it was only through the diligence of constant scouting and traps in the forest that had enabled them to survive thus far. Aodh had only been gone for a month but it felt much longer. Tadgh and his men were in total fear and awe of the three witches who seemed to be able to communicate without the need for words.

15

Although all three had been pregnant when Aodh had departed one, Anchorat had given birth. Tadgh and his men had begun to celebrate as the newly born boy was brought to the entrance of the cave. In their innocence they had believed the witches had brought the child there for them to acknowledge it as a child of their lord, Aodh, but when the new mother smashed the newly born baby's skull against a rock they knew otherwise. After they had buried the baby, as Morwenna requested, his men had pressed Tadgh to discover the reason. It was with extreme trepidation that Tadgh approached the Queen as she drank the green foul smelling concoction of nettles and mandrake leaf.

"Your majesty?" She lowered the beaker and peered over the steaming rim at the fearful warrior who had begun to wish that his men had not suggested this impertinence. "The men wondered, we all wondered, well, was the child deformed, or sick in some way?"

She nodded and Tadgh breathed a sigh of relief. Sickly babies were often left to die, perhaps not murdered but it was an understandable act and in many ways a kindness. "He was deformed for it was a male child and there will be no male children born here." She stroked her swollen stomach. "This one will be a female but if the Mother is unhappy with us as she was with Anchorat then it too will die."

As he trotted down the trail he shook his head. He had tried to explain it to his men but he could see that they were as perplexed as he was. Perhaps when Aodh returned he would be able to explain, Aodh could always explain things to the men that they found difficult to understand. Especially when the subject matter was women. Tadgh had wanted to ask more questions but the look on Morwenna's face had frightened him so much that he had decided to be discreet and depart.

As he reached the edge of the forest and the clearing he paused and sniffed the air, like an animal would. He knew the smells as

16

well as the sights and sounds of this new kingdom. He had learned that smells, especially strange smells, carried huge distances and he had found it the best way to discover strangers. So far they had only had to kill and dispose of four hapless travellers who were heading from Glanibanta to the coast. He suspected that, as spring became summer, the numbers of travellers would increase but he was determined to keep their presence a secret, at least until Aodh returned and it became the leader's responsibility.

He suddenly stopped. There was a new smell; it was a mixture of garlic, oil and leather, only one creature carried that combination of scents- Romans. He dropped on to his hands and knees and began to crawl through the undergrowth down the hillside towards the rough and twisted track which wound its way along the valley sides. Tadgh made not a sound as he felt his way along the ground which was mercifully free of either dead leaves or branches both of which would have exposed him to a sharp eared sentry. His silence enabled him to hear the chatter of the legionaries and the crunch of their nail soled caligae. As soon as he heard them he froze. He knew from their voices that they were close but he was far enough from the trail and camouflaged by the bushes to avoid detection. The closer their voices came the greater the tension the warrior felt and unanswered questions rattled around his head. How many were there? Were they looking for them? Did it presage an invasion of this land? As the small group trooped along the path below him he almost breathed a sigh of relief. They were not a patrol hunting for rebels; the mule and tools told him that they were building something. When they had travelled some distance down the path away from him he began to back track their route; only by doing so would he know if they were alone or part of a larger force.

Their trail was clear for an expert tracker such as Tadgh and he smiled with satisfaction when he found the signs of their camp at the deserted fort at Glanibanta. As he trotted back to the cave he pondered on the problem. They were obviously a detachment from a larger force and as such would have to report back at some point. What if they were paving the way for a legion? That would mean that the hidden sanctuary of the cave would be at risk and with it the life of the Queen. She was heavily pregnant and Tadgh knew enough about women to realise that it would be a bad time to move her. He had to delay any departure and that meant eliminating the detachment. There was no legion close by and it might buy them the time for the babies to be born and for Aodh to return from Caledonia.

Morwenna's keen eyes bored into Tadgh and he had the frightening feeling that she was reading his thoughts. Her words confirmed this. "There is a problem Tadgh?"

"Romans your majesty. Only a detachment at the moment but it means a larger force will soon be here and in your condition..." The words hung in the air.

"Do not fear for us Tadgh for the Mother protects us and we are not the weak vessels which are men but it is not convenient for us to move at the moment. What do you suggest?"

"There are only seven of them and I have twenty warriors. We could ambush them and dispose of their bodies in the lake. Eventually they would be missed but they would have to look all along the trail to find out where they had gone"

"How much time would that give us?"

Tadgh shrugged for whatever answer he gave would come back to haunt him. "Three or four weeks would be as long as I would care to take the risk."

"By which time Aodh and his Caledonii brethren should be here. Do it."

So the fate of the old Optio and his six young comrades was sealed. Tadgh and his warriors armed themselves for combat for the first time since the first snows had fallen. All of them were glad to be doing that which they loved, hunting Romans. It would not be a fair combat, twenty against seven, but they all remembered the battles where they had been pitted against the mighty legions and seen comrades mowed down by the arrows and artillery of an army which liked to fight at a distance; the Brigante way was face to face and toe to toe, look the man in the eye when you killed him. This would be partial revenge.

They found the detachment unloading their equipment at the edge of a wood. The land before them dropped gently to a small lake and then rose to a mighty pass towards the west. Tadgh nodded to himself. They were obviously measuring for a road and this would be a camp once they had finished their work. He gestured for half of his men to spread north while he took the remainder south. They needed to attack from both sides at the same time. There was no hurry or rush needed, the detachment was going nowhere and Tadgh took his time, confident that Brennus, his brother, who led the other group, would attack once Tadgh had launched his assault. The leader knew that his men wanted to slay the Romans in single combat, as he would, but he had the Queen to think of. He could not afford any losses amongst his twenty men and he had fought the Romans enough to respect them as warriors. Even old men like the crested leader of this detachment would be a good soldier with the deadly gladius. His men had their bows ready and when he nodded nine arrows flew through the air. As Tadgh watched them he saw another flight from the north. One legionary shouted a belated warning and managed to grab his shield but for the rest it was a swift death as two arrows hit each man. The legionary took one in the leg but still bravely grabbed his sword ready to defend himself.

Tadgh ran across the open ground with his mighty war hammer in his hand. The legionary had to crouch slightly because of the arrow in his leg but he pull his shield close to his face and held the gladius angled upwards ready to slash at the unprotected body of the wild warrior who was racing rapidly towards him. Tadgh had fought enough Romans to understand their tactics. In a line the legion was unbeatable as each man protected his comrade to his left with his shield. The man at the end of each line was normally the best warrior. Here the young legionary was isolated and Tadgh almost felt sorry for him as he smashed the war hammer against the shield. The blow broke the young man's arm and both the shattered shield and broken arm dropped uselessly to his side. He bravely held out his sword but it was no protection from the next blow which smashed into the side of his skull driving the metal cheek guards into the brain of the young legionary who died instantly. "You died well boy. Gather the weapons and then throw the bodies and other equipment into the lake. Put the weapons on the mules and then get rid of any evidence that there was a fight here."

Later, as they walked back to the cave Tadgh looked around the site; it was as though nothing had occurred and the seven men had never existed. Their armour had dragged the bodies to the bottom of the murky lake and would never be discovered. They would be reported as a lost detachment in the empty wilds of Britannia, a memory only to their comrades in the Ninth and a tale told to terrify new recruits in the inns at Eboracum.

Livius looked at the twenty volunteers before him and suppressed the urge to embrace every one of the remaining troopers from Marcus' Horse who had chosen to join his Exploratores. Julius had stayed on before he returned to Rome to help the young officer with the training of the new unit. It had taken him but two days to be able to decide that Livius knew what he was doing. "You understand the idea better than I young Livius. I would be thinking of charges and movements of vast numbers of men. You have grasped the concept of subtlety and concealment in a way which is foreign to me and that is not an insult. That is me giving you the respect of one leader to another. You do not need me but the legions need you."

So Livius stood before the twenty warriors looking at the unit which had been created but five days earlier. Each man was a trained cavalryman and Livius had had no need to worry about horsemanship or weapon training. He knew that they were all excellent trackers but what he needed to instil in each man was the belief that he could operate as an individual, without an officer to give orders and instructions. He knew they had the ability but he needed to give them the belief and now, after five days he was well on the way to that aim. The powers above him had decided that training was no longer necessary and they needed the new skills of the Explorates before the invasion of the north could begin in earnest.

He rode down the line of troopers looking each man in the face. It pleased him that they returned his look and in each face he saw respect. It was what he had hoped for rather than expected as a right. He knew that officers had to earn that respect from men whose lives were held in their fragile hands.

"Men this is new to all of us. We are going somewhere we have never been before, not the land but the job. I know each of you and I know that you will meet that challenge. We are too few and already others are being trained to join us but they are not Marcus' Horse and they do not have your experience." He smiled as each man seemed to grow in the saddle, proud of his association with that proud ala. "We have no more time for training and we will be leaving tomorrow to undertake a new life which will be more dangerous and more hazardous than that which went before. You will notice that we do not have the spear and shield. You will also notice that your armour is now carried on the spare horse. We are not Marcus' Horse, at least not in

21

name nor in the way we work, just in the heart, the honour and the memory of lost comrades. We now wear leather armour and use bows and swords. We no longer operate in turmae but in pockets of five men and even that may be split. I am the only optio but each of you is a chosen man, chosen by me. Each of you is equal and decisions on the field will be made by all. You men have intelligence as well as ability and you will use them both." He paused to let his words sink in. He too was dubious about the success or failure they could expect. All men expected a leader to make decisions but each man was, in effect, a leader and he hoped they would fulfil the potential he knew they had. "My servant will deliver each group their orders tonight. Read them and learn them then destroy them. Your orders will determine how long you are away from Eboracum. I will be operating in the west close to Glanibanta. I tell you this not because I expect that you will need that information but because it is important that you know where I will be." He raised his sword, "May the Allfather be with you. Marcus' Horse!"

Each man roared proudly back, "Marcus' Horse!"

The next day Livius took his five-man patrol west. The spare horse carried spears and armour in case they needed it but Livius was sure that when this first patrol was over they would be irrelevant. In the weeks since he had been tasked with the creation of the unit he had thought long and hard about how it would work and decided that charges and individual combats were a thing of the past. They would have to be invisible, spectres, ghosts who were never seen only sensed. He hoped that the other fifteen men sent out on their patrols would not have to be sacrificed to enable others to learn from their mistakes. He was determined that his patrol would learn and learn quickly. When he had chosen his orders it appeared the most difficult and the simplest of the four tasks. Engineers were scouting a new road in the west and Livius was to aid their task by scouting ahead of them. He had chosen the assignment because it operated the furthest from Eboracum and that made it dangerous but he knew the area well and finally it was the last area in which Morwenna had been seen. If he was to find that arch fiend it would be there.

As they rode west along familiar roads Livius placed himself at the back of the small column so that he could assess the men with whom he would be working over the next months. Cassius had been his first choice. He would be an optio as soon as they mustered more men. He was older than Livius and extremely dependable. He was rarely flustered and always made uncannily good decisions. In many ways he was a good luck omen.

Rufius was out in front and he was the youngest of the group. He was also the most recent recruit and the one about whom Livius knew the least but he had shown an enthusiasm and eagerness for combat which reminded Livius of Decurion Macro who had also been the one who desired to be the first into combat and the last from it. He also seemed to have Gaelwyn's ability to follow tracks over stones.

Decius was the hothead; a fierce warrior who was abrasive in the group but also fiercely loyal. He had incurred the wrath of many officers outside of Marcus' Horse for the fights caused when he felt that the name of the ala had been slurred. He was as loyal a man as one could want but Livius knew that he needed more self-control and then he would be a good trooper. If he thought first and then acted he would live longer.

Agrippa was, like Cassius an older man and Brigante to boot. He had been chosen by Livius for one reason and one reason only, Gaelwyn the old Brigante scout had rated him as a good tracker and that praise was enough to elevate the older, quieter man in Livius' opinion.

Finally there was the enigma, Metellus. Without doubt he was the best educated of the six and even Livius felt illiterate next to him. He would quote poetry both Latin and native with ease. He could speak almost every language with great facility and yet he was the deadliest man with a bow that Livius had ever seen, he could even outshoot Macro and that was unheard of. As they trotted westwards the decurion reflected that if he failed with this group of men then the Exploratores as a concept was already dead.

He wondered what old Prefect, Marcus, would think of him if he could see him now. He looked like the other troopers with no sign of rank. Like his troopers he wore no helmet, it was attached to his saddle. The leather armour was covered by a dirty and nondescript tunic which gave Livius and the others the look of bandits fallen on hard times. Of course their Roman mounts and their healthy bodies would have left no one in any doubt as to who they were but Livius had encouraged his men to let their beards and hair grow; they would make them look more like the natives than Roman. He also planned on splitting up his group; six men were too large or too small a number. He planned to operate in threes with a ten mile gap between them.

He found himself oddly excited by the assignment and, when Julius had told him the devastating news about the ala Livius had thought that his world had ended; now he saw that the Parcae had a different plan for him and a new future. His first stop on his first patrol would be close to Morbium for he wanted to seek the advice of Gaelwyn, Marcus and Gaius; the three warriors he respected more than any other.

Cato and Marcus had ridden over to the farmstead of Ailis and Gaius to give them the news of Marcus' Horse. The bonds of friendship were so deep that they were, in effect, an extended family. The three boys Decius Gaius Aurelius his brother Marcus and their adopted brother Decius Macro Culleo were always eager to hear the stories these revered warriors told. Decius Gaius was no longer a boy. He had now seen fourteen summers and was becoming a man. He and his father were very close in every way, looks, manners, the way they spoke and Decius modelled himself on the father who was also his hero. It was obvious to his mother that he would follow in his father's footsteps and run the farm. The two younger boys were more like brothers than had they had the same parents. They were born very close together and, when Macro's mother, the witch Morwenna had abandoned him, Ailis had fed and cared for both boys. They were both her sons. Now they were still young men enjoying young men's adventures. They dogged Gaelwyn, desperate to learn how to become hunters and warriors. The old man feigned annoyance at their demands but in reality he loved training young minds and bodies. The two of them were fast becoming the best trackers and hunters for miles around.

When they saw the two riders approaching the three boys ran from the field in which they had been working; mending fences could wait but the chance to eavesdrop the conversations of their elders was a treat not to be missed. By the time they crashed through the villa door Cato and Marcus were sat with Gaelwyn and their father around the family table.

"Stop! Where do you think you are going?" Ailis' voice was raised slightly but it stopped the three of them in their tracks. They hung their heads in silence. The four men grinned at their discomfort. "You know the rules; when you come from the fields you wash your hands and take off your sandals."

Young Marcus Gaius looked pleadingly at his father who grinned and shook his head. "If you think I am going to argue with your mother think again. Go and wash your hands."

They would have flashed their grubby paws through the water had Ailis not stood with arms folded and a stern expression making sure that they did a good job. After checking them back and front she nodded her assent and they raced into the room.

Gaius, their father was speaking, "So the ala is no more eh?"

25

Cato shook his head. "To be honest Gaius it would have been a new ala anyway. After the retirements and deaths there were but a handful of men left."

"I wonder what Ulpius would have thought?"

"He had no sentiment about the ala. It was the people in it he cared for, besides from what Cato says Marcus' Horse still lives with Livius and the Exploratores."

"Uncle Marcus, what are Exploratores?"

"Well young Decius Macro Culleo, now that you are clean enough to listen to your elders I will tell you. They are a new cavalry unit attached to the legions. They will operate secretly sometimes behind enemy lines and they will scout and track Rome's enemies."

Gaelwyn snorted. "Scouts! They couldn't find their arse if they didn't fart!"

The boys giggled. "Uncle Gaelwyn!"

"Sorry Ailis but they were never very good at tracking."

"To be fair Gaelwyn they were never as good as you but then few were." Mollified by Gaius' words the old man nodded.

"So Livius is out on patrol then?"

"Well Marcus he was about to leave with his men when I left the fortress. It looked strange to me, the whole force is but twenty one men, not even a turma but they have to do the job of an ala."

"Sounds interesting anyway."

"Sounds perfect!" Marcus Gaius' voice had yet to break and the squeak he made caused the adults to stare at the blushing young boy. "Well it would. Don't you fancy it too Decius?"

Macro's son was a smaller version of his dead father with broad shoulders and he grinned and nodded his affirmation. Gaelwyn found himself thinking he was actually looking at Macro. "Well you are too young. They wouldn't be able to have you for at least ten years."

The four men looked at each other not wishing to contradict the she-wolf protecting her cubs but they knew that they had been warriors when barely fourteen summers old. It would be two years at the most that Ailis would have her boys with her. The disappointment on their faces almost made Marcus laugh out loud.

Suddenly Gaelwyn's hunting dog rose and growled. The four men grabbed their weapons from beside the door and raced out. The growling meant strangers and after Ailis and the boys had been kidnapped by a raiding band of barbarians they took no chances. The four adults and three boys formed a half circle of steel around the door as the horsemen trotted into the yard.

"Well that is a nice welcome for an old comrade!"

"Livius! Your ears must have been burning for we were just talking of you."

"Well if my men can use your barn I will join you."

Gaius shook his head. "They are my old comrades too. They can join us. Wife we have company for supper."

Chapter 3

"An unexpected visit Livius."

"I do have an ulterior motive Marcus. I called at your farm first and your man told us you had left already." he paused and then gestured at the line of horses standing in the yard. "These are fine horses and they look like Roman horses. We need to look less Roman and somehow..."

"Wilder?"

"I was thinking more Brigante."

Gaelwyn snorted. "As though that could ever happen."

Gaius smiled. "It could uncle."

"How? Your short hair and womanish faces mark you as Romans even at a thousand paces."

"He is right Gaius and I have told my men to grow their hair and beards. Our tunics are old and worn. We do not carry shields but the horses..."

"The horses look the same; they look Roman."

"Exactly Pref... er Marcus. Could we exchange them for seven of yours?"

Marcus looked at Cato who nodded. "We have some that would just suit. They are a variety of colours and sizes but the only problem I can foresee is that they are not as well trained as I would like. We can pick them up tomorrow if you like."

Sighing with relief Livius shook his head. "That is no bad thing Sergeant for we do not need them to be able to ride knee to knee and we can train our own mounts as we head west."

Gaius looked up suddenly animated. "West? Towards the land of the lakes and..." they all flashed a glance at an entranced Decius Macro Culleo, son of Macro and Morwenna, who seemed oblivious to their sudden interest in his face.

"Yes Gaius. The Ninth are to build a road west and a fort for the Gauls to guard that side of the country."

"And Glanibanta? Our old hunting ground?"

"Yes Marcus that is to be re-invested with auxiliaries. I think the new Governor has actually read the reports we wrote and realises the potential in the west and the dangers."

Ailis returned with a pot which she planted unceremoniously in the middle of the table. "Enough of plans and strategies Gaius, we have guests who are politely listening but from their faces want to eat."

The Exploratores started to bluster and deny their hunger but Gaius laughed." This is why we should have women with the army. They are far more sensible and practical than we warriors. Of course they are hungry and thirsty too I expect. Decius and Marcus go and bring in the beakers Decius Gaius, bring in the wine."

After the meal, which Livius realised might be the last decent food they ate in a long time, they discussed how the Exploratores might operate. "Your problem Livius is that of communication. If you discover something how will you let your superiors know?"

"Good point Marcus, ever the strategist. It is one reason why I chose groups of five troopers. Two can return with the information whilst the others continue to scout. It may be that, in the future, we take an extra horse with us."

"I still think that the mail armour is a waste of time and will slow you down."

"You never did like armour did you Gaelwyn? We may still need to fight and I have seen how armour can save a trooper. It is worth the small discomfort. Besides I can think of situations where we need to look Roman, with helmets, crests and spears. When this first patrol is ended I will ask each of the patrols what they could suggest to improve the way we work."

"That is a good idea. Just listening to you I can see that it is a major change."

The group of warriors watched the glowing fire and drank their wine comfortable and happy, knowing that, possibly for the last time in a while they were safe. As with all good soldiers they had learned to take comfort when possible for most of their lives would be a cold and hard existence with little food.

Marcus Gaius spoke up. "Uncle Livius I would like to be an Explorate."

"Me too," burst out Decius Macro, desperate not to be left out.

The men laughed and then stopped when they heard the crash from the kitchen. "You are too young and all this nonsense ends now. To bed, now, the three of you!"

Their complaints and pleas fell on deaf ears and when Ailis returned with a stormy look upon her face the men had the good grace to look downwards except for a defiant Gaelwyn who looked his niece firmly in the eye. "I am surprised at you Gaius, encouraging your sons to join the army!"

"I didn't."

"You laughed which is as bad."

"They will make good scouts Ailis. They are the best trackers I have ever trained."

"Uncle they are bairns."

Sadly shaking his head Gaelwyn murmured, "It is a wild frontier now Ailis and they will be fighting soon, whether that is defending the farm of fighting Rome's enemies it will happen and I would rather they were with someone like Livius who can at least think a little, than a jumped up aristocrat who doesn't know his arse from his elbow."

"Thank you for that Gaelwyn it is the nicest thing you have ever said to me but fear not Ailis. Even if they wished to join there will be no recruitment until next year at the earliest and even then I think they would be too young."

Mollified Ailis turned to leave pausing only when Gaius spoke. "It might at least give them a focus wife if we said that when they were older we would consider it. They might apply themselves to their reading and writing if Livius said that was a condition of joining."

Her slumped shoulders told them all that although she accepted the inevitable she was not happy about it, "Very well but I will have the final say."

The next day as Marcus led Cato and Livius' patrol east to exchange horses, Gaius put his arm around his wife's shoulders. "You cannot protect the boys forever. Marcus and Decius want to be warriors." He kissed her gently on the side of the head, "Decius is like his father and Marcus wants to be like me. You cannot change that."

"But they are so young!" She buried her tearful face in Gaius' shoulder.

"When I fought the Brigante and the Caledonii I fought warriors younger than the boys and they had been fighting for years. Marcus and Decius could do worse than joining Livius for they would not have to fight in pitched battles."

"But they would be alone and amongst enemies."

"When the Caledonii took you I then realised that we all live on the edge of a precipice. It is easier to fall than to stay safe. They are both good trackers and excellent warriors. I would back the two of them against anyone and we will have two more years for Gaelwyn to make them even better." He turned Ailis so that she was facing him. "You are Brigante. Brigante are warriors and your husband wields the Sword of Cartimandua. Decius will run the farm but Marcus will wield the sword; it is his destiny. Would you deny him that destiny?"

She shook her head and angrily faced her husband, "Allfather but I hate it when you are right! I may have to suffer it but I do not have to enjoy it."

Gaelwyn appeared from around the corner of the villa. "You will see niece, it will all turn out well. Your son will be a greater warrior than his father and as good a tracker and scout as his uncle."

Turning back into the kitchen she snorted, "I do not know how your head fits through this door it is so big and you are so full of…"

Gaius laughed. "She is the only one Gaelwyn who ever bests you."

Sniffing as he took his dog to the stables Gaelwyn retorted, "Which is why I never married. I wanted to win some arguments at least."

"Tadgh!"

Racing into the cave the warrior wondered what new task he was to be given. "Yes your majesty?"

"My waters have broken my time has come."

Pleased that he knew this routine he nodded, "Certainly your majesty." Leaving the cave he shouted to his men. "Half of you down to the road, the rest in your positions." Morwenna had made it quite clear that the men were to be at least one hundred paces from the cave while they were birthing and Tadgh had decided that, as an extra precaution, he would have a circle of men further out to give them extra warning.

As they waited one of the older men turned to Tadgh. "I pray to the Allfather that it is a girl." Tadgh nodded, adding his silent wish to his comrades. The men were deeply upset by the killing of the healthy boys. The buried bodies were a constant reminder of Morwenna's power. To warriors it seemed alien to kill a healthy male but Morwenna's formidable will prevented any show of dissent. There was silence from the cave. It was as though the three witches had decided not to show any weakness to men who they thought were the weaker species. Morwenna and her acolytes' ruthless disposal of the babies had persuaded the warriors that perhaps women were the stronger of the species.

32

As Maban called out to Tadgh he could feel his heart racing. Would he have to witness a baby's brains being splattered on the rocks or would he be able to sleep comfortably at night? "It is a girl. We need meat. Go."

As Maban returned to the cave Tadgh smiled and thanked the Allfather. "It is a girl!" His warriors shared his happiness and every man smiled and breathed a little easier. "We hunt. Brennus stay here with four men and guard the women."

By the time they had returned with the meat Morwenna was sitting out side the cave feeding the child. Although she looked pale there was a serene smile on her face and a power which seemed to glow from her body. Tadgh laid the doe on the ground before her and Maban took out a blade which was razor sharp. Slicing open the dead animal's stomach she reached inside and removed the heart, liver and kidneys. Even while she was feeding the child Morwenna was fed chunks of raw heart taken from the deer. She seemed to care not as the blood ran down her neck onto her naked breast and anointed the baby's head. This accident caused Anchorat and Maban to screech with delight. Maban turned to Tadgh. "You may have the rest of the animal."

Dismissed, Tadgh dragged the carcass down to the lower level where they would cook it. The men had all averted their eyes from the witch feeding the child but when they heard the screech and then saw the blood splattered child they all made the sign against evil. Morwenna might be their mistress but she terrified them.

The meat was sending powerful aromas wafting around the camp as Brennus returned with the outlying scouts. They all salivated as they saw the beast on the open fire. The sun was just dipping behind the hillside and Tadgh was thinking that the day had, so far, turned out far better than he had hoped when suddenly they heard the sound of a horse's neigh and the crack of hooves on the rock lined path. Every man went to his weapons as the

33

seven riders emerged from the trees two hundred paces away. The leader, a mighty bare chested warrior with blue tattoos rode to within a hundred paces of the shelf below the cave. In his hand he held a sack stained with a darkness which did not bode well. "I am Corin, a messenger from the mighty King of the Caledonii, Lulach. I have a message for the witch Morwenna." He hurled the sack and it landed thirty paces from Tadgh who stood with sword extended. "This is what the king thinks of those who betray and desert him. There will be no alliance between the Brigante and the Caledonii and the witch should stay in her cave for if she ever ventures north she will die." Turning he galloped back to the woods before any of Tadgh's men could shoot an arrow.

Brennus walked up to the sack and brought it back to Tadgh. Above him on the ledge near to the cave they could see the three witches, Morwenna still holding the blood covered babe. She held their gaze for a moment and then spoke in a voice which seemed to echo across the hillside. "Open it and let me see my husband."

Loosening the sack the eyeless skull of Aodh dropped to the ground. Brennus made the sign against evil as he wondered how she had known that it was her husband's skull. Tadgh looked at the face of his one time leader. Although the eyes were gone the rotting lips were parted in a rictus grin which suggested he had suffered greatly at the end. "Bring it to me." Tadgh climbed up to the cave and reverently place Aodh's head at Morwenna's feet. The Queen of the Brigante took the babe from her nipple and turned its face to the skull on the ground. "There Genovefa is your father, treacherously murdered by the Caledonii. We will, my daughter, have our revenge." Staring at Tadgh she said, "Bury him with the others and then we must talk. We have plans to make."

As he took the head to the graves of the babies Tadgh wondered again about the power of Morwenna who had shown no emotion at the loss of her husband. He had no idea how he and his twenty men could fight a whole nation but he knew that Morwenna would have her own ideas and plans and, chillingly, they would probably result in success.

Centurion looked with dismay at the vast expanse of sand and swamp which stretched out before them. They had headed west as soon as they could and had made good time. Now his leader would have to rethink their direction they would take for there was no way they could risk the mules and their valuable cargo over such treacherous land. Looking northwards Centurion could see only one route and that would take them through the land of the lakes which meant closer to Rome and the Brigante. It was the worst of all possible outcomes. His face betrayed him as he rode up to the column of laden pack mules.

"I assume we can no longer head west."

"Soft sand, marsh and swamps as far as the eye can see. It looks like we will have to head north."

Decius looked around for some sort of sanctuary in which they could shelter. He saw a small copse in the lee of a hill. "Let's head over there." As they led their strings of animals Decius realised that he had too few loyal men to rely on. With just Tiny and Centurion he could ill afford for two of them to scout ahead for he needed one of them with the mercenary soldiers who had betrayed him once. If he just sent one ahead then they were in danger of being ambushed or attacked. The hills were clearly visible and he knew that most of the entrances ran south to north which meant he had to find the westernmost valley and hope that there was a path or a pass to the west. Tomorrow he would leave Tiny and Centurion to guide his gold north while he sought out a safe route.

It was a miserable dawn when Decius set off. It was the first piece of good fortune he had had for it hid him from prying eyes. He had given Centurion instructions to head directly north whilst he went north west determined to stay as close to the west as he could. He saw the sands which barred their way and, infuriatingly, he could see the dim shape of a peninsula to the west. Reluctantly he dragged his horse towards the north and found his passage north constantly barred by obstacles which the mules could not navigate. He was being edged inexorably east. As he rode over a small col he saw to his dismay a wall of rock rearing to the east leaving him no option but to head north up a wide narrow valley. The land to the west also rose steeply but at least they had their route into the land of the lakes.

From the col he could see woods clinging precariously to the sides of the rocky walls leaving very little open ground. It would make their passage difficult but also hide their presence. He decided to wait at the rocky outcrop and await the arrival of his men. At least he had a plan, not necessarily a good plan but at least a plan which had some chance of success. He reluctantly returned to the others. They would have to travel together. If they did find a route west he did not have to want to waste time seeking his men. It was easier when he returned for he knew where he was going.

The further up the valley that they travelled the more worried Centurion and Decius became. Ahead of them they could see a huge lake to the west as far as the eye could see whilst to the east was a steeply rising mass of rocks; not that they wished to go to the east but they could not and they found themselves being funnelled ever northwards. To add to their misery they were running short of food. "I know that you do not want to hear this but we need to stop and rest. The mules need grazing and of that there is plenty and we need food. The lake must we well stocked with fish and the land looks to be full of game."

Decius looked around him and could find no answer to Centurion's powerful argument and yet it felt wrong to stop. What if they were discovered? Everyone they might meet was a potential enemy. This was not a defensible site and yet for the small number of men he had at his disposal where was defensible with the number of animals and the amount of gold he had to protect? Centurion was right.

"There looks to be a stream which cuts away from the lake. We will build a camp there and use a palisade to protect us."

Centurion sighed with relief. He had been afraid the headstrong young leader would ignore his advice. "I will get Tiny to organise the palisade and I think one of the men has experience of fishing. Once we have the mules protected I will take two men to hunt. A week is all we need and that will allow us to scout ahead."

"Thank you Centurion."

As Centurion organised the men he reflected that perhaps he was getting too old for this sort of work. They had so much gold that a luxurious existence was within touching distance and he did not want that dream jeopardised. What if his caution made him hesitate the next time he was in combat? When he had been with the legion he had never expected to survive for survival meant more of the same but now he could be a rich man with servants and guards; it was a disquieting thought for someone not given to such sentiment.

Even Decius felt happier after the first three days. His hunger had been eased and the mules were looking much healthier. This land was truly beautiful and, were he not a hunted man, he could have easily lived there. Once again he looked at the gold stacked in the middle of the camp to avoid putting too great a strain on the animals. Of course the strain on the men was even greater and Decius had felt some moments of consternation when he saw some of the looks the men cast at the glowing pile. Even Centurion looked a little twitchy.

He gathered them around. "Men I have a question to ask you. Should we bury some of the gold here as a safeguard against anything happening to us and the rest of the gold before we leave Britannia?"

He knew that the question was unexpected and he chewed on the piece of venison as he watched their faces. Tiny looked totally confused for he had never had his opinion sought. Centurion was weighing up the benefits and problems whilst the others were working out if they could manage to extract more gold than they were due this way. He gave them a suitably long time and then rose to his feet, spitting out the piece of gristle he had found.

"We have fifty mules left and some of them will not survive the mountains. If we bury the gold from ten of the mules we still have a fortune left for each man but we also have enough gold to come back to should we need it. The mules will have less to carry and we will move faster. Each man has an equal vote in this so think carefully when I ask you to vote."

Decius was very devious. He had learned to play games of strategy as a young man and he excelled at them. He could foresee him returning at some time to Britannia but most of the men would lose their gold and, probably, die as soon as they were in Gaul whereas he would not. This was like banking a fifth of the money and reserving it for himself. He knew that, with the exception of Tiny, each man would be thinking the same thoughts but none of them was as ruthless as their leader.

"Time for a vote." He saw seven hands raised. Only Tiny looked confused. He saw the huge man looking pleadingly at him and he nodded. Tiny's hand rose in the air. "It is done. Let us dig a hole, bury it and then each man remember where we buried it for tomorrow we eradicate every trace of the digging."

Livius felt better with their new horses and having talked through with Marcus and Gaius the best way to operate, it was almost as though talking it through clarified his thinking. He had split the team into three pairs and they travelled parallel routes five miles apart. This made them more inconspicuous and allowed them to cover more ground. Each night they gathered together for a common camp both for security and to secure information. As they headed towards the spine of the island life was good as they knew the land intimately and they began to develop their techniques and methods in the knowledge that there were few enemies. Once they reached the high lands they knew that things would change but their confidence was growing. Livius was delighted when Cassius found one of the camps made by the engineers who were ahead of them, surveying the route for the road. "Excellent Cassius. We now know their path. Your task tomorrow is to find where they went and find their next camp."

Decius could not contain himself. "But sir that's not fair. The camp is weeks old! How will we find their trail?"

Livius was pleased when he saw the others smile. "That is the trick Decius to find those signs that are almost invisible after all we are Exploratores. They had to build fires to cook and then there will be the marks of their equipment in the ground."

The young man looked around in exasperation. Metellus leaned over and said quietly, "Should be fun eh? At least we haven't got to polish armour!"

Chapter 4

Tadgh waited patiently outside the cave. It had been a week since the baby had been born and two weeks since they had disposed of the patrol of engineers. He knew they had another week but Morwenna had not spoken of her plans. It was obvious to the warrior that the Caledonii were not going to help and that meant that the Queen had an army of twenty. If the Romans came, and Tadgh knew that they would come, then their cavalry would easily capture them and it would be crucifixion for all of them. His men had been visibly upset, not only at the fact of Aodh's death but the more disturbing knowledge that Morwenna seemed to know it before they did. Having a witch for a leader did not inspire confidence in warriors who like to know what they were facing. Tadgh would not have dreamed of asking any questions but he was stoic enough to know that Morwenna would either read his mind or work out that he was worried.

He sat on the rock outside the cave and chewed on a piece of dried venison. Eventually Morwenna appeared alone. "You are worried Tadgh?"

"I am concerned your majesty. We cannot stay here for the Romans will, at some point discover that they have lost their party of soldiers. We have a very small army and no aid coming from the north …"

"You are a good leader Tadgh but I am not only a good Queen but a witch so powerful that you cannot imagine the power at my disposal. Fear not for there are footsteps heading this way which will solve all our problems and will give us an army better equipped than any you have seen, including the Romans." Her eyes bored into his and her sinuous voice seemed to enchant him. "You do believe me don't you?"

Suddenly it all became clear. He was serving a servant of the Mother. All would be well. His fears had been groundless. "Yes your majesty. I am sorry I doubted you."

She smiled and placed her hand on his head which seemed to cool and make his thinking clear in an instant. "You are mortal and you do not have the gift of speaking to the Mother as I have for you are merely a man. Never fear Tadgh. Aodh's death was foretold and was necessary. It was part of the Mother's greater plan. This is not the end, this is just the beginning."

*

High on the fells just beyond the small settlement of Lavatris, Livius and his small patrol camped in a small dell hidden from the main road. Glancing around their faces he could see a dramatic change from the neat troopers who had left Eboracum a week ago. Their faces had more than stubble; they had the untidy straggles of beards. Those of Agrippa and Cassius were flecked with grey. Their hair was growing but a close inspection would still have revealed them as Romans. The biggest change was in the smell. Livius had told them not to bathe and their sweat had intermingled with that of their mounts making them reek, not unusual in the barbarians but unheard of in a Roman ala. At first they had found this difficult to countenance but as they became used to it they found it could be ignored as soon they all had the same rank aroma.

"What did you find?"

Cassius looked across the fire at the decurion. "The Brigante hereabouts want nothing to do with Morwenna. They see us, the Romans, as a good thing. They are all doing well."

"But there has been no sign of the rebels since before the first snows."

Livius smiled for Metellus always thought beyond the obvious. "And Agrippa what news of the engineers?"

"They passed through here about four weeks ago," he grinned at Decius, "well done for spotting their camp young Decius." The young man gave a happy smile as he blushed but he was pleased with the praise. It meant he was improving; he would soon be accepted. "No sign of any other patrols."

"I think we are the first to venture across since the rising last year." He peered westwards. "I hope the engineers are safe for if there are no rebels here where are they? They cannot be close to Brocauum for the Batavians have a cohort based there and they patrol the road north to Luguvalium. There is little further south and even fewer warriors."

"The land of the lakes again eh sir?"

"You are right Metellus. It always comes back to the land of the lakes. Perhaps that is why the Governor is bringing the Ninth across to build a road and garrison some forts."

Metellus chewed his hard tack and gestured west. "The rebels were defeated but we never found their leaders. The settlements on this side of the divide are hostile to them."

Agrippa snorted, "Can you blame them? Think of the men folk who died needlessly in the battles last year."

"You are right; it was mainly the young men who died and old men who remain. What a sad waste."

Livius shrugged, "Hindsight is always accurate Cassius and it is a hard lesson to learn. Perhaps there will be no rebels hereabouts because there are no warriors left."

"But there must have been rebels, and not the leaders, who escaped. Where did they go? Are they the bandits we hear about in every settlement we visit? The ones who rob those on the road and steal livestock?"

"Probably Metellus and it shows how important our task is. Well our new method of riding in pairs and covering more ground appears to work. Tomorrow night we camp just outside Bravoniacum."

Cassius looked up. "That is a long ride."

"True but I am keen to catch up with these engineers. I fear they may need our protection. Agrippa, take your party into Veteris and gauge the opinion. I will visit Bravoniacum."

Decius looked with satisfaction at the burial site for the gold. They had spent the previous day digging a deep pit and lining it with wood. Centurion and one of the mercenaries had kept watch whilst the others toiled. Even Decius had dirtied his hands for it was a momentous decision. When they had buried the gold they had place rocks over the top and then covered it with the turf they had removed. Finally Tiny led the herd of mules across it allowing them to graze and defecate. When Centurion returned he could not identify exactly where the treasure was buried.

"Tell me where the gold is buried, Centurion."

Centurion searched all over and then spat on the ground. "I know it must be within a hundred paces of here but I could not lay my hands on it."

He laughed and walked to the exact spot. "It is buried beneath here. There is turf laid on rocks laid on the gold."

Centurion gave one of his cavernous smiles. "I know now."

"Good. We all know where it is and now we can move faster. Any animals which become lame we eat for we now have spare beasts and we will not need to seek food as we did here." They had salted some fish for the journey and made jerky from the venison. The lakes had a plentiful supply of fresh water and Decius was confident they would reach the settlements on the coast within the week.

As they led their strings of animals along the lakeside Decius watched his mercenaries carefully for any sign of disloyalty. The loyalty of Tiny and Centurion was not in question but he now had to watch the others for he saw the backwards glances as they left the buried gold. Decius knew, however, that he would be less likely to have his throat cut in the night for instead any of them who felt he had had enough would just slip away back to the lake and dig up the treasure. It had been a small price to pay to avoid a treacherous death.

Centurion trotted back to the column, his face showing that he had encountered a problem. Decius held his hand up and halted the column. "There is a Roman fort ahead."

"Occupied?"

Centurion shook his head. "It looks to be deserted."

"Is it at the head of the lake?"

The look of surprise on Centurion's face was matched by his voice, "Yes. How did you know?"

"It is Glanibanta. I know where we are now. If we head up past the fort we find two lakes. The route west is to the south of the southernmost lake. There is an old signal tower where we can camp north of the Roman fort." Centurion looked questioningly at Decius who shrugged. "My brother was in Marcus' Horse and he told me of it the last time I spoke with him."

"I didn't know he was in the cavalry."

"My uncle wanted us both to be able to help him to rule, Livius was the military choice and I was the one selected, as the elder brother, as the one for the business."

"Wise choice, for Marcus' Horse has suffered many casualties in the wars in the north. Do you know if he is still alive?"

"I do not know and I do not care. I would hope that he is dead for, if alive, he would recognise me immediately and that might upset our plans eh Centurion?"

"Even with the beard and the long hair?"

"We are brothers; we would know each other believe me."

The signal tower provided a perfect camp site with the river and the woods bordering three sides. The grass enabled them to let the mules and horses graze. Even the surly six seemed happier and there were smiles around the camp fire as they feasted on

44

freshly caught trout, the fragrant smoke spiralling into the summer sky.

It was Brennus who saw the smoke and reported immediately to Tadgh. Since Aodh's remains had been returned there had been not only a sombre atmosphere but a heightened sense of danger. They were a vulnerable group and could not resist an attack by an aggressive enemy and in these lands everyone else was a foe. Tadgh had allies he could call on but they were spread through the vast land that was Brigantia.

"Were they Romans?"

"I did not go close for I was alone."

"You did well. We will take a small group and scout them towards twilight." Detailing twelve of his warriors to closely guard the Queen Tadgh led Brennus and his other seven warriors down the trail to the tower. One advantage they had was the familiarity with this land; they knew it intimately and could traverse it even on a moonless night. They were also able to travel silently knowing that the bubbling river would mask any noise which they might inadvertently make. They waded through the shallow waters and hid in the shelter of the low scrubby bank. Their muddied and blackened faces peered over to see a huge herd of mules most of them with heavy saddlebags. The group spent a few moments gathering in the scene and then Tadgh led them back across the river where they could share information.

"No more than ten men."

"I only counted nine."

"Some may have been in the woods on the far side."

"No Brennus I think not. They looked far too relaxed. What were the mules carrying I wonder?"

"I have never seen so many mules at least not without a Roman guarding them."

"And these were not Romans."

"Not Roman army that is certain."

"Could they be deserters?"

"Possibly. You four stay here and watch them. Let me know if they move or if others appear. This is news for the Queen."

When Morwenna was informed of the arrival of the mules and their cargo she seemed neither surprised nor unhappy. She looked Tadgh firmly in the eyes and fixed him with her most powerful stare. "Could you capture the men and their cargo?"

The Brigante warrior looked up with a look of astonishment on his face. "Capture? We could kill them majesty and take whatever their cargo contains but why capture?"

For a moment he regretted his answer as it reeked of insubordination and the questioning of her orders but instead she nodded. "I can understand why you would be surprised but think Tadgh, are these Romans?" he shook his head. "Brigante? Traders?"

Again he shook his head and ventured, "If I were to guess anything it would be deserters or bandits."

"And as such would make welcome additions to this would be army of rebels," she swept her arm around the remaining warriors and the cave. Whatever is on the mules there is a great deal of it if there are as many animals as you say. We need to build an army and build it swiftly before the Romans come to build their roads, and their forts. We need to inspire the people to, once again, rebel against the Roman overlords. If we can build up an army we can gain allies. The Selgovae and Carvetii are ripe for rebellion and the land north of here is sparsely garrisoned." She held his shoulders in her pale, slim hands and repeated, "I ask you again, could you capture them?"

Taking a deep breath the warrior answered. "If we wait until they are asleep we could but we would have to kill the sentry they will inevitably leave on guard."

"You have answered my question. Do it. And Tadgh…"

"Yes majesty?"

"Take all your men, we need to guarantee success. We need no sentries tonight, the Mother will watch."

"Yes majesty."

It was a moonless night and Decius was sufficiently confident about his men and their temporary loyalty to allow one of the mercenaries to stand the second watch which allowed Centurion and himself more sleeping time. He was certain that he would hear either horses or mules if the man decided to leave and return to the buried gold. The problem he had was that they were too close to the gold yet and one of his men could return and dig it up. As they moved closer to the coast the problem might decrease but the man who deserted would have more time to dig up the gold.

Tadgh had sent Brennus with ten warriors to the far side of the camp; they had trekked around the edge of the lake and were even now waiting silently in the thick woods. The sentry was silhouetted against the fire on Brennus' side and it would be his lieutenant's task to kill the sentry. Tadgh and his group were tasked with the five men on their side of the fire which would leave just three men for Brennus to deal with. Brennus and Tadgh had already identified the two major problems that they would have to overcome, the huge warrior and the greybeard. They were on Brennus' side. Despite his promise to the Queen about capture the clubs they would use to render their victims unconscious were big enough to cave a man's skull in but Tadgh was taking no chances.

As they slipped over the river bank they knew that any noise they made would be hidden by the river roar but Tadgh was aware that the mules might smell them; that was the danger. They slid across the damp grass like serpents slithering ever closer to their sleeping prey. The sounds of the river faded and were replaced by the creak of mule harness and the spit and crackle of logs on the fire. Tadgh kept glancing at the sentry who was crouched by the fire picking at pieces of food still remaining on the bones by the fire. When they were twenty paces from the camp they halted and although Tadgh could not see Brennus he knew that his brother and his party would be close to the sentry. Each pair of warriors had identified their target and waited with bated breath for the arrow in the back which would signal the attack.

Whether the guard heard something or just stretched they would never know but the arrow caught him in the lower back. Even as he started to scream the twenty one warriors raced across the open ground. Tadgh drew back his club ready to hit any victim who evaded his men's attacks. He watched with horror as the huge warrior they had feared shook off his blows and punched one of Brennus' men so hard that they heard his jaw break. The giant was the only one who had given any resistance and Tadgh raced towards his unprotected back and smashed the club into the back of his unprotected head. He slumped slowly to his knees and Brennus hit him again in the face with his weapon rendering Tiny unconscious at last.

The prisoners were all tightly trussed and tied, unceremoniously on their horses. The wounded warrior was also given a horse and they quickly led the mules and prisoners back to the cave.

It was almost dawn when they finally dragged the obstinate pack animals up the narrow trail and hobbled them in the lee of the cave. The horses were also hobbled and the prisoners left where they were. Tadgh was desperate to know what the saddlebags and packs contained but he knew better than to open them before Morwenna had sanctioned the action. She surprised all of them by first ministering to the wounded warrior who was soon sleeping having taken a potion, his injured jaw bandaged and held as he slept.

"You have done well my fine and worthy warriors, especially you Tadgh, as I knew you would. We will guard these men until I have had time to talk to them and persuade them to join our little band. Now let us see what the Mother has brought to us." She gestured for one of the bags to be opened. The sun was just breaking over the hills to the east and whether it was an accident or Morwenna had planned it the result was that as the gold spilled out of the pack the shafts of sunlight hit it making the smelted gold glitter almost blindingly brightly.

The Brigante looked at each other but Tadgh noticed no surprise on the witches' faces. Brennus articulated the thought that was in all their heads. "Were we lucky? Was that the only bag of gold or are…?"

Morwenna smiled her secret smile. "Select another bag each from a mule of your choosing and let us see." Brennus did so and whooped with joy when he found more gold. Having discovered their bounty and their salvation they capered around like children each one holding the gold to their chests. When Morwenna's voice spoke it spoke with authority and a command which could not be denied. "Now we will stack all of the gold at the back of the cave. When that has been done you will build a wall of the rock in the cave in front of it. Then take the mules down to the lower level."

Tadgh looked at the Queen with increasing respect. She had a plan and he thought he could discern what it was. The gold was her hold over these, possibly, unwilling volunteers; she had devised a way to make them cooperate. "Come on you lazy bastards get working. You two take the gold and then the rest of you form a chain. Brother you and I will start to build the wall. Come on then move!"

The bright spring sun was already up when Decius finally awoke with a head that felt like he had been drinking for a week. He tried to move his hands and found them bound. He found he could not lift his back and he could see, below the belly of a horse, his feet. They had been captured but by whom. He tried to speak and found his throat parched and it came out as a croak, "Who…"

He heard a silkily smooth female voice purr, "Ah one is awake and, looking at his clothes ,I would think that this is the leader. Release him but hold his arms while we talk."

Decius saw the knife slice through the bonds and then he was roughly taken from the back of the horse and turned around. He saw immediately that they were not Romans but Brigante and, from their armour and weapons, they were part of the rebel army.

"Turn him so that he can see me."

As his face was turned he almost fainted with surprise for he beheld the most beautiful woman he had ever seen. Her red hair cascaded down her back and he could see her breasts as she was feeing a baby. They were pure white but his eyes were drawn to the green eyes which bored into his. "I am Morwenna Queen of the Brigante and priestess of the Mother. You have two choices and they are clear choices, join us and live, refuse and die." He tried to turn his head to see where his men and the mules were. "Only one of your men was killed the rest are bound as you were. The mules are gone as is, "she paused to emphasise her words, "as is the gold. We thank you for acquiring it for us and it is now part of our war chest. So I will ask again. Do you wish to join us and live or refuse and die?"

Ever the pragmatist there was only one answer he could give. "Your majesty I would be delighted to join your rebellion."

She came closer to him and hissed. "When you know me a little better you will come to learn that I do not appreciate sarcasm and insubordination results in death but you have just met me so you have had your one chance. When your men are given the same choice they will not have that chance. Now release him."

When the warriors took away their support his weakened legs gave way and he sank to the floor. His chin was grasped and a scarred warrior grinned into his face. "I am Tadgh and I serve the

Queen. You only live whilst my Queen allows it, remember that. Also remember that it would be very easy to hamstring you to prevent your escape and we would do that in an instant if we thought you might flee. A cripple could still serve us eh?"

"So you see..." she looked at him.

"Decius Lucullus Sallustius."

"So you see Decius Lucullus Sallustius it is your choice to be either a hamstrung slave or a warrior in my mighty army."

Decius was disappointed in the size of the force which had captured him and his men but he was confident enough to believe that, somehow, he could subvert it to his own ends. The witch thought she was swallowing him but he would become the predator. The fact that she was a woman meant that she would soon succumb to his charms, every woman did. As his men became conscious he knew he had to persuade them to join the rebels. The two he was most concerned with were Centurion and Tiny. In Centurion he had someone who understood military organisation and in Tiny he had someone who would defend him, even at the cost of his own life.

Centurion was the first to come to consciousness an hour or so after Decius. His angry face contorted as he struggled. Decius put his face close to his lieutenant's ear and whispered. "We have been captured by the Queen of the Brigante and her warriors. They have taken the gold. We will go along with them or they will kill us. Do you understand?" Glancing at the faces of the fierce Brigante and back to Decius he slowly nodded. He had always had a quick mind and he could see that they were not in a position to resist. What disconcerted Decius was the look on Morwenna's face; it was as though she had known what he had said to his comrade. She was an unknown quantity. He preferred women like his aunt and mistress Aula Sallustius who could be manipulated with a smile and a touch. This woman was of a different order and he would have to tread carefully until he worked out how best to charm and seduce her.

Finally it only remained for Tiny to wake and he showed no sign of doing so. The sun had passed its peak and Tadgh went to the Queen. "I think this one might have been struck a little too hard." Sliding his sword out from its scabbard he continued, "perhaps I should…"

Morwenna shook her head. "No not yet. Maban, Anchorat." The acolytes joined their mistress and held hands in a circle around the giant whose breathing was laboured and whose face looked deathly grey. Even Decius felt that the big man was going to die. Firstly Morwenna cleaned the wounds of blood and then rubbed on some of the perfumed salve. The three women were oblivious to the others and walked around Tiny's body, chanting, their voices a murmur and the sweat from their exertions pouring down their faces. Suddenly they stopped their incantation and Anchorat placed her hands around the dying man's head. Morwenna placed her lips around Tiny's mouth and began to breathe in and out. Maban placed her hands on his chest and began to push down whilst murmuring a rhythmic chant and Anchorat held her hands over the wounds on his head. Suddenly they all saw Tiny's body convulse and the three women stepped back. As his eyes opened Tadgh and the Brigante warriors gave the sign against evil.

Centurion looked at Decius and shook his head he turned to Decius and whispered, "I think we would have been better off had we run into Romans. This is witchcraft and no good can come of it."

Shrugging philosophically Decius replied, "The die has been cast and the Allfather has determined that this is our fate. Let us help Tiny and then see if we can find a way out of this." As the two men went to help Tiny to his feet Decius had already begun to formulate a plan- the Queen was a woman and it would be a simple task to seduce her and control this rebellion. With the gold at his disposal he could buy an army and create his own kingdom. He could buy what his uncle had dreamed of, his own heritage and lands.

Chapter 5

Livius and his three Explorates donned helmets when they entered Brocauum for there was a garrison there. Drusus and his group would circulate amongst the taverns in the vicus to pick up gossip. The guards at the gate were intrigued by the four riders who halted at the Porta Praetorium. Neither the optio nor the auxiliary recognised the uniform although it was obvious that they were soldiers.

"Decurion Livius Lucullus Sallustius of the Exploratores section of the Ninth Legion. I am here to speak with the Prefect."

"Enter sir," the optio was intrigued and, as they entered through the Porta Praetorium, could not resist the question. "Sir what is an Explorate? I have never heard of such a unit."

Smiling Livius leaned down and said, "Confidentially until this month neither had I optio. We are scouts and we are looking for an engineering party. Has one visited here recently?"

"No sir. You are the first visitors from the east since the snows."

Saluting the optio Livius rode on. He turned to Marius who rode on his right, "It is as I thought Drusus, the engineers would have headed south west towards Glanibanta."

"That is a hard road sir. The paths there are very steep."

"Aye. The legions will find that a difficult road to build."

They halted outside the Praetorium where a small party had gathered to greet these new visitors. Livius recognised the centurion from the rebellion. The huge veteran grinned from ear to ear causing the young auxiliary to stare. He had never seen First Spear smile let alone grin. "Decurion Livius! I didn't recognise you in," he gestured at the clothes they were wearing. "Has Marcus' Horse run out of funds now?"

Dismounting and handing the reins to Marius Livius shook his head, "No Centurion Cursus, Marcus' Horse is no more; it has been disbanded."

The grin left the auxiliary centurion's face. "I did not know." His face darkened and he lowered his voice. "Why was this? Has something untoward happened?" The question was not an innocent one. If a legion, cohort or ala disgraced itself it would be disbanded and its men sent to other units.

"No Hirtius nothing like that. There were too few of us to muster even a turma."

Cursus stepped back to look at Livius' garb. "Well may I ask what in the name of the Allfather are you?"

Livius leaned in and led the centurion to one side. "If we could go and meet with the Prefect I can tell you both."

"The Prefect has taken a patrol to Luguvalium. I am in temporary charge. Come let us go into the office." The clerk stood to his feet when they entered. "Go and fetch us some wine and then see to the troopers outside." When the man had left Livius and Cursus sat. "You have my interest young Livius. What are you then?"

"We are scouts, sort of."

"Sort of scouts eh? Still in the dark. Scouts for who?"

"The Ninth."

"Are they close by?"

"No we serve as intelligence gatherers which is why we look as we do. Even now three of my men are in the vicus gathering information. We were chosen because we no longer look Roman and we can find out more informally than formally. This is the first time I have looked as you see me for a while. Normally I look like a bandit or a deserter."

Cursus laughed. "I have to say I would have been suspicious of you had I not recognised you. I will be interested in any information you gather from the Carvetii in the town."

"You shall have it but what is your opinion of the rebellion and what news do you have?"

"There has been no trouble since last year but they are not a happy people. They do not like our presence."

"But we both know that it is necessary for this was one of the centres of the rebellion."

"Exactly but we have heard nothing of the Queen who led it. Perhaps she is dead."

The clerk returned with the wine and after he left Livius shook his head. "No we have heard nothing and I am sure that we would have heard if Morwenna had died. Have you any idea where she and her army could be?"

"I am not sure that she has an army. We destroyed most of them at the battle of Morbium. My guess is that she fled north to the savages."

"Could be." His tone implied that he was doubtful about that. He swallowed off his wine. "The other reason we are here is to find a patrol of engineers which headed west after the last snows. They are surveying a new road for the Ninth who will be following us."

"They didn't pass here. Perhaps they went further south. If they did they could be in trouble."

"Why is that?"

"We have few travellers from that direction but those who do travel from the south speak of bandits and groups of survivors from the rebel army. When your lot were on patrol that didn't happen but they can out run my lads and our task is to stop the northern savages from invading again so they pretty much have a free rein."

"So the frontier is not safe then?"

"No it is like a tinderbox. Luguvalium is always being attacked, only small scale stuff but it means we have to keep our patrols larger than we would like. It is why the Prefect is out with two centuries on a patrol up the road. I will be glad when the Ninth get here. A legion as a back up is always handy."

"Well I can't see them getting over for a month or so, longer if I can't find this patrol. Well I will go and find my other men. I will send Marius back with any information we gather."

Later that morning as the patrol gathered to share information Livius became concerned. Drusus had a troubled look on his face. "You had better tell the lads in the fort that the town is unhappy. There are a bunch of troublemakers. We did as you suggested and let them think that we were deserters from the Roman army and they welcomed us with open arms. They suggested we head south west to the big forest where they reckoned we would find like minded men. They all have weapons hidden and are waiting for the chance to rise again. They thought that if we were deserters there may be more. It seemed to encourage them to open up."

"Any leaders here then?"

"No they were a little cagey about that but they know the routine well. They told us to avoid the road to Luguvalium because the Prefect was there with a big patrol and they know the routines in the fort."

"Well done Drusus. Marcus, go back and tell the Centurion what Drusus said and tell him I suggest changing his routines perhaps have a few searches." Marius nodded and left. "We had better head south west. I am less than happy about this patrol of engineers. If they ran into a big group of deserters or rebels they would not stand a chance."

"How come they only sent a small patrol?"

"The Governor thought we had rid the land of the rebels and thought it was safe. His priority is the road so that we can use the Classis Britannica on this side of the island as well as the other."

*

Morwenna and Tadgh walked through the woods with Decius. Tiny had taken just one night to recover and accepted the new situation with his normal stoicism. After a more pleasant night's sleep Decius had begun formulating his plans to take over the

57

group. When he was asked to accompany Tadgh and Morwenna he had been suspicious. Would he suffer a knife in the back? He did not like to be without the support and protection of Tiny and Centurion but he was now, effectively, a prisoner and would have to go along with his captors.

"You have a huge amount of treasure there how did you come by it?"

Morwenna's question was a loaded one but Decius could see no advantage in lying. He would lie when necessary but this occasion did not merit a lie. "I was in charge of the Wyddfa gold mines." His focus was fixed on Tadgh and he did not see the sudden spark of interest in Morwenna's green eyes.

"Did you exhaust the mines then?"

Laughing Decius shook his head. "We could have dug for another twenty years and not exhausted them."

"Then why did you stop?"

He shrugged, "Rome was becoming a little too interested in what I was taking."

"I see. You were taking for Rome but keeping most of it for yourself. Very enterprising. And now it has been taken from you by me."

He stopped and faced Morwenna looking at her shrewdly. "Yes but you have a plan for me otherwise we would have all died around our camp fire and you would not have done as much to save Tiny."

"Do you see Tadgh; you did not smash the intelligence from this thief. No Decius we have a reason for saving your life. You and your men look resourceful and I need resourceful men. I need more resourceful men to enable us to continue with the rebellion. Your gold will fund that."

"What is in it for me?"

Tadgh's hand went to his sword, "Your life you dog!"

"No Tadgh he is quite right and I would suspect that if our new friends did not benefit from our new arrangement then we would soon lose them. Am I not right?"

Spreading his hands Decius nodded, "We would need persuasion. My men are mercenaries and work for money not ideals."

"Good for they are the kind of men I can use. Here is the honey for you to sweeten the deal. When you have helped me to raise an army and rid this part of Britannia of my enemies I will return your money to you and help you to escape this land." Decius began to nod his agreement. "There is however another condition, before I allow you to go you will take me and Tadgh to this gold mine so that we may extract more of the treasure of Wyddfa."

Decius was more than interested. Perhaps he could delay taking over the group until they were back at Wyddfa. If he had Morwenna's army he could get even more gold and it would be easier to rid himself of Tadgh and his thugs in a land he was familiar with. "You have my support and that of my men."

"Good."

"And of course as an equal, my men and I will have our weapons returned."

Morwenna stared deep into his eyes and Decius found himself almost blinking with the power. "Of course but do not betray me for I am a priestess of the Mother and I can see into your black and treacherous heart."

Internally Decius shuddered although outwardly he appeared calm. Had he misjudged the woman before him? He would have to go along with her, at least for the foreseeable future; especially until he had found where she had buried the gold. "My men and I will be loyal. Your majesty." Tadgh's snort of derision spoke volumes and he led them back up the hill. The relief on the faces of Centurion and Tiny, as they walked back into the encampment touched Decius. He could see them exchange a look as they both nodded at each other. It was obvious to Decius that they thought he had been taken away for a quick execution. He would have to speak to them privately as soon as possible. The others were just battle fodder as far as Decius was concerned but he needed his two most loyal comrades to help him to escape.

Morwenna addressed the camp. "Tomorrow we begin to buy weapons and men. Today we rest and," here she looked at Decius' men, "recuperate. Sallustius you sit with me while I feed the child. I would learn more of your story," she glanced up at Tiny and Centurion lurking nearby, "and tell your giants that you are safe while you are in my land."

Decius smiled and turned to Centurion and Tiny. "Do not worry. Later we will talk." Centurion saw the look in Decius' eye and nodded, leading Tiny to the fire and the food.

"Sallustius?" Was that not the name of the Governor of Britannia?" She paused to place the babe on the nipple and to gauge the effect of her next comment, "the one executed for treason."

"He was my uncle and was the grandson of Cunobelinus the last king of Britannia and he was executed for naming a lance after himself."

She smiled. "And you believe that no more than any other British prince. He would have rebelled had he not been discovered."

Decius shook his head, "I don't know but it is irrelevant now. He is dead."

"You of course are of the royal bloodline as am I. Are you not?"

"I suppose we are but does it matter now that the Romans rule both your lands and mine?"

"What was taken can be returned." Already an idea was forming in Morwenna's mind. A child born to the two of them would have a much wider appeal to the people of Britannia; uniting two of the more important tribes in a single dynasty. It could even be a boy. She almost chuckled at the thought of The Mother weaving her strands and plans to create such a possible future. The Mother had brought Decius to her and she had thought it was for the gold but now she could see another motive just as powerful. She leaned over and said quietly, "When it is night time come to my cave I would speak further with you."

"Your wish is my command. I will obey you in all things." He walked back to his comrades bemused. Was she flirting with him? Perhaps he had been wrong and she was not as distant as he had thought. His charms and attraction must still be working on women, as they normally did. When he reached the fire and the food he was quite cheerful. He playfully punched Tiny's enormous bicep. "It is good to see you awake. We thought for a while that you had gone to the Allfather."

"When the time is right Tadgh will feel a much heavier blow from me. Tiny does not forget."

Decius leaned in conspiratorially, "Well for the time being let us play nicely with our hosts. There will be a time for revenge but for a while, at least, we will go along with them and be keen and loyal rebels." He turned to Centurion. "Have you found the gold yet?"

"So far they have not let us move away from the area around the cave entrance. I glanced down the cave and could not see it and the ground here is too rocky. "He gestured around them. "The Romans must have used this as a quarry for their fort and tower. They must have put it somewhere else but it will be close."

"I know it will be hard but let us be friendly towards the warriors. It may be that they will tell us what we wish to know if we can gain their favour."

"It will be hard. Tiny and I would just like ten minutes alone with some of those who attacked us."

"As would I but look at the situation. We are safer here than we were. The gold is safe even though we know not where it is and we can sleep at night without the worry of having our throats slit. Our day will come. The Queen wants us to take her back to the mines at Wyddfa."

Centurion looked surprised. "What? Now?"

"No later, when we have raised an army."

"Isn't that risky returning there?"

"No for they must have searched already and assumed we have fled and besides when we return we will have an army with us. We will be safe."

"And once in the mines…"

"Exactly. So let us make the best of this. Build up our strength. Arm ourselves and find where the gold is. Then we can make our move."

The land south of Brocauum was teeming with bandits and deserters. They preyed on the small isolated hamlets and the merchants bringing goods to the forts and new settlements close to the border. It was a hand to mouth existence but at least they were free from the Roman yoke. Their weapons and equipment were so poor that they could not take on soldiers but anything else was fair game. The ten bandits were returning from a fruitless raid on the road between Luguvalium and Brocauum. The Prefect's patrol had prevented them from replenishing their supplies at the Roman's expense. When they saw Drusus and his five men making their way along the lakeside they saw an opportunity to return with plunder. The six horses and whatever food and weapons they might have would be welcome additions to the band's resources. The leader, a deserter from Gaul called Alerix was a little worried that the men looked to be deserters, as they were, for they rode like cavalrymen even though they looked like bandits. However he thought they could be taken as he had the advantage of the woods in which to hide and ambush. His men's bows stood a good chance of taking at least two or even three men out and the others would be overwhelmed by his ten men.

They moved swiftly through the woods, travelling faster than the horsemen who seemed in no hurry. They took up their ambush position and were twenty paces from the lakeside, well hidden by the brush and dead trees. The horsemen came along in a long line and Alerix had placed himself at the end so that he would be the one to initiate the attack with his bow. He had pulled the feathers next to his ear when suddenly the men they were ambushing all slipped to the other side of their horses and the man next to him fell gurgling to his death with an arrow protruding from his neck. Even as he continued his turn to face this new onslaught he saw three more of his men fall to arrows from the unseen foe. Catching a glimpse of a movement he began to turn but the sword from behind sliced though his neck leaving him to wonder as his life blood seeped from him how the hunter had become the hunted,

"Thank you for that Drusus. Your timing was excellent."

As Drusus wiped the blood from the dead deserter from his blade he shrugged. "Thank you and next time someone else can be the bait. They were poor ambushers, we knew where they were the whole time."

"Which is why they deserted; they weren't very good soldiers." Cassius waved from the far end of the line as the last of the bandits was despatched.

"It is a shame we couldn't have taken any of them prisoner."

"I know Metellus but it was too great a risk that one could have escaped and brought others here."

"At least we might have found out if there are others and where they are."

"True but I think from their direction of travel it is south east of here and we are heading west. It is a good job that Rufius has such sharp eyes and spotted them this morning."

Agrippa nodded as he searched the body for weapons and gold. "True he is a good tracker, almost in Gaelwyn's class." He nodded at the dead deserter. "A Gaul by the look of him. He still has some of the auxiliary armour."

"Yes and a couple of others are Brigante. Looks like there is a little army here. As soon as we get to Glanibanta I will send a message to Cursus. If Eboracum can spare them then the Gallic Horse might be able to root them out of their little den in the woods." They led their horses to the lake. "We will camp tonight down there at the end of the lake. It looks like we will have to take watches tonight. This may well be the main route the bandits use."

"They could have caught the engineers."

"No Drusus. There were at least eight armoured legionaries. These ten would have stood no chance against them. I think that we will either find the engineers alive or they ran into a much bigger force than this and we will find their whitening bones."

Decius wondered what lay in store for him when he approached the cave. Tadgh was just leaving when he saw Decius approaching. He deliberately walked at Decius and made no attempt to move out of his way. When Decius moved to the left Tadgh shunted him into the rock wall and as the young man lay on the floor he glared down at him. A disembodied voice from the cave echoed, "Tadgh!" and the Brigante warrior reluctantly carried on walking to the main camp. Rising to his feet and dusting himself off Decius entered the glowing cave. It was the first time he had been in the cave and he was surprised how big it was. There was a large pool of water in the middle and Decius could see a glow from a fire in a smaller cave off to the left. Assuming that was where Morwenna was he made his way nervously towards the glow. Sheepskins and deer pelts lined the alcove in which a naked Morwenna with a naked Maban next to her reclined. The soft glow from the fire made them both appear to be a pulsing pinkish red. Morwenna's long red hair cascaded down to her breasts and she waved him over to her. Maban slid over to allow him to sit between them and Morwenna took his chin in her hand and kissed him long and hard on the lips.

Decius was in a dilemma; it was a pleasurable experience but, as the man, he had normally initiated such lovemaking. The fact they there were no words uttered made it even more disconcerting. When Maban began to undress him and kiss the back of his neck as she did so he stiffened and tried to back away.

"Peace Decius. Relax. Is this not pleasurable?"

"Yes but..."

"Yes but it is not the woman's role to start such love making? This is my land and my rules. Tonight my acolyte and I will pleasure you; each other and you will pleasure us both. Tomorrow night Anchorat will replace Maban. We will do this until we are with child. This is not a discussion it is a command and what did you say before? Your wish is my command, well this is my wish. Accede to it."

Decius found himself naked and between two beautiful women. Aula Sallustius had been a beautiful woman but she had been approaching middle age; these two were perfection with blemish free skin and no sign of any unwanted flesh. The smells in the cave and around the herb fuelled fire were intoxicating and made it easy for him to succumb to the two beautiful women. Even as the thought came into his head he asked himself why he was fighting this. Nothing bad could come from it and how many men would object to two women making love to them? "You are my mistress and I bow to your will."

Maban giggled and Morwenna said huskily, "The bowing will come later."

Chapter 6

Drusus waved from the top of the pass to attract Livius' attention and his column of six men kicked their mounts into action. Cato had chosen the horses well and the journey across to the west had enabled them to train each horse to its new master. They responded instantly to commands and would run all day on the meagre rations they carried. Of course they knew horses and looked after them well. They had acquired some shrivelled apples in Brocauum and the treats had further endeared the masters with their mounts. Racing along the valley bottom horses and riders were as one, enjoying the freedom, however temporary.

Livius reined in his horse, Star, flushed with the pleasure of riding and the beauty of the morning. This life was a total change from the rigid camp building and static patrols of Marcus' Horse. This was almost a pleasure. "Yes Drusus?"

"Found their camp and their trail. It looks like it was wet when they left for their hobnails are still visible in the mud. They are heading west. It looks like you were right it will be Glanibanta."

Turning in his saddle he whistled and soon the other five riders rode in. They had decided to call them section one, two and three. Drusus' patrol was section two and Marius had section three. Drusus and Marius had just naturally taken charge and as all soldiers needed a structure and a hierarchy it seemed to be the best way. "Marius send two of your men back to Brocauum. Tell them of the deserters we killed and that the engineers are heading west. They will then need to return to the legion which should be somewhere near to Morbium I am afraid I can't be any clearer. When they have reported what we have found to the Prefect they should return here. You and the others can make a camp here and rest while we push on to Glanibanta. If we find the engineers we will return and if there is any problem or we need to go further west we will inform you."

Grinning Marius snapped, "Yes Sir!"

Livius shook his head. "I forgot, you love fishing. I suspect you will be sat on the lake until I return."

"No sir, we will patrol and hunt and….. yes sir, I will be fishing."

"Seriously be careful Marius, there are other deserters around and this is the main route. They may come looking for their lost comrades. If they do either hide or come for us."

"I will sir. I won't let you down."

"I never thought that you would Marius."

As the two sections headed off to follow the trail discovered by Drusus, Livius said, "Until we get to Glanibanta we will keep the two sections together. This is getting very close to the place those Brigante fled to after the battle at Morbium."

"If I might suggest a couple of scouts on the flanks then sir?"

"Good idea. Rufius, Decius take the left and right flanks. Scouting. The two younger men grinned and galloped off."

Agrippa snorted. "That is the last we will see of them for a while."

"Yes Agrippa but think of the peace and the quiet."

"There is that sir. That is why you are an officer and I a mere trooper. You think of the bigger picture."

It was pleasant to be riding in the verdant and green valleys of the lakes. "This is good land Drusus. When peace finally comes this would be a good place to raise a family and to farm."

"Don't know about farming sir. There are rocks right below the surface."

"You are right. I remember trying to build a camp. But it is so beautiful around here."

"I suppose it could be used for grazing but it is such an awful place to get to."

"I know which is why this road of the Ninth is so important. I am no engineer Drusus but I do not know why they would come this way. There are more twists and turns than an eel in a trap."

"I know sir unless the optio in charge was eliminating this as a route."

"I can't see that. He would be making a lot of work for himself. Well I suppose we can ask him when we find him."

Drusus looked across to the west and the darkening clouds rising above the wall of rock. If he and his men are still alive."

"Ever the optimist eh Drusus. Come on let's pick up the pace. We may be able to camp at Glanibanta tonight. Always a little safer when you have wooden walls around you."

"I still don't know why it was abandoned sir, twice."

"Me neither. From what Prefect Marcus told me a lot of good men died to build it in the first place and if we had had men here in the last rebellion then even more lives would have been saved. I am not sure that Rome wants Britannia."

"Don't let the Emperor's spies hear you sir."

Livius looked at Drusus wondering if he was joking but the trooper had a serious look on his face. "Drusus if I cannot trust these men then I am a poor judge of men and would deserve any punishment Rome could mete out but all of us are from Britannia Drusus, perhaps we have a prejudiced view. It is our home and we want to hold it."

"Yes sir but Prefect Marcus and Decurion Gaius, they came from across the sea and they love Britannia as much as we do."

"One day Drusus, Rome will come to regard Britannia as a frontier worth defending and protecting. Until then it is up to us."

They managed to reach the camp before dark and the sharp eyes of Rufius picked up the trail of the engineers. "Looks like they camped here and then headed west."

Drusus and Livius looked at the tracks. Metellus knelt down. "There were others here, not Romans and they came after the engineers."

"That does not bode well for we have seen no people apart from the deserters."

"Yes sir and it looks like whoever it was trailed them."

"Well done Metellus. Well we can do no more tonight but I think we will all take a turn at being on watch. It will only be an hour each. My section first Drusus. Rufius first hour, then Agrippa, Decius, Cassius and then you wake me. I'll wake you Drusus."

"You don't have to stand a watch sir. You are an officer."

"Yes Drusus but remember we are making up the rules as we go along. I am not as tired as the rest and that means I do not need the sleep as much as the rest do so we all share the hardship. Besides it is good to endure a little discomfort."

"Then you joined the right army sir."

"Thank you Metellus your wit is always appreciated."

Livius regretted his decision when Cassius shook his shoulder. "You can go back to sleep if you like sir, Drusus said…"

"No and thank you Cassius. Anything to report?"

"No sir quiet as. Not even an owl."

"Good. Get some sleep. I have a feeling tomorrow could be a long day."

He turned away from the glowing embers of the fire to accustom his eyes to the night and within a few heartbeats he could see things clearer even in the darkening gloom. It was a clear cold night and he wrapped his cloak tightly about him. He wandered over to the horse lines; he knew that they would be tight and secure but a horseman afoot was a waste of time as Decurion Princeps Decius Flavius had always told him. As he came back to the fire he looked up at the wall of rock and rubbed his eyes. It seemed that there was a glow from half way up the rock. Perhaps it was his eyes or imagination. He rubbed his eyes and looked again. Just as suddenly as it had appeared, it disappeared. He was now glad that he had chosen a watch for that was an anomaly and, after they had found the engineers, he would have to investigate.

Livius gathered them all around the dead fire the following morning as they chewed their biscuits and ate their dried hard tack. "Today will be an important day. We may find the engineers or at least get a better idea of where they went but last night I saw a glow up there. He pointed away to the rocky outcrop peering above the tree line. Did anyone else see it?"

Metellus nodded. "I thought I saw something but it only appeared for a short time and then vanished. " He shrugged. "I couldn't work out what it was and put it down to my imagination. If you had not said anything then I would have forgotten it."

"The same thing happened with me. It is an important lesson for all of us. We are Exploratores. Nothing is irrelevant and nothing should be ignored."

"Sorry sir."

"Nothing to be sorry about Metellus. I nearly ignored it but we are all learning here. What we do will be a model for everyone who follows us. Remember that."

Half under his breath Agrippa muttered, "If we ever do get back."

"Thank you Agrippa your confidence in my command overwhelms me."

"No sir I didn't mean I…" When everyone, including Livius, burst out laughing he stormed off muttering to his horse. "A baby sitter that's what I am. Looking after children and they aren't even mine!"

"Right I want two of your lads out scouting today Drusus and keep your ears open as well as your eyes. The red glow came from over there," he pointed north, "so that will be a danger area for us all and today we wear helmets. There are no locals which means that if we meet anyone it will in all likelihood be an enemy. If you want your mail on it would not be a bad idea."

"You wearing it sir?"

71

Livius looked at the young men who depended on him and his decision making. It was a responsibility. "Yes Cassius I am." He smiled as each man dismounted and retrieved his mail from the pack animals.

The two pack horses moved much better without their loads and the two sections made good time along the trail which wound around the edge of the lake. After their noon rest Livius changed the scouts, just to keep them fresh. "Looks like more men were following here sir."

"Right Rufius take the point and follow the trail."

The site of the slaughter was obvious to the keen eyes of the patrol. Despite the Brigante attempts to mask the massacre there was just too much evidence in the darkened and bloodstained grass.

"Well Drusus at least we know where the engineers ended their survey."

"Yes sir but where are they? Prisoners? There are no bodies, or even bits of bodies to be seen."

"Sir!"

"Yes Metellus?"

"Up here there is a trail heading west. Looks like something was dragged and carried. I can see mule prints as well."

"Right Drusus, take your section along the trail. My section we will ride parallel but to the north. Watch for tracks and be aware of ambushes from the north."

The tension was so palpable they thought they could see and taste it in the air. Somewhere ahead was either their engineer patrol or their enemies and they were a long way from help. The trees and bushes which had seemed so alive with birds and squirrels the previous day now seemed foreboding and threatening as though each one was hiding an enemy or a dark secret. Even their mounts seemed apprehensive and picked their way gingerly along the trail. The one good aspect was that it was largely straight which meant they were heading somewhere. The land rose a little and Rufius, who was on point gestured down to where Livius could see Drusus walking his horse down to a small lake.

By the time Livius' section had reached the side of the still and shining water Drusus was wading out. "Found something?"

"I think we have the engineers, sir." Drusus dragged the naked corpse from the shallow waters into which it had been thrown. It was the optio who had been the heaviest of the patrol and the Brigante had not managed to throw him far enough into the lake. Drusus pointed. "You can see shapes sir, probably the others shall we get them?"

Livius knew that it was his decision. While they were helping the dead they were vulnerable and could be attacked. He saw a small hill rising to the east about two hundred paces away. "Decius and Rufius get on that hill and keep watch. Let me know if you see anything and I mean anything." He dismounted and began to take off his helmet and mail. "The rest of you, let's be quick about this. We will give them an honourable funeral but I don't want us to join them so soon."

Working as a team with a common purpose to do for others what they hoped their comrades would do for them, they dragged out the naked and mutilated bodies. All of them had had their manhood removed and some of the younger legionaries had had their eyes and noses removed. The hardened looks on the faces of his men was not lost on Livius. They would remember this and they would fight even harder.

When the bodies were laid out they all looked to Livius. A funeral pyre would have been the most obvious choice but it would attract attention. "We will have to bury them. Drusus get your section to bring stones and rocks. My section we will dig one grave and they will spend eternity together."

73

Working with a common purpose they cut the turf with their swords and gathered together a pile of stone and rocks. They were soon able to lay the men together in a sad line. Once the stones were laid on top and the turf replaced it looked like just another bump in the land. It would, at least, keep wild animals off them. They stood in a half circle as Livius spoke words over them. "You were faithful unto death and you will be together in the hereafter. May the Allfather welcome you and we will see you when our time comes brothers."

Turning to his horse Livius began to put on his mail and helmet. "Now let us see where they went after this." He whistled and waved for the two scouts to join them. When they did so he addressed them all. "Normally the Brigante like to take heads and show the world what tough bastards they are. Here they didn't. They have something to hide. We will follow the trail carefully. Our job is not to fight an enemy but to find him. No death or glory to revenge those poor bastards. Whoever killed them is not to be underestimated. Even engineering legionaries are tough."

"Romans! Horsemen and they are following the trail of the others."

The sentry had seen the column of riders as they left the fort. Tadgh had a sentry placed where he could see the fort and yet not be seen. Since they had acquired Decius' horses it made communication much better.

"Take two men and find them but do not let them see you."

Tadgh raced into the cave. "Majesty there are Roman horsemen nearby. Do we fight?"

She slowly shook her head. "No get Decius' men to drive most of the mules down the path towards the two lakes. Stampede them if necessary and then bring everyone else into the cave with their arms. Perhaps we can make them believe we fled north."

74

Decius was in the cave. "You will have to send Centurion and one of your more reliable men otherwise my other men might just run."

"Is that a bad thing? You told me you could not trust them. Do not tell them that the Romans are here give them some gold and tell them to take the mules north to Brocauum to buy grain."

"But if we give them gold and the mules."

"Exactly they will just go and when the Romans follow them we will leave and find another base."

"Where will I get gold?" asked Decius innocently.

She reached under the sheepskins of the bed and brought out one of the packs. "Give them this and pretend that we trust them."

The mercenaries looked slyly at each other when Decius gave them their instructions. "Take the mules and head north past the two lakes. Turn east at the main road and head for Brocauum. There is enough money to buy enough grain for the animals and for us to grind for flour. Do not let me down. Since Scarface you have not betrayed me. Do not start now!"

Protesting their innocence they took the gold and began driving the mules across the shale and stone which littered the hillside below the cave. The mules were as keen as their drovers and, without the gold bags they skittered and slid their way down. The mercenaries rode six of the biggest mules and drove the rest before them. Decius smiled to himself. They were getting away as fast as possible. If the Romans came from the lake, as Tadgh had said, then they would not be able to miss the tracks of the mules. Even as he helped to gather their belongings and secrete them in the cave, Decius wondered just what was in the lake. Could that be where they had hidden the gold? When the Romans had either gone or been disposed of he would have to go to the lake and find out. According to Tadgh the Roman cavalry had been on their way to the lake and that was over two miles away. They had time.

Livius and the patrol spread out on a wide front to make sure that they could find the trail. Whoever had killed the legionaries had taken the engineer's mule and its distinctive hoof prints were easy to spot. They were keen to avoid an ambush and followed at what to Livius seemed like a snail's pace but he knew was the right speed, cautious. The engineers had been killed some time ago and the only reason they could follow the trail was that it had not rained since the massacre.

Rufius raised his arm and Livius walked slowly to join him. The young scout spoke quietly but confidently. "Look sir. There are more hoof prints. We have a herd and they have been moved recently. He picked up a still steaming piece of mule shit.

"I'll take your word for it, Rufius."

"Been round animals my entire life sir. And it seems to me that this is where the glow was last night."

Livius looked around. The boy could be right. He could see, about half a mile away, what looked to be an overhang, and possibly a cave. He signalled for the others to join them. "Looks like they have left recently. Perhaps last night..."

Rufius shook his head. "No more than an hour ago sir. We've got 'em."

"They have mules so they will be mounted. The trail is so wide that even a blind man could follow it but they could be setting up an ambush so be careful."

Rufius breathed a sigh of relief when he saw the wide swathe of open grass before him. There was nowhere for an enemy to hide and the land slowly dropped away to a large rocky shelf which was below a steep rocky face. It was quite obvious to the young scout which way the mules had gone for there were many of the rocks overturned showing a darker face. The scout halted below the cliff. There looked to be a ledge which jutted out and could hide enemies. He unslung his bow and notched an arrow as he waited for the rest of the patrol to catch up.

"Well done Rufius. See anything? "

"No sir. Just not taking any chances." He gestured with his head. "You can see which way they went. "

"Right, let's follow and then we can come back here afterwards. I don't want these bastards to escape."

Livius' words carried up to the cave although they were distorted by the rock face. They confirmed Tadgh's worst fears. The Romans would return. He would suggest that they ambush the patrol to the Queen but he was not certain that she would want to take the risk. What Tadgh did not want was to traipse around this wild land with three women and a baby but that was the future. He leaned forward to hear when they left.

Cassius took over the scouting duties and his keen eye soon spotted the movement in the distance. "There they are sir. I can see them. There must be fifty mules at least."

As the decurion crested the rise he could see them for himself and the riders who were urging them along at a great pace. "Drusus they are riding along the far side of the lake. You keep on after them and I will take my section to the left of the lake that way we can cut them off."

"Right sir."

"And Drusus."

"Yes sir?"

"Try to get a couple of prisoners but take no risks we don't know how many others are hiding in these hills."

The mercenaries felt that they had pulled a fast one with Decius. They had no intention of heading for Brocauum, instead they would continue north and bypass Luguvalium. They would sell the mules, share the profits and then go their separate ways. None of them owed any loyalty to any man but they shared a need for self preservation. They had more chance of survival together. It was Ban who led them now. He was the biggest and certainly the toughest of the last of the mercenaries. He was not a stupid man and knew that there was some reason why they had let them leave so profitably. He could discern no reason but the fact that they wanted them to go to Brocauum, with a Roman garrison meant that was the one place they would not go.

The mules were slowing and Taile shouted over, "We should slow or even rest, we cannot maintain this pace."

Ban shook his head angrily. "No we push them on. If any die it matters not. We need to get far away from that bitch as soon as possible." All of them feared the Queen and her powers. Fighting men was one thing but fighting magic was quite another. Even had they not been given the opportunity they had, all of them would have deserted Decius sooner rather than later. Ban glanced to his left and the open expanse of the lake. To his horror he saw sunlight glinting off helmets and the helmets were atop horses and moving parallel to them. Romans! No wonder they had been given the gold; they were bait. He cursed Morwenna and Decius to Hades but he now had to hurry even more. "Roman cavalry to your left!"

The fear spread through the men like wildfire and they whipped their slow moving mules even more. Ban now understood why they had not been given horses. They wanted them to be caught. He loosened the sword in its scabbard. He hoped that the cavalry was not the auxiliary cavalry with the bows and javelins or any stand they made would be a short one. He could see the head of the lake approaching and saw that the Romans would have to cross a stream and a swamp that, perhaps, would give them the edge. "Take the mules to the right, away from the lake!" A plan was forming in his mind. When they reached the head of the lake he would leave the exhausted mules and just take the one with the bag of gold. They could then ride up through the woods and abandon their mules when the going became too difficult. The high peak could be crossed by men but not horses. The Roman cavalry would have to slow down to negotiate the mules and that might just give them the time they needed.

Already the first of the mules were entering the woods and slowing down. "Ride through them!" His men needed no urging as they saw what they assumed were the scouts of a larger cavalry force hurtling towards them. The mules began to struggle as they climbed up the steep banks of the woods and that suited Ban for mules were better at climbing than cavalry mounts. It was as they cleared the tree line and scrambled along a rocky bank that Ban saw the second column; they had been flanked but all was still not lost for soon they would leave the mules and climb on foot. When Ban saw the first mule stumble he yelled. "Leave the mules and climb on foot." His men obeyed instantly and, grabbing the bag of gold Ban led them up the rocky slope. They could all feel the air being ripped from their throats and their legs soon burned with the exertion. As he glanced over his shoulder he saw that his plan had, at least in part, worked and the cavalry scouts too were now afoot.

Livius had to admire the ingenuity of the enemy who had conspired to thwart his plans. They could not know how fit the Exploratores were nor that their bows could reach men two hundred paces away. Livius took his bow from his shoulder and saw that his men were doing the same. He drew an arrow and halted. As soon as he shot his arrow into the air ten others followed. One lucky arrow hit the man who had climbed the highest and he tumbled down taking the man who had the large bag over his shoulder down with him and the two tumbled down the slope. A second man was mortally pierced by two arrows whilst a third was hit in the leg. The other two continued to climb but as the first three had all been hit these were the closest to the Romans.

"Drusus take your men and secure the prisoners we'll take these two." The last two were now panicking and increasingly lost their footing. Once again the men of Decius' section drew their bows and this time all six arrows found their mark and the two of them died instantly. "Cassius search them and get their weapons. Agrippa; help him. The rest of you down the hill."

He turned in time to see one of Drusus' men reach the wounded and unwounded man. Perhaps he thought they were both wounded but his lack of care cost him his life as the unwounded man plunged his sword into his throat and he took off down the hill. The rest of Drusus' section drew their bows and the killer fell to the ground with four arrows in him.

Drusus was kneeling over the boy who had died when Livius reached him. "I am sorry Drusus. Our first casualty."

"He was just a boy sir. I'll kill the other bastard!"

Livius grabbed his arm. "No you won't Drusus, you will carry the boy down and bury him while I question the prisoner." Nodding, Drusus picked up the corpse and walked slowly and sadly down the hill.

When Livius found the prisoner he was still alive but only just. The arrow had entered his back and looked to be in his stomach, a death wound. During the fall he had also shattered both his legs. The man looked at Livius his eyes pleading. "The pain. Have you anything for the pain?"

"Sorry just water. Here." He gave him his water skin and watched as the man swallowed a draught. It did not help the pain indeed it seemed to aggravate it. "You are going to die. You know that?" The man looked at his legs and nodded. "You have two choices. Answer my questions and I will give you a soldier's death or else I leave you here to be eaten by the animals. Which is it to be?"

The man owed no allegiance to a leader who had used him as bait and as he nodded he coughed up blood and croaked, "Questions."

"Who are you?"

"Guard for the gold."

"What gold?"

"The gold my master stole from the mountains."

"And who is your master?"

"Decius Sallustius."

Livius almost froze with shock and anger but he knew he only had a short time as the man's life was rapidly ebbing away and he needed his questions answered before the man became unconscious. "Where is your camp?" The man's eyes closed and Livius had to shake him. "The camp where is it?"

"Cave near the rocks."

"Who else is there?"

"Witch queen."

Before Livius could ask any more questions the wounded man coughed up a mighty pool of blood and then fell unconscious at Livius' feet. He would answer no more questions. "I am true to my word. " He drew his sword and slit the man's throat. Walking down the hill his mind was filled with so many thoughts it was a wonder he did not fall down the steep slope. His brother was here and his mortal enemy Morwenna. The one question he had not asked was how many men did she have?

Chapter 7

As they watched the Romans race after the fleeing mules both Decius and Tadgh were working out how best to escape and the quickest method. Morwenna had also ventured to the ledge to watch the flight of the bait. She seemed satisfied with what she saw. The two rivals for Morwenna's affection faced her, both waiting for the other to make a suggestion so that it could be mocked and their own idea accepted. The High Priestess of the Mother did not allow them the time for she knew what she intended and had made her own decision.

"We outnumber them. Prepare an ambush and when we have weakened them further we will leave for the coast."

Tadgh looked at Decius and then back at the Queen. "But the gold?"

"We will take it with us. We still have some mules and your men have strong backs. It is but one day to the coast."

Decius gestured towards the now unseen Romans. "These are Romans how can we weaken them?"

"They will not expect an ambush and I can count, Decius there were only eleven warriors. We outnumber them two to one and if you noticed they had neither shields nor spears. This is not Marcus' Horse."

Now that the decision was made Tadgh threw himself into the task of making it work. "You take your two lads and I will send Brennus and some of mine." He pointed to the part of the path which curved below the ledge. "There are lots of stones there. Build a wall and when they are below you then you push the rocks on to them. I will wait in the woods on the other side of the path with my men and we will trap them."

"If they come that way. They may not be as stupid as you think."

"Brennus and some of my lads will wait up the hill in case they try to flank us. You and your two brutes should be able to push down a few rocks eh?"

Decius resented having to take orders from a tattooed, long haired barbarian but he had no other suggestion to make. Whilst he could fight he did not have a strategic mind or an understanding of war. The time for a confrontation with Tadgh would come but it would be when he knew where the gold was and they were safely away from the Romans. "Very well." He turned to Morwenna. "And when we get to the coast, what then?"

"You have too many doubts Decius. Trust me for I see beyond the seas. There is a sanctuary across the water."

"Not Mona. The Romans have a garrison there."

"No not the Holy Island but we will return there one day. Get on with your wall building we have work to do." With that enigmatic comment she disappeared into the cave with Maban and Anchorat.

"Centurion, Tiny! We have a wall to build." There were many stones left from the quarrying of the stone and, with Brennus and his nine men, the wall was soon man high. Brennus and his men had not spoken a word and they trotted off to guard the flank as soon as it was completed. Decius had to admire Tadgh's plan; the wall effectively appeared like part of the cliff and, if they had not been there before, would assume it was a natural feature. The only other approach was through the woods up a steep path and, there too, rolling rocks would disrupt any assault.

Centurion wandered over and offered Decius a piece of mule meat roasted the previous night. "Well it looks like we all have a bigger share of the gold we buried."

Decius pointed to the far hillside where they could see mules milling around. "They could escape."

Centurion snorted. "Those maggots were worm meat as soon as they left here. Roman cavalry in the open can catch anyone.

He," Centurion pointed at Tadgh who was toiling below them to make a barrier against horses, "knows what he is about. Even a turma couldn't dislodge us from here and those eleven men stand no chance."

Decius had to respect the old soldier's view. "But they will be armoured."

"So are we but they have no shields and their horses will be blown. This is a steep hill. No we will beat them and we will escape but where will we be going afterwards do you think?"

"Across the sea somewhere. Away from Rome. I am not sure. Caledonia? Scotland?"

"From what these Brigante told me the Queen is not welcome in Caledonia."

"Ireland then. Allfather but that is a wild country."

"Aye and a poor one. A good place to buy warriors perhaps." Decius nodded. Perhaps this witch queen knew her business.

Livius gathered his nine men to the head of the lake. They now had three spare horses having buried their only loss. All the way down the fells he had been remembering the ill advised pursuit by Prefect Julius of the man who had betrayed and killed his brother. It had resulted, ultimately, in the destruction of Marcus' Horse as well as the death of Decurion Macro. As much as Livius wanted revenge and wanted to capture his brother he was mindful of his responsibilities. He would not hazard his command for a personal vendetta. "Drusus, take one man and two of the spare horses. Find Marius and ask him to meet us at the cave. You ride and find the legion. Tell the prefect that we have found the engineers, Morwenna and the man who stole the Emperor's gold. Have your man go to Brocauum and give the same information to Centurion Cursus."

"What will you do sir?" Drusus knew of Decius' brother and worried that his superior might do something stupid.

"We don't know how many they have so we will do what Exploratores are supposed to do and follow. This is our first real lesson Drusus. We no long fight, we find. Now go, time is of the essence."

"May the Allfather be with you." He and his chosen man stripped the supplies from the two horses and headed swiftly south towards Drusus.

Decius looked at his section and the two troopers from Drusus' section. "Cassius you take the two lads from Drusus' section and back track the mules to this cave the man spoke of. Do not approach it, just find it."

"You think they will be waiting?"

"Cassius, we have fought this witch before. She is like a snake. Would you put your hand in a hole where you thought there was a snake? No. and neither will we. All we have to do is to find the snake and watch it. I will head to the." He pointed at the long ridge which rose above the lakeside. "There we can't be ambushed and we can look down upon them. I will use the mirror to signal you. Three flashes will mean retreat to Glanibanta and five mean join us."

"Just two choices then?"

"It is just part of the learning process Cassius. We need to work out a way of communicating and when this is over it will be one of my priorities. Two flashes is an acknowledgement that the message is understood."

Nodding Cassius rode off leaving Livius and his men the hard slog up the hill to the top of the ridge. He took them on the far side of the hill so that only their heads were visible and would not be seen from below. The cave was hidden from view because of the overhang and the best place to see it was from across the valley at the same level. As none of the Romans had ever been on the slopes on the other side they had no idea where the cave was situated. The decurion hoped he had impressed on Cassius the

85

need for caution. They had no idea how big the rebel army was although Livius suspected that it was small or they would have been attacked earlier. The Queen had been at the cave since the rebellion and Livius was under no illusions, it would be fortified and defended. The woman had cunning, just as her mother had had, as both Macro and Decius Flavius had discovered at the cost of their lives. Below them, by the lake Cassius and his two companions went in and out of sight as they negotiated trees, rocks and around headlands but Livius made sure they kept pace with them. It was important that they arrive simultaneously.

At the cave the progress of Cassius was also being observed. "I can only see three of them. You don't think those maggots killed the rest do you?"

Centurion snorted, "If they killed one it would be a miracle. No these Romans are being cautious. The others will appear believe me."

Decius threw a stone to attract Tadgh's attention. When the Brigante looked around Decius held up three fingers and pointed to the lake. Tadgh nodded to show he understood. The Brigante warrior would not make the mistake of underestimating these Romans. He hoped they would come up the path but he knew that they might not be that lucky. He scanned the skyline. If he were the Roman leader he would come from the heights. Of course the overhang from the cave meant that it could only be assaulted from the front and his men could prevent that. Tadgh knew, however that they could make life difficult for those in the cave if they did control the ridge.

Brennus and his men felt exposed. He had chosen a small hollow just above the path down to the cave which afforded them a little shelter and made them difficult to see but if the horsemen rode towards them then his small band would be out numbered. He had made it clear to his men that, if they saw the horses, their job was to retreat to Tadgh who had other plans for the enemy. He was confident that the horses would not be able to climb down the steep path and they would be safe. His sharpest eared scout heard them before he saw them and he pointed, like a hunting dog. Brennus signalled the men to slither backwards. He had already identified a better place to attack them and that was where the fell top path twisted around the rocky side of the cave. It was very steep and would have to be traversed gingerly even by foot soldiers and, more importantly could only take one horse at a time. It would be a killing ground.

Rufius Verena and Decius Galba, as the youngest and keenest scouts, were on point. They were ten paces apart. It was the keen eyes of Rufius who saw the Brigante making their way down the hill and he held up his arm and pointed forward. Livius trotted up with the others. Decius Galba, who was ever reckless, galloped his horse on, ignoring Livius' standing orders for he was keen to catch one of the Brigante and show his courage.

Livius cursed. "Damn the boy." He could not risk a shout in case they had not heard Decius but he would have to support the foolish pursuit. He had planned on scouting afoot when closer but Decius had taken that decision from him. Decius leaned forward in his saddle his sword held out. Suddenly the sky opened and his mount slithered and slipped to a halt, falling on its haunches as it crashed into the hollow. While the stop saved the lives of both man and beast it made them an easy target for the waiting Brigante who fired their arrows at the young trooper. His mail and helmet saved his life for the arrows bounced off. One struck him in the forearm and he yelled in pain as he wheeled his mount around. His horse needed no urging to flee the storm of arrows and he reared up as one lucky shot caught him close to his tail.

Livius halted the patrol in a line and drew their bows when they saw the wounded trooper racing back. "Steady lads and shoot over Decius." Some of the more eager Brigante started to follow Decius but a volley of arrows dissuaded them and Decius made it safely to the patrol.

"Sorry sir. Forgot your orders."

"I will chew you out later. Metellus see to him." In the absence of a capsarius Metellus doubled as medical orderly and doctor. While Agrippa saw to the horse Metellus began to bind the wounded arm. "Well we know where they are. You stay here while I go to signal Cassius."

Taking his sword from its scabbard and polishing it on the cloak which was over Star's neck he rode to the skyline. He saw Cassius looking up at the skyline and the noises there. One of Drusus' men was on point and the other close behind him. Livius flashed the sword into the sun and the light glinting attracted Cassius' attention and he stopped. It saved his life. The other two continued forward and suddenly an avalanche descended on them as the trap was sprung. Neither the horses nor the riders stood a chance on the steep slope. They were swept down the hill as bigger and bigger rocks crashed down on them. When the noise and the rocks had finished the four bodies could been seen below them. They were undoubtedly dead.

Livius flashed the sword three times and was gratified to see two in return. Cassius backed his horse away from the blocked path and, as soon as he could, he turned around and galloped away. The arrows which followed him were fired from too great a distance and fell harmlessly behind him. "Right we know where the cave is. Rufius, find us a safe way down to the lake. We will see if we can see the cave from lower down. When we get to the lake Agrippa, take Decius to the fort and wait for Cassius although I think he will be there before you."

"But sir…" Decius Galba began.

Agrippa silenced him. "If you don't shut your mouth I'll stitch it shut. Listen to the decurion, unlike you he knows what he is doing."

"Sorry sir."

"Listen son we haven't got the luxury of thirty men. We have a handful and every one of you is valuable. We have no more spare horses and we are many miles from help. We have to learn but learn quickly."

Morwenna appeared pleased. "We now know where they are."

"Aye I have told Brennus to leave two of his men by the cliff top but I don't think they will try that way again. I have four men watching the lower path. That is where they will come next time."

"It will take them some time to negotiate the hill and find the path. It is time to take the gold. We leave at dusk."

Both Tadgh and Decius were taken aback. "But the Romans are still there."

"Yes Tadgh and we have seen their numbers. Two more lie dead a third lies wounded. Do you fear six men on horses? We have one minor wound. There are nearly thirty of us."

Decius murmured, "But we have three women and a baby."

Morwenna turned on him, her eyes angry and she hissed at him. "Never doubt me or my women. We have killed more men than you my preening cockerel." Tadgh hid a smile as Decius physically shrank from her attack. "Now get the gold and load the mules." Turning back to Tadgh she spat, "We have one journey to make. To Itunocelum and then we take a boat. I do not care if they follow us. They cannot stop us and once we are at sea they will have no idea where we have gone. By this time tomorrow we will be safe."

Morwenna was right and it was late afternoon by the time Livius and his two remaining scouts reached the path. They could see the overhang and knew where the cave was from that. The path invited them up to the cave but Livius knew it was an invitation to death. The dead troopers and horses were a reminder and his men could see their bodies on the slopes above them. Any burial and honours would have to wait until the enemy had departed. He turned to Rufius and Metellus. In many ways he could not have a better pair of companions for Metellus was the most intelligent and thought of his men whilst Rufius was the quickest and undoubtedly the best tracker. He led them away from the path and dismounted. "Take off your helmets and blacken your faces with the soil." They each tied their mounts securely to a tree. Livius had toyed with the idea of hobbling them but he worried that, if they needed a quick escape that would slow them down.

He pointed to the left. "We are going up through the trees that way. The rocks where the bodies are is too steep and besides the rocks would alert them. The path will be watched and I think we have the best chance through those trees. Rufius you have the sharpest ears and eyes, you take the right, closest to the path. Metellus take the left. Keep your swords sheathed we will need both hands to negotiate the slope and remember we are not here to kill, we are here to find." He was gratified to see a nod from each man. "We will wait until it is twilight and then go up. Eat while we wait." Prefect Marcus had impressed on the young Livius that a man on a full stomach fought better than a hungry man and any edge he could get, he would take.

The dark was behind them as they began their ascent. The last glow of the setting sun illuminated the ridgeline highlighting any movement. Livius had waited far enough from the cave to prevent their discovery but it also meant that he had no idea what was going on. Vague doubts had plagued him. Were they coming for him? Were the Brigante scouts, who knew the land far better than he even now filtering through the woods? It had been relief which had flooded through him when they finally began to make their way through the pine forest. They were careful to avoid making noise on the soft pine floor but that meant that their progress was, perforce, slow.

Rufius held up his hand, a lighter shade in the dark and they paused. As Livius peered ahead he could see a lightening which indicated that the woods were ending and they were close to the rocky face. Gesturing for them to remain where they were Rufius crept forward and suddenly disappeared from view. Livius was reminded of Gaelwyn who had this disconcerting habit of disappearing and then, just as suddenly, reappearing. Rufius did the same. Livius had counted in his head when the boy was away and he had reached almost five hundred before he did so.

"They've gone. There is no one up there."

Even though it was dark the area around the cave entrance was lighter than the woods. Leaving Metellus on watch Rufius and Livius entered the cave and the decurion risked lighting a brush torch from his tinderbox. As soon as he entered the cave with his lighted torch he could see why the glow in the sky had appeared and then vanished when watching from Glanibanta; someone had been moving around in the cave.

"It's enormous sir and look," Rufius raced towards the back where it looked as though an enormous wall had once stood.

"I wonder if that is where they had the gold the prisoner mentioned?" All around they could see the discarded detritus which followed a hasty escape.

The sharp eyes of Rufius spotted something and called Livius over. "Sir, they have a baby."

"How in the name of the Allfather do you know that?"

Rufius grinned. "I have six sisters and trust me sir, this is baby shit." He held his torch over it. " It has a lovely green quality don't you think?"

Shaking his head he said, "I'll take your word for it. You seem the section expert on shit whether it be baby or mule. Nothing left in here to see, let's find their trail outside." When they came out

91

and extinguished the light their world became suddenly black. "Anything Metellus?"

"No sir. It is as black as a witch's heart out here."

"Hardly the best simile Metellus."

"No sir but the most appropriate."

"Right Rufius go and find the trail. Metellus ride back and bring the others here. I will fetch our horses. We are camping here tonight."

The next day began with a damp fog which clung to the fell sides and their clothes. Their horses looked like spectres cloaked in white. Livius had had his men up before dawn. Not only did he have his section back together he also had three more men, Marius and three of his section. Most importantly they had a fit horse for Decius who had had the good grace to take the ribbing and teasing from the others."I passed the message on to the centurion sir and he was going to send patrols into the woods. Other than that it has been quiet."

Livius felt much more confident now that he had ten troopers once more. The trail was quite clear; the mules and so many humans could not fail but to leave a trail. "What worries me sir is that they don't seem bothered. They are not hiding the trail."

"I know Metellus but, at the moment I can't see where they could ambush us." The land was a wide valley but Livius could see a col high up in the hills where he would have to be more circumspect. "At least we must be travelling faster than they are let's push on."

Marius and his section were taking the scouting role as their horses had had a good rest. As they approached the high pass Livius sent Rufius with Marius to scout for an ambush. He was relieved when they waved back that it was safe. Passing the top Metellus observed, "Good place for a fort sir. I reckon if those poor sods hadn't been slaughtered we would have found them here laying out the foundations."

92

"You are probably right Metellus," Livius realised that the Exploratores could make life easier for the engineers by finding such sites more quickly than the foot soldiers.

"Sir come and look at this."

Marius shout brought the rest up the last incline at a trot. At the top they beheld the sight of the sea not ten miles away. The sun had burned through the fog and it was a gloriously sunny day. "Not the view sir, look there. Your man Rufius has good eyes."

When Livius shaded his eyes against the sun and focussed he could see, in the distance the column snaking its way along the rough path. "Well done, we have found her."

"Yes sir but one of my lads, Julius knows the area. There is a port there. I reckon the bitch is leaving Britannia."

Livius heard someone mutter," Good riddance."

Shaking his head sadly the decurion said, "I am afraid not. She has a fortune in gold and could go to Ireland or Caledonia and bring back an even bigger army."

"Yes sir but we only have ten men we couldn't stop them."

"You are right Drusus. It would take a turma and that is just what we haven't got. Let us push on and hope that there are no boats for her."

The pursuing Romans had been seen but it did not worry Morwenna. "Even if they were a hundred paces behind us I would not worry. No we are safe and now that your men have found the boats we are safe." Six of Tadgh's men under Brennus had ridden through the night and secured the boats beached on the sand in the small settlement. Any question of ownership was soon settled at the point of a sword.

Tadgh and Decius had declared a silent truce on the trek from the cave as they knew they would have to work together, for a while at least, and they had discussed what might happen. It fell to Tadgh to broach the subject and risk the wrath of the red head. "Where are we going then your majesty? Ireland or Caledonia?"

She beamed triumphantly, "Neither. I will tell you once we are at sea for I do not want the Romans to know where we are going."

"You can trust us."

Her eyes widened and she snapped. "And you will obey me! You will find out once we are on board."

The boats were drawn up on the sandy beach but even landsmen like Tadgh and Decius could see that there would be no room for the mules. The Queen did not seem concerned by that. "We only need the gold. Leave the mules as payment for the use of the boats."

When the headman had that explained to him he became slightly mollified but the death of three of his young men by Brennus, had made him bitter. He could see that he would have to go along with these invaders but once he had taken them away he would let the Romans know where they were. This was a time when he needed the Romans.

With two villagers in each boat to sail them, the ten vessels were fully laden. The headman, in whose boat Morwenna, her acolytes and Tadgh were travelling, expressed his doubts."If we hit a strong sea up near Caledonia…"

"Do not worry, we are not sailing far."

Shrugging he cast off. He assumed she wanted conveying a little way down the coast. He too had seen the pursuing Romans and thought that she was merely escaping her enemies. When he returned home he would soon tell them. "Which course then?"He spoke dismissively to the young red head. What did women know of the sea?

Her answer silenced him. "South west. There is an island. Do you know it?"

"Mona?"

She slapped him hard across the face and as he stiffened he felt Tadgh's knife at his throat. "Do not play games with me or you will die. You know there is an isle closer than that."

94

He nodded his face reddening, "You mean Manavia?"

"Yes land us on the north east coast and then go home suitably rewarded."

Back at the settlement Livius watched the flotilla heading southwest. Marius nodded, "Ireland then?"

"Possibly. We will remain here today. The headman's wife said he should be back tomorrow. We will wait here until then. When we know where they have gone we will return to Brocauum. Hopefully Drusus will be there with the legion."

The refugees were mightily relieved that the voyage was a short one and thanked the Allfather for their safe arrival. As a villager from each boat held them against the gentle bumping of the tide they disembarked. Unseen by the headman Tadgh nodded to one man in each boat and, when almost all of the passengers had reached dry land two warriors slit the throats of the sailors. No one would tell the tale of the voyage of the Brigante Queen and her gold. As the stripped bodies floated away on the tide, the boats were drawn up high on to the beach and Morwenna began her journey. The first steps to reclaiming her throne.

Livius waited three days for the return of the headman and would have waited longer had not the tide brought in the body of one of the villagers, a young boy of ten, his gashed throat seeming to grin mockingly at his mother who had lost her husband and her only son in such a short time. Her sobs wracked her body, her life now in ruins.

"Well the bitch and my brother have escaped but we will meet again. Let us return to the legion and report our failure."

Metellus shook his head. "No sir, not failure but success."

"How do you make a success out of this cock up, Metellus?"

"Simple sir. Our job was to find the engineers and locate the Queen. We found both of them and as a bonus you know where the Emperor's gold is. Remember sir we are not Marcus' Horse, we are Exploratores."

Part Two
The Deserters and the Irish
Chapter 8

The days were drawing in again when Decurion Princeps
Livius Lucullus Sallustius of the Exploratores attached to the
Ninth Legion approached the office of the Prefect and Tribune.
As he waited outside for his meeting he reflected on the past
months. Metellus had been correct; his superiors had regarded the
patrol as a huge success. As Prefect Fulvius had told him, "At
least we know where the bitch is, and that is not in Britannia."

Livius realised that he was probably worrying too much. His
superiors knew far more about the wider picture but he couldn't
help wondering what mischief she could get up to with the gold
she had at her disposal. The Prefect had been less happy with the
loss of the gold but he placed the blame for that on the Gallic
Auxiliaries who had been sent to the mine to intercept his brother
before he had fled.

Still his success had meant that they had recruited more
Exploratores and he was quite touched by how many men
transferred from other alae after his first patrol. They now
numbered thirty Exploratores and three officers. Marius and
Drusus had been made up to Decurions once Livius had explained
the need for someone to take charge and that, of course
necessitated a promotion for him. The patrol had also shown the
limitations of the unit. The wound suffered by Decius Galba had
been on his left arm, his shield arm. It had been Metellus' idea to
have thick hide arms fitted to their leather armour. They were
made in two pieces and hinged at the elbow allowing them
freedom of movement but giving them some protection.

They had also spent some time working out signals with both
mirrors and smoke so that they could communicate over a larger

area. They still operated in groups of five but within that organisation they could disperse to cover a larger area. Finally he had taken every trooper, for three days, to Gaius' farm where Gaelwyn showed all of them how to track more effectively. Even the grumpy old man had been impressed by Rufius' skill and would not believe that the Trinovante did not have Brigante blood coursing through his veins. The training had taken place the previous week and it had really helped to bond the Exploratores as a team. As they listen to the stories of Marcus' Horse told by a very frail and aging Marcus, he could see them understand how they could be greater together than individually.

When Gaius had brought out the Sword of Cartimandua they all gasped at its beauty but more than that they all saw, in their minds, the famous Ulpius wielding it to kill the last king of the Brigante, Venutius. The three boys of Macro and Gaius had sat equally enthralled and Livius realised his age when he saw that Decius Gaius was as tall as he and a man grown. The younger boys had also developed into healthy young warriors keen to join the Exploratores. It had saddened Livius to see the tears in Ailis' eyes as she heard them plead to be allowed to join. When Livius had said that they could in the spring, with their mother's permission, he had seen a mixture of joy that they were not going yet but a dread that they would eventually be taken from her. The boys themselves were just pleased to see the nod of approval from their father.

It had been as they had been leaving that Gaius approached him carrying a sack cloth. Gaius was looking grey and drawn; not for the first time Livius wondered if his old mentor Marcus and his old commander Gaius would see another summer. They had certainly aged in the past year but the death of Macro and the journey to rescue Ailis and the three boys, years earlier had taken its toll.

Gaius came close to Livius to speak with him. "Here is the Sword of Cartimandua. I give it to you to hold and use in trust until my boys are of an age to use it. I know that I shall never carry it into battle again."

"But Gaius it is the sword I would be afraid…"

Gaius smiled and Livius could see that the years had made gaps in his teeth that showed his age more than his grey hair. "No Livius. When Marcus gave it into my possession I felt as you do now but the sword has a power. Use it and hold it for it carries within it a power that can even defeat witches such as Fainch and Morwenna. It is a force for good not evil and besides if it was still around the house the boys, especially Decius Macro might be tempted to use it."

"I will look after it with my life old friend."

"And one more thing. I may not see you for some time but when the boys join you, you will watch over them will you not?"

"I will care for them as you and Marcus cared for me when I joined the illustrious ala. They will be as my sons and Gaius.."

"Yes Livius?"

"They will live and prosper for I can see in them the spirits of their fathers."

"May the Allfather watch over you."

He glanced down at the mighty sword hanging from his baldric. He had to admit that Gaius was right. He felt naked without it by his side and, unlike his old spatha, he cleaned and polished it each day. To the men he commanded it seemed to add to his stature and he had had to order them not to keep trying to touch it as though it was a good luck omen. It was a fine sword and the Brigante warriors who had joined the Exploratores felt it was a sign that the Allfather was on the side of the Romans.

The door opened and the sentry said, "You can go in now sir."

99

The Prefect and the Tribune were sat with First Spear looking at a map of Britannia. "Ah Livius good of you to join us."

He smiled Tribune Didius had made it sound like an invitation to a party, still he was an old fashioned man and gave particular attention to Livius as he was a close friend of his old Prefect Julius Demetrius. "I am pleased to be here sir. My men are fully trained and champing at the bit."

First Spear grunted, "As are we all."

"Quite Centurion Lartius and now we can get down to it." He pointed to a spot on the map. "This is the place you think would make a good fort?"

Livius took a deep breath; his idea could become policy. "Yes sir it is at the head of a steep pass. It would prevent an enemy force attacking from the sea and is but a day's march from Glanibanta. There is much stone around the site."

"Good. We intend to build the main road to go to Brocauum and thence to Luguvalium but we will build a smaller road to link Glanibanta to Brocauum and another one to this place, er what is the name."

Livius ventured, "Mediobogdum?"

"That's it and at some future date we will extend the road to the coast to enable the fleet to supply us but as we have no port there we will not afford our enemies a back door to the province eh?"

"No sir."

"Now your Exploratores will be operating south and west of the road and fort building. The Gallic Horse based at Luguvalium can patrol but they will largely be keeping a watch north of the Stanegate. I am afraid there are no units operating south of there until Deva and Mamucium. It is our vulnerable spot." He shrugged apologetically. "It appears to be pacified. But an army could freely operate there and we would not know it. The Legion will base itself at Glanibanta and build the road north. The

100

auxiliaries from Brocauum will build it south from their fort and, hopefully, First Spear ,they will meet in the middle." The Tribune smiled at his little joke.

"We had better or I will have those Batavian's balls roasted on a skewer."

"Er quite. As you know the area better than most you will need to keep, what do you call your units?"

"A section sir. A bit like a maniple in a legion."

"Quite. Well keep a section with the road builders. That still leaves you with a sufficient number of men eh?"

"Yes sir. That won't be a problem. Er any news of Morwenna?"

"No we have some Speculatores in Caledonia and they have seen neither hide nor hair of the bitch." The prefect looked as disappointed as Livius felt. If they knew where she was they could plan. This way she could appear anywhere.

The Tribune suddenly smiled. "Perhaps she drowned eh, went to Neptune?"

"We should be so lucky."

"Yes First Spear I fear you are right. No news I am afraid but no news is good news eh. Well any questions?"

"The Speculatores, are there any operating south of us. I would hate to spy on our own spies."

The Tribune laughed, "Very good, very witty. No we keep our spies in enemy territory. Technically the land to the south of us is part of the Roman Empire so you will be our only spies."

"In that case sir. "He stood and saluted. "First Spear I shall see you in Glanibanta."

First Spear grunted a vague goodbye and, when the door had closed, turned to the other two."Bit of a dandy that one isn't he with his fancy sword?"

The Prefect shook his head. "You have not been in the province long, First Spear but that young man is of the British royal blood line. He fought in Marcus' Horse with General Agricola and even spent some time in Emperor Vespasian's jail under sentence of death so the last thing you can call him is a dandy. He is older than he looks and believe me he is a tough soldier. And the fancy sword you noticed is actually the Sword of Cartimandua and is revered by the Brigante. It may yet sway them to support Rome."

Lartius held up his hand, "Say no more. Even I heard of Marcus' Horse on the German frontier. I wish we still had them."

"So do I First Spear, they saved the Ninth on more than one occasion but unfortunately the ravages of war killed so many that the Exploratores here represent the last fifteen men who remain of Marcus' Horse."

Manavia was a hive of activity. When they had arrived in the early summer Decius Lucullus Sallustius had been quite worried. He had never heard of the island and feared attacks from the wild Irish. Maban had taken something of a shine to the well muscled soldier and she had taken him to one side. "When the Romans destroyed the holy groves on Mona, the last of the priests and warriors fled to this island and have remained here hidden ever since. This is the safest place in the whole of Britannia. Once my lady has contacted the Druids then we can begin to build your army."

Once the Druids had arrived he was amazed at the reverence with which they held the young woman. As High Priestess she ruled beyond lands, she ruled thoughts and ideas. He also saw, for the first time, the joy she could demonstrate. When her three daughters were brought out she positively glowed. All three were young priestesses and her latest baby was taken away to be initiated into the cult. Morwenna was more powerful than he had imagined. He and his two companions were left to their own devices for the first week and they used the time to explore the rocky little island. It was not very big but they discovered that, on a clear day, they could see the land of the lakes. If they returned they would not have far to go.

Centurion had asked the question of Decius that had been on his mind since they had reached the safety of the island, "Why not go to Gaul with the gold?"

The answer had been quite simple, the Druids guarded the gold. They regarded it as their own property, their gold as it came from the holy mountain of Wyddfa. Morwenna could use it but they had no chance of acquiring it. Morwenna had not reneged on her promise for she said that when she returned to her land they would have gold but it was obvious to Decius that he would have to go to war to actually get his hands on it. Once he discovered that he threw himself into the art of becoming a better soldier, training every day with Centurion and Tiny building both muscles and skills.

A week after he had arrived he was summoned to a meeting with the High Priest and Morwenna. He felt quite intimidated when he entered the myrtled grove, laden with mistletoe. The two of them sat on wicker chairs and Decius was forced to sit at their feet like a child. He found himself unable to meet the stare and glare from the white haired druid whose beard almost reached his knees. He had no idea why he had been brought to see them and he noticed a playful smile dancing around the lips of Morwenna. The silence seemed to span an eon and he was desperate for someone to break the eerie emptiness and speak. Finally the druid did and he turned to speak to the priestess. His voice was deep and sonorous, echoing despite the fact that they were out in the open. "You are right priestess his mind is full of contradictions. He wants power and yet he wants to remain hidden. He has yet to find his true desire and his destiny remains unrevealed."

Decius started at the thought that someone had been inside his head. How did he know what he had been thinking?

"He is like a piece of clay oh wise one. He has yet to be formed. The Mother brought him to us with the Wyddfa gold so there must be something hidden that we do not know and cannot see."

The druid nodded. "We are grateful son of Cunobelinus for you are the small stone which begins the avalanche. I will leave you with the Mother and she will tell you of the plans we have made." He paused and put his bony hand on Decius' head. "You are bound to us now and part of us. You will grow and reap great rewards from this but remember too as well as the benefits there are responsibilities. You cannot betray us as you betrayed your uncle and your mistress. You cannot abandon us as easily you abandoned your men. You are bound to us beyond earthly and material ties."

With that he left, leaving Decius wondering how he knew for no-one else knew about Aula. He was shocked and in fear for the threat from the druid was a very real one. Decius was not deceived by the age of the druid, the man had a power about him and any thoughts of betrayal receded to the back of his mind. "He is a wondrous creature is he not? He was here when the first Romans came with Julius Caesar and he has fought them since that time. They say he can never die as long as the Romans remain on Mona."

Decius believed her and yet found it incredible; Caesar had landed one hundred and fifty years ago! The meeting had not been what he had expected and it had changed his life. He shook his head to regain his composure and rose to sit on the wicker seat. Morwenna put her hand between him and the seat and shook her head. She rose and put her long cool fingers in his hand. "Let us walk along the shore and I will tell you of the plans."

He was like a child and merely did as he was told. The voyage to the island had changed his life completely. Centurion had been right when he had said that they had lost control of their own destinies. It was as though he had left the world he had known and entered a new and dark world filled with powers he did not understand.

Morwenna squeezed his fingers, as though to wake him and ran the back of a nail down his cheek. "Listen Decius we have decided that we will invade Brigantia after the winter solstice. But we need the people to be ready. Tadgh has gone to buy Irish soldiers to fight for us while Brennus will train those who live on the island."

"Do you want me to…?"

She placed her finger on his lips. "I want you to listen and then obey. We need the Brigante to be unhappy with Roman rule so that they will beg us to lead them. To do that we need the Roman army to treat the Brigante ruthlessly." He went to speak again and she pressed her finger on his lips once more. "There are many Roman deserters in Britannia. We want you and your men to recruit them and build a small army. We have Roman armour and weapons which we have been gathering since the first invasion. The men you lead will look like Roman soldiers; you will look like a Roman leader. You will harass and steal from every settlement on the west coast, avoiding, of course Roman garrisons. When the people are suitably enraged we will come to their aid and you can bring your men to rejoin the rebellion." She led him to a rocky outcrop close to the water and they sat down. She put his head on her lap and leaning down kissed him full on the lips. "Now you may talk and ask me the hundreds of questions racing around in your head and I will answer them then we can make love."

Decius didn't know where to start. "How will we find the deserters and raise the army? If they are deserters they will be hidden and wish to stay hidden."

"Our spies have told us of taverns in the vicus at Deva which are frequented by deserters. You will start there and we will give you gold to pay them." She paused and stroked his hairline gently. "I did forget to mention that any money, gold or treasure you capture whilst hurting the people is yours to keep. You have a share of your own gold but this would be in addition, call it a bonus for loyalty and hard work."

He rapidly worked out that he could be very rich very soon. "We will need a base from which to operate."

"I am sure there is somewhere south of the land of the lakes. You passed through that land did you not see anywhere that would have been suitable?"

He suddenly remembered a couple of sites where he and the mules had camped that were many miles away from other occupied areas. The question was, how did she know? He opened his eyes and looked up at her. "You will have to trust me with your gold. What is to stop me running away with it? To disappear into Britannia?"

"Firstly you will not because you fear the wise one. Secondly you know I would come for you and you fear me but the main reason I am confident is your greed and your lust for riches. It was that lust for gold which made you abandon your lover. You know you will be richer with us than alone."

He could not argue with her for he knew that she was right. "I will need more men that I can rely on than Centurion and Tiny if I am to lead an army of...How many men do you want me to find?"

She shrugged. "Two centuries? Perhaps two hundred men."

"It would be difficult to find two hundred deserters." He touched her mouth with his fingers, "but I am sure that I could find other, equally able men of equally dubious backgrounds, to fill the new legion. But I will need either Brennus or Tadgh to help me control them." He pulled her head down to kiss her. "And now I believe you said something about making love?"

106

Surprisingly Centurion and Tiny both went enthusiastically along with the idea. "It seems safer than Gaul. I mean we don't speak the language in Gaul do we? At least here we know what's what. We know the country and we know the people. Deva is alright and I know a few taverns near Mamucium. I don't think we'll have a problem recruiting we just need somewhere to hide 'em."

"I told the Queen there were a few places south of Glanibanta that would work. The land there is mercifully free from patrols."

"It was free from patrols. Now it may not be but we'll have to cross that bridge when we come to it. Have they said when we can see the armour and uniforms?"

"Tomorrow but I am not hopeful, I mean how much armour could they had collected?"

Even Centurion was impressed with what they found. Admittedly some of the armour was old and rusted and much needed repair but there was enough equipment to fit out a cohort. They would not fool a Roman but the Brigante of the west had not seen many Roman soldiers and would assume that was how they dressed. "Get it cleaned up and it will work."

Centurion selected his own armour and said, "We'll let our recruits do it. It will make them realise that they are part of an army and it helps if a man looks after his own gear."

Brennus had been told he would be accompanying them to Deva. He looked disdainfully at the mail and shields. "A Brigante does not need such things," he said as he threw the moulded cuirass to the ground.

"I know," laughed Centurion, "but for the next few weeks you are a Roman which also means," he winked at Tiny who knew what was coming, "you have to cut your hair and shave your beard off."

Cursing in Brigante he stormed off to see Tadgh who had returned with two hundred wild Irishmen the day before. As they left they grinned at Brennus who sulked like a child having been told by Tadgh he had to look Roman.

When they left the next day on the small cog which the druids used to acquire supplies, the four men looked like Romans. All had worn the uniform of a centurion the previous day and passed inspection. As they watched the island recede in the distance they were all wearing the togas of the rich Romano-British middle classes. Decius felt very much at home as it was the dress he had grown up with. The other three shifted uncomfortably in the crisp white togas and sandals having only worn military garb for years. They had with them some of the Brigante of Brennus' band. They would be responsible for guarding the armour and their base. For the other four the next week would be a dangerous and a difficult time as they moved amongst the lowest class of criminals, the outlaws. As he watched Manavia slip slowly away he remembered his last embrace with Morwenna. Lying between Maban and Anchorat she had whispered in his ear. "You are fecund are you not? All three of us are with child. If mine is a boy we have an heir to our thrones."

"And if it is a girl?"

"Then she will join her sisters and become priestesses of the Mother and one of them will become as I am High Priestess."

He was to be a father. Not that any sentiment came into that thought. He cared not for the future but it was a sobering thought that, when he returned to Manavia, or when Morwenna joined him there would be a child who would continue after he had turned to dust. He found himself wanting to share that idea with someone; not Centurion and Tiny. He realised, shockingly, that he wanted to tell his brother; the fool who followed the eagle and was on the opposite side of this conflict. The Roman Parcae were devious indeed. He shrugged his shoulders as though to rid himself of the thought; what would be would be. He could only control his own path and he would do so.

The ship brought them south east to a huge empty beach backed by a pine forest growing out of sand dunes speckled with straggly grass. The druids, the ship's captain and Decius had all discussed the landing site and the refuge at length. Although Decius did not know the area well he knew that the landing site was forty miles from Mamucium and Deva, the two Roman bases in the area and that it was deserted. No-one lived there as the sandy soil could not support farms and the huge beaches deterred fishing. They had decided to find a place with water in the shallow pine forest and build a round house in which to store the armour and gold. Brennus, still muttering about his close cropped hair stayed with the Brigante while Decius and his two companions left to find animals and their first recruits. They only had a month in which to raise their band of cutthroats and they would have to begin their raids within two weeks.

Centurion led them across the deserted low lying land. There were few hills and few forests. Roads were non–existent and the country was as different as it was possible to be from the lands near Wyddfa and the land of the lakes. The lack of hills, however, made travelling simple. They had some good fortune on the first night. As they camped in the lee of a hill fifteen miles from their landing site, they saw the glow of a fire in a small copse less than a mile away. When they drew closer they saw that it was a merchant and his slave. More important was the horse and the mule. Transport. The two hapless travellers stood no chance against the ruthless killers who fell on them and savagely ended their lives. They discovered some gold sewn into the merchant's breeks and a pack with the black jet mined close to Streonshal. The man had been heading for Mona where he would have received top price for the precious stone valued by the remaining druids who hid there. It gave them a reason to travel to an inn; they had a cover story. As they ate the merchant's meal which his dead slave had so thoughtfully prepared Decius smiled. Perhaps there was something to this religion which Morwenna followed for good fortune seemed to be with them. Already they were richer and safer as a result of their chance encounter, if chance it was.

The animals made the journey swifter as Decius could ride and his two companions found it easy to jog alongside. Centurion took them south to the recently built Roman bridge which crossed the Seteia Fluvia. It was half way between Mamucium and Deva but more importantly it had no garrison. A small vicus had grown up at this important crossing and there were many inns. Its proximity to the mountains of Wyddfa and the hills which divided the land to the east meant that it was frequented not only by travellers but those seeking an escape to a wild place.

They reached it on the evening of the second day. They found the inn which Centurion said was the most respectable. As a trader it would have been the one Decius should have chosen. Once he was ensconced then Centurion and Tiny would find the more dangerous ones to secure the services of the cut throats, low life and villains they sought. The inn keeper's eyes almost popped out his head when the rich merchant entered and paid for a room and stabling in advance. He was not surprised that the well heeled traveller wished for his slaves to sleep in the stable for how else did one become rich other than by watching the denari?

Leaving Decius to enjoy a hot meal and wine Centurion nodded and took Tiny across the river to the less respectable side of the vicus. Both wore leather cuirasses beneath their tunics and were armed with daggers strapped to their legs and gladii beneath their tunics. The men they were seeking were desperate men and the two warriors were under no illusions. They might have to break a couple of heads before they could get the men they sought. As they paused outside the first inn, a dimly lit timber built building with a low buzz of noise Centurion took a deep breath and said to Tiny, "Ready?" The big man nodded,

110

"Remember just watch my back and let me do the talking." Tiny grunted. Both knew that talking was not his strength. Just before they entered he dropped his cudgel under the small elder bush which had sprung up there.

Chapter 9

The noise stopped as soon as they entered and every eye was drawn to them. Centurion took in the hands reaching beneath the rough hewn tables obviously for weapons. The cheap tallow candles gave off more smoke than light adding to the murk. There was only one empty table and it was close to the door which led off the main room. Centurion sighed with relief for it was against a wall, their backs would be safe. They sat down and waited the eerie silence making even Centurion uncomfortable. A scarred one eyed man shuffled over and stared at them, his one eye moving from one to the other. "Ale and food." The man did not move but held out his hand. Centurion held out one coin. When the innkeeper tried to take it Centurion grabbed his wrist. "We hope to be frequent visitors but we expect good service. Do you understand, soldier?"

The man's one eye widened. Centurion had recognised the tattoo on the top of his arm. "I serve good beer and food you will be safe." Turning he gave an imperceptible nod and the room began talking again. "Nice welcome eh Tiny?"

Tiny nodded at a group of men who were sat by the door. "They look like ex-soldiers." Centurion nodded his agreement. The four men had shorter hair than the Brigante wore and each wore the unmistakeable caligae which marked them as Roman soldiers.

"I'll leave first. When they follow you know what to do." Tiny nodded.

The food, when it came, was at least edible, a local game stew with black bread. The innkeeper had been right, the beer was acceptable. As he turned to leave, Centurion held out another small coin. "Who were you with then?"

Taking the money he lowered his head to keep his words for the two men alone. "Second Augusta."

"Tough legion. Who did this to you?"

Spitting into the glowing fire he snapped, "Fucking Silures bastards. Who did you serve with?"

"The Ninth."

"They are north of here now eh."

"A little too close for my liking. I'll be heading south in a few days."

"Like that eh?"

Centurion's hand went to his blade. "You have a problem with that?"

Chuckling the man turned to return to his kitchen, "Let's just say you are not alone here."

As they finished their meal Centurion winked at Tiny, "Well we came to the right place. Time to recruit." He stood and drained his beaker. Tiny looked up and shook his head. Centurion shrugged and left, their little play acting finished. Tiny waited until the four men purposefully left the inn and followed Centurion a few minutes later. He emptied his beaker and then he too left. He could see Centurion striding towards the bridge and the four men walking furtively behind. Pausing only to retrieve the cudgel he had hidden under a bush he moved surprisingly quietly for a big man to close the distance between him and the four would be assailants. He smiled for he could see what they planned. They would take Centurion at the bridge, rob him and then dispose of his body in the water. He knew that Centurion would know this and would be prepared. As Centurion reached the bridge he whirled around, his gladius extended in his hand.

The four ex-soldiers were taken aback; they had thought they had an easy victim. Their leader spread his arms wide and smiled, "Friend there is no need for swords but you are obviously a man with money while we are poor old soldiers. All we want is your purse and then you can be on your way. It is not too much to ask is it? To help those who made Rome great?"

113

Throwing his head back and laughing Centurion hissed, "Scum sucking leeches like you probably ran in the first attack. Piss off!"

The leader's smile disappeared and he and his companions pulled out their pugeos. "Then we'll do it the hard way. You might have a sword but we are four against one."

He got no further as Tiny smashed his cudgel into the back of the head and said, "Two."

As the other three looked at the new assailant Centurion punched the pommel of his sword into the face of a second attacker, "Against two."

The last two found the tips of two razor sharp gladii held to their necks. "Spare us please!"

"I am not sure we have the right men here Tiny. You two pick up your mates and take them across the river." He pointed. "Behind that stable there."

As soon as they entered the stable Centurion threw them four lengths of rope. "Hobble yourselves and then your friends." One of them looked as though he was going to object and Centurion leaned in and said in his ear, "It does not matter to me if you are awake or not and my friend here is very handy with a cudgel as you can see." The man looked at the erstwhile leader whose head was leaking blood. They complied.

The soldier who had been hit by Centurion's sword came to and Centurion pricked his neck with the point of his gladius as his eyes opened. "Just a reminder friend that we hold your pathetic lives cheaply. Now you will be wondering why we have made your acquaintance this evening. Obviously you have no money so we are not robbers. What else can you offer us? And before you start to worry in case we are bum bandits we aren't. No we want you because you are all deserters." The one who had been hit by the sword opened his mouth to protest. "And we are not here to return you for punishment. Tiny and I had the pleasure of serving with the Imperial army until we decided to go into business for ourselves and we would like to offer you the opportunity to join our enterprise." He allowed them a few moments for the idea to sink in. They exchanged looks and then looked back at Centurion. "Good you are interested. Well here it is. We are starting up, what would you call it Tiny, ah yes, a little army." Tiny nodded and grinned his toothy lopsided grin. It was not a pleasant sight. "You will be fed, clothed and paid in gold." He saw their eyes light up. Stabbing his gladius into the ground he took four denari from his purse and dropped them from one hand to the other slowly. "This would be your first pay. All you have to do is agree to join us."

They looked at each other and then the one with the injured jaw said, "What if we don't want to join you? What if we are loyal citizens of the Empire?"

"Then I would have misjudged you. Incidentally I rarely do that but if that were the case then my friend here would knock you on the head and return you to the tavern."

Once again they looked at each but before they could come up with another answer their leader began to come to. "Perhaps this is the moment when my friend and I retire to the door so that you can explain the situation to your headstrong friend and then you can give us your answer."

They moved out of earshot but close enough to prevent the hobbled soldiers from escaping. The conversation was punctuated by gestures at Tiny and Centurion. Finally, after the discussion, they turned to face their captors. The leader spoke. "My men have told me of your offer. I am Nuada, once chosen man in the Tungrians. I would be lying if I didn't say I was interested but there are some questions which need answering."

"Go ahead, Nuada, and we will tell you our names when you have accepted our offer."

"How much is the pay?"

"An excellent question. There will be a denarius a week," he held his hand up to stop their protest, "plus a share in the profits and there will be many profits."

"Fair enough. Second question. What do we have to do to earn this money?"

"Be soldiers and follow orders. What you did for Rome but this time we are working for ourselves."

"So we are likely to come up against Romans?"

"I like the way you think, Nuada. You have a keen sense of self preservation and I will not lie to you. There will be times when we will have to fight Romans. However it will not be the legions and we will never fight unless we outnumber them. Our foes will, generally, be unarmed, perhaps merchants perhaps farmers, maybe miners."

"So we will be bandits?"

"If you would like to view it that way. We prefer the term freedom fighters for we are, after all, fighting for our freedom."

"A few moments?"

"Go ahead." As they talked Centurion turned to Tiny. "We have them." Tiny nodded.

Nuada spoke. "We agree."

As an answer Centurion nodded to Tiny who slit their bonds. At the same time he placed a coin in each of their hands. "Now would you like to start earning money?"

Nuada grinned evilly. "Who do we have to kill?"

"No-one yet. We are keen to recruit more men of your ilk. If the four of you know other like minded freedom fighters then we will give you one denarius for every five you bring and they will each receive one denarius as you did."

"That sounds good to me. When do you want these men?"

"By tomorrow. Meet us here after dark and say your goodbyes for we will be moving on after that."

"Right we will see you then er…"

"You can call me Centurion and this is Tiny."

"Right until tomorrow. Nuada led his men towards the door; as he neared Tiny he swung his fist in a roundhouse punch aimed at Tiny's head. The giant had seen the signs and had been expecting it, his huge fist enclosed Nuada's hand and he began to squeeze.

"Silly boy, Tiny was following my orders when he hit you. Drop him Tiny." Tiny released the hand which was white and almost drained of blood. "If you want to take Tiny on then be my guest but next time I won't stop him and I will be short one soldier. Understand?"

Nodding Nuada turned to Tiny, "Sorry. "

After the four had gone they returned to the inn where Decius still sat. "Well?"

"Better than we could have hoped. We have four and they are bringing their friends tomorrow."

"Good then tomorrow I will head for Mamucium to sell the jet. When you have the others Tiny can take them to Brennus for training and you can meet me in Mamucium."

Decius spent the night in a tavern close to the fortress of Mamucium. The fort was not as big as either Deva or Eboracum but the vicus was a large one. It was the biggest settlement travellers came across once they had crossed the divide. For that reason the taverns were busier and more expensive than the others they had encountered. It also had a better clientele and Decius soon found a trader who was willing to buy the jet from him. Decius knew that the trader was robbing him but as the gold he received was pure profit he did not mind. He had an ulterior motive. The trader was so pleased to have made such a killing that he was happy to tell this stranger of the best routes, most populous settlements, and the richest traders in the area. Soon Decius had an accurate picture of the commerce in the region. More importantly he discovered the patrol routes used by the Gallic auxiliaries. He was relieved that they were foot soldiers for it made contact less likely. Later that night when he withdrew to his room he took out a wax tablet and made notes about the routes and places. He didn't think he would forget them but it was better to be careful as his uncle had found out to his cost.

The following morning he waited at the western end of the road into the vicus. He knew that Centurion would get there as soon as he could and it allowed him the opportunity to plan where they would begin their reign of terror. He knew it was important to start as far away from the forts as possible. He had found that the traders used two main routes into Mamucium, one from Luguvalium and one from Eboracum. He was loath to use the one from Eboracum because it was further away from his base, the land of the lakes and the sea. He also knew that the nearest troops were at Luguvalium and they were busy with the northern barbarians and Deva where the Twentieth Valeria was still trying to control the Silures and Ordovices. They would begin their attacks on the north south road west of the divide.

When he saw Centurion striding along the road looking weary he realised that they would have to buy a horse, or steal one as soon as possible. "How did it go?"

"They brought thirty men so it is a good start. Tiny took them off to Brennus. He will join us tomorrow."

"How will he know where to meet us?"

"There is a tavern not far from here. It has a sign showing a white horse, he will meet us there."

"One of your places?"

"Yes but this time I know the tavern keeper, he served with me."

"Isn't that dangerous? He will know you are a deserter."

"I saved his life and besides he was never a lover of Rome. He was flogged more than once and a man never forgets that. Besides he lost an arm fighting for Rome and didn't receive a pension."

"How did he get the tavern then?"

118

"The lads liked him and when he was injured we collected some money for him. That is another reason why he owes me but most importantly he still keeps in touch with other likeminded soldiers."

Nautius Naevius had been a big man when a soldier. Since taking the tavern he had almost exploded into the fattest man Decius had ever seen. For all that he had a sharp eye. He greeted Centurion like a long lost brother, "Gaius! Where have you come from? I haven't seen you for years."

"Oh here and there. This is my friend er Decius."

"Any friend of Gaius is a friend of mine Decius." He looked at him shrewdly, "But I suspect the reason my friend has only given me one name is because I may know your family name." he held his hand up. "I don't need to know the details. Now are you staying?"

"We hope to."

"I can offer you good rates."

Grinning Centurion came back. "You may charge us full rates as long as we get what we want."

"Whatever you want. Women, girls," he glanced at Decius, "boys?"

Centurion put his arm out to restrain the red faced Decius, "Nautius is known for his wicked sense of humour. He means no offence, do you old friend?"

"Of course not. Well you have me intrigued. Come I will show you your room and then you can tell me of the services you require."

Being morning the tavern was quiet as Nautius explained, "The kind who frequent my tavern like to work in the dark if you understand my meaning. They are the kind of men who don't like too many questions."

Decius and Centurion exchanged looks. They had agreed that Centurion would do the negotiation while Decius held the money.

119

"Sounds like our sort of men." Centurion checked that there was no one within earshot. "We are looking for ex-soldiers who don't mind getting their hands bloody if you catch my drift."

Nautius nodded. "Are you bothered at all about their backgrounds? I mean I know some lads, a bit like you Gaius, who left the Empire, shall we say under a cloud?"

"They would be perfect."

"And how long would you want them for? A little job? Perhaps longer?"

"Indefinitely! Clothes, weapons and food provided."

"Pay?"

"Share of the profits and a regular income." He leaned forward. "A lot more than Rome pays."

"And for me?"

"One denarius for every ten men you find."

"One for five."

Spitting on his hand Centurion held it forward. The innkeeper did the same and, as they clasped hands said,"Done!"

"Nice bit of business there, have a drink Gaius and you too Decius." They both raised their freshly filled beakers. As they put them down Nautius said innocently, "Shame about your uncle though. It was good to have someone with such powerful connections."

Decius hand went to his sword but Centurion restrained him. Nautius spread his arms, "Your secret is safe with me I was just letting you know what a valuable source of information I am, your new partner."

Decius leaned over. "Be careful what you do with that information or you could lose more than a hand."

Three days later Decius left Centurion and the recently arrived Tiny to collect the new men and then they all headed back to the camp. He had been away for five days but he was pleased with the progress Brennus had made. The thirty men had been put to work building their quarters and some rough defences aimed at slowing up and deterring an attacker with deadfalls and man traps. Decius nodded to himself. Brennus had made the camp hard to see and he did not think it would be discovered accidentally.

He called Brennus over to him as he rode in. "Good job Brennus." The Brigante shrugged the compliment off. "How about the men?"

"They are alright but I would not trust them."

"That is the point isn't it Brennus we don't need to trust them as long as they are being paid and I think the sooner we begin to get some money the better."

"You are beginning?"

"We are beginning. I think I know where we can make some easy and quick money, even with the number of men we have recruited and it will help us to see how they work. Have they been fitted out with armour and weapons yet?"

"Later today."

"Do it now. We head out tonight. I know where there will be horses and gold." Although he expressed surprise Tadgh and Morwenna had impressed on the Brigante that for good or bad Decius was in charge. It suited Brennus for any mistakes were not his.

He had allowed the men to rest in the afternoon following their arming. He knew from his time with the Brigante that warriors like to accustom themselves to weapons and armour. As these thirty were the first they had received the best equipment; later recruits would not fare as well. Decius and Brennus had taken centurion uniform and, following Brennus' advice; they had given Nuada that of an optio. "He is a leader and better to have him leading for us than causing trouble in the ranks." Decius had no argument to Brennus' logic and had agreed.

It was moonrise when he gathered them together. Although they had no tents yet Decius knew they would have to acquire them soon. He addressed them. "Tonight we are going for a little walk. About twenty or so miles. I want to be at the road by mid morning. There will be a caravan of traders heading north and we are going to relieve them of everything. Your first payday is tomorrow. As far as anyone is concerned we are the Second Pannonian Auxilia."

Nuada spoke up," Does that unit actually exist?"

"No idea but if we use it often enough then people will believe it is. Tomorrow we kill everyone but when we are in settlements we try not to kill but we take everything. Clear?" The grins and nods told him that they were happy with their new working practices and they set off cheerfully.

By the middle of the night they were less cheerful and they were showing the effect of their lack of exercise and marching. Decius was pleased that he had worked out with Tiny and Centurion and he kept a hard pace. He had decided on this excursion not only for the rewards but also as a training exercise. These thirty men would, in effect become his elite force. They were the best armed and they would have had the most training. He intended to over reward them. He was quite happy to buy loyalty. They found the empty fortlet exactly where he had been told by the merchant to expect it.

"Right men let us occupy this fort as though it belongs to us. When the caravan reaches us I want them to approach it feeling safe. They will see Roman soldiers whom they will assume have re-garrisoned the fortlet and they will expect to be safe. We need to take any livestock alive but the men are there to be killed. Brennus take ten men to the northern end of the road to cut them off. I will be in the middle. Nuada take five men to the southern end. This isn't Rome so just rest until you hear the order, then you behave as Roman soldiers."

The men took him at his word. Any regular Roman centurion would have had an apoplectic fit if he had seen them lounging

122

about. Decius climbed the small watch tower to enable him to see down the road. He saw the smudge turn into mounted men and he shouted down, "They are here! In position and remember we are Roman."

By the time he had descended they were all in position and their appearance made him think that they might just pull this off. They looked like Roman soldiers. Admittedly they were not identically dressed but it would have taken keen military trained eyes to discern the differences. As the column of men and animals wound its way slowly along the road Decius could see that it was bigger than he had hoped. There were ten mules, a wagon and eight mounted men. Four of the men were armed which suggested to Decius that they were hired guards.

The leader of the caravan was the man who had spoken to Decius in Mamucium. He smiled and waved genially as he rode towards Decius. Something about Decius caused him to frown and he shook his head as though he was mistaken. As soon as the last guard had passed Nuada and the leader was almost level with him Decius shouted, "Now!"

Thrusting upwards with his gladius Decius struck the first blow and he stabbed the leader who managed a, "You!" before he fell, a bloody, dying heap.

Decius' soldiers had taken no chances with the hired guards and each one had had two attackers. He was surprised to see that two of the guards had not been killed but were being tightly held by Nuada and his men. He frowned as he walked up to them. They had disobeyed his first order. "Before you get yourself excited," Nuada paused before emphasising his next word, "sir! We know these two. They are good lads who fought with us and I think they might like to join us." He shrugged, "If they don't then I will kill 'em myself."

"Very well, optio. You may explain while Brennus and I check what we have."

The wagon contained wine, food, caligae and mail armour which were obviously intended for Luguvalium. The mules were carrying blankets and tunics. Decius almost danced for joy. They would look more like Romans now. The bodies of the fat merchants and traders brought even greater bounty. They must have sold the jet and their other goods at Mamucium and were being paid to deliver supplies to the army. Even Brennus looked pleased. "If all our attacks result in this Brennus then we will all be rich men."

Brennus spat, "You will be rich. I am not a bandit I am a Brigante warrior and I fight for honour not gold."

"Your loss. More for us." Nuada strode up and Decius noticed that the two guards were not bound and still had their weapons. "I take it you would like to join us?"

The men grinned, "It would be an honour to serve in the Second Pannonians sir."

They left the bodies where they lay. When the next patrol found them they would look for a small bandit group not the Roman column which headed south eastwards. Now that they had horses Decius was able to ride and send scouts out. One of them returned. "Sir there is a settlement ahead. Looks like a ripe plum to me sir. Cattle, sheep and they look prosperous."

"Lead on." Turning in his saddle he shouted, "We have a settlement. We are now tax collectors. Avoid killing but take what you can. Follow my lead."

As they approached the village he could see that it stood at the foot of a palisaded hill. Obviously they had a hill fort in which to retreat but as they had only seen Romans approaching they had stayed in their settlement nestling close to a stream and a small lake.

The headman walked up to them. He was a greybeard and looked happy to see them. "Welcome sir I am…"

"I am Centurion Octavius of the Second Pannonians and I am here to collect your unpaid taxes."

The headman spread his arms. "But sir it is not yet tax time."

"It is now." Decius kicked him hard in the face and he fell unconscious at his feet. "Listen to me. Rome has given you the benefit of protection and now you must pay for it." Turning to Brennus he shouted," Collect the taxes centurion!"

By the time they left the settlement most of the men had been hit and left bleeding. None of the livestock had been left and the gold they had buried beneath their huts had been uncovered and taken. They left a community shocked into a wailing acceptance of the injustice of Rome. Decius had no doubt that, when the headman awoke, he would complain to Mamucium but, more importantly, would complain to neighbouring hamlets and so the word would spread. Rather than heading in a direct line to their camp he headed north for a while to confuse any pursuit. When they rode into camp triumphantly Centurion and Tiny were there already with another group of men. "I see it worked then?"

"It worked like you wouldn't believe. We will all soon be rich men."

Chapter 10

Livius and his new decurions had settled on a new routine as they travelled west; they rode in pairs. It made life much easier and quicker yet enabled them to cover large areas. Each section or as they now called them, maniples, using the legionary term met up each night to camp and exchange information. This enabled them to send a rider back to the legion if necessary otherwise they could carry on with their patrol. The Prefect liked this as no news was good news. Livius found himself grinning; it was highly inappropriate a demeanour for what was in effect the senior cavalryman in the legion but he could not help himself. He had a perfect job. He was riding in the most beautiful country a man could ever see, for it was still summer, and he was with comrades who felt more like friends than inferiors. He noticed as they rode through the valleys that, now that the Batavians had rid the forests of bandits there were more farms and they waved happily to the visible sign of Rome, Livius and his men.

The engineers who followed Livius were also happy for Livius knew the country so well that their job was made much easier and the road was already built close to Glanibanta. Livius knew they had to be close to Mediobogdum before the first snows fell for then the ground would be too hard to work. If they could manage that then the auxiliaries could build their fort and be snugly housed for the winter. It would also mean that Livius and his men could winter in Glanibanta and he was also looking forward to that.

Rufius was riding next to him. Since they had come west he had chosen the youngest member of the maniple to be his partner. The others had self selected their partners leaving Rufius alone. He was a quiet young man and Livius had taken him under his wing. He remembered when he had ridden with Marcus Maximunius and how that had helped him, how the older man had passed on his experience, wisdom and knowledge to the young, callow trooper. Perhaps he could do the same for Rufius. He saw, in the young man, much of himself when he was young; the keen enthusiasm, the desperation to do well and the deep loyalty to his comrades. "Well Rufius does the land look familiar?"

"Yes sir. It seems like yesterday." They were riding north of Glanibanta and both anticipating viewing the site of their skirmish where they had lost the first members of the Explorates. Livius had decided to ride up the path to the cave in daylight. He knew that the road would not be coming this way but he wanted to spend the night there and explore the cave while it was still daylight.

"Rufius just ride by the lake and find the route from that direction."

"Yes sir," snapped Rufius who rode off, keen to impress.

Livius smiled seeing a younger version of himself. He had asked him to try the other route so that he could discover if it was passable following the man made avalanche. He found the path very steep and remembered how difficult it had been in the dark; even in the daylight it was not an easy journey. He wondered if it might be possible to place a signal tower here. The path twisted savagely from side to side with a rocky cliff and trees forming a thick barrier. Suddenly he emerged into daylight and he could see where the rocks had fallen killing his two men. Drusus had come back himself to bury the men of his section after they had watched Morwenna sail away to safety. Now there was just a jumble of rocks and the whitened bones of horses to mark the site of their deaths. He let Star's reins drop. The horse was so well trained that he would just wander to find grazing, returning at Livius' whistle. He could see the remains of the camp which had been here, the blackened rocks where the fire had been, the pile of bones from the animals they had eaten, and the dried shrivelled droppings from the mules. It looked nothing like a Roman camp which was always ordered and organised. It showed that no matter how numerous they were and no matter how cunning, they were still barbarians and Livius knew that the organised Roman war machine would, eventually, grind them down. The Emperor Trajan appeared to be busy in the east but the officers of the Ninth were hopeful that, if he came west he could finish off the work so nearly completed by General Agricola twenty years or so earlier.

He was just about to go into the cave when he heard the clatter of hooves on rocks. Rufius' head appeared, almost magically and his grinning young face beamed at his superior. "That was a ride."

"Was it hard?"

"Very. The rocks are so small that they constantly move beneath the hooves. It is a good job that Blackie is nimble on her feet or we would have ended up at the bottom of the valley." Rufius dismounted and nuzzled his horse, "Good girl!" Neighing she wandered off to join Star who had found some tussocks of grass on which to graze.

"So the only way up now is the way I came?"

"I suppose sure footed auxiliaries might be able to manage it but they would make a lot of noise."

Rufius was a clever young man. He had understood what went behind the question rather than just the question. He would make an excellent officer for he was already a perfect Exploratore; someone who could use intelligence to bring back useful information. "We'll explore the cave and then camp here tonight."

"Will the others be joining us?"

"Perhaps I told them either Glanibanta or here. I suspect they will choose Glanibanta as it is more comfortable."

"Oh I don't know sir. This looks like a dry cave, plenty of water and grazing for the animals. We can even light a fire in the cave."

"Let's do that. It looks like rain and it will illuminate the interior later."

The fire did indeed throw light throughout the whole cave. It was more than a cave it was a whole cavern system and they explored the rear where the wall had once been. "I would love to know why they built the wall."

"Hiding something? Perhaps a separate room, I mean they had the Queen with them."

"The Queen, Rufius is a witch, and I don't think that she would worry about others. I suspect that she and her women occupied the whole of the cave and left the men outside. We now know there were only thirty or so of them anyway."

As they returned to the fire and the hares which were roasting Rufius asked, "Do you think she has gone for good then sir?"

"No. Her mother, the witch Fainch, plagued the province for over twenty years until Marcus Maximunius finally caught up with her and had her crucified. We will have to do the same for her daughter. You must never underestimate her Rufius. She has more faces than a dozen actors. She can smile and appear innocent while stabbing you in the back. The old Decurion Princeps of Marcus' Horse found that to his cost."

"She is that dangerous then?"

" Far more dangerous than any man I have ever fought."

Rufius turned the hares over while he plucked up the courage to ask the question which had rattled around in his head since they had set off from Brocauum. "Sir someone at the fort said that she was with your brother. Is that right?"

"I am sorry to say yes. My uncle sent my brother Decius to look after Wyddfa's gold while I learned to be a cavalryman. I suspect he was seduced by the gold and the desire for riches."

"What will you do if we catch him?"

"It isn't an 'if' Rufius, it is a when. When we catch him he will be tried and punished for his crimes."

"Crucifixion then?"

"Probably." Livius wanted the subject changing for he found the thought of his brother as a traitor disturbing. " Anyway are those hares ready yet?"

Two weeks after beginning their raids Decius was pleased with the results they had achieved. They had over a hundred and fifty men under arms with more arriving every day. Nuada and Centurion vetted them just in case the Romans had sent in spies but the authorities seemed blind to the insurrection happening in such a quiet part of the province. The auxiliary patrols along the main road were increased but the first raid by Decius had just been opportunist. His mission, as Morwenna and the Wise One had said, was to upset and annoy the people. Now that they had more men at their disposal they could send out more columns to increase the chaos.

Decius and Brennus were in the main hut with Centurion deciding where the next raids should take place when the messenger arrived. They kept a watch close to the beach to warn them of Roman naval activity and to alert them to the arrival of their own boats. This was just such an occasion. The man was not only out of breath he was also very excited. "It is the Queen! She is at the beach and wishes to see you my lord and General Decius."

Brennus and Decius did not waste time wondering why the Queen had come they knew that she would not want to be kept waiting. They both sprang on the backs of their horses without waiting for them to be saddled. When they arrived at the beach Morwenna was sat on a wicker seat with the boat hauled up on the sand. Around her stood ten tall warriors each one with sword and shield. She looked heavily pregnant. As they slithered to a halt the ten warriors came menacingly forward, their swords pointed at the two men. Morwenna held up her hand, "They are friends."

The swords were sheathed but Brennus could not resist walking up to the largest one and spitting in the sand near him, daring him to action. "I see you are still as belligerent as ever Brennus."

"Sorry your majesty."

"And General Decius, how fine you look in your uniform. Where did the title come from?" she asked teasingly.

Decius shuffled for he was embarrassed. "It was the men they thought…"

Decius had forgotten how enchanting her laugh could be and when she laughed it made him look up and smile. "I am not unhappy about it, just surprised. I did not see you being seduced by uniforms and titles. Perhaps I should be jealous." She turned to her guards. "Go and guard the trees or something. I am quite safe with these two." They wandered off reluctantly. "Tadgh feels I need protection now that the child, our child, is growing so well." Decius smiled at the term, 'our child'. "How go the raids?"

"Well we have a hundred and fifty men. We acquired some new mail and caligae and the people are becoming unhappy. There is a great deal of unrest with Rome. We are increasing the raids from tomorrow."

"Good. I have news for you." She peered closely at his face to gauge his reaction. "I come to tell you that we will be bringing our army over before winter."

"But that means we may be fighting during winter."

"Yes General but what you do not know is that in this part of the land the winters are milder than in the east, the north or even further south, near Wyddfa. It will hurt the Romans more than we and will allow us to build up our strength. The other reason is to give new orders to Brennus." Brennus looked surprised at being included in what had appeared to be an almost private conversation. "You can stop being a Roman now Brennus and become a Brigante once more." He gave such a loud whoop that

131

the guards looked around and began to move back to the beach until Morwenna waved them back. "When a settlement has been raided you must visit it as a Brigante who has been displaced by the Romans in the east. Tell them that this is what they did to you and how they sold your village into slavery. Embroider the story as much as you wish. But you need to be convincing. Find any Brigante warriors who are willing to fight against Rome and have them join your army. Not this army here but a second one which you will build further north. General Decius will supply you with gold and any non-Roman weapons. Do you have them?"

"Yes many. We disarm any village we find. It aggravates the situation."

"Good. Take your Brigante, Brennus to build your camp. You have built one which worked for the deserters. It should be easier with your own people."

"It will indeed." He suddenly looked worried. "But I do not have long do I?"

"We have a thousand warriors ready to come over for the rebellion. Many Brigante fled to the island and to Ireland. They wish to return. We have also used the gold you provided to buy Irish warriors. Your new Brigante will join with us and we will use our Roman army too." She paused and looked again at Decius' face. "Decius, will they fight for us?"

"No," he said bluntly, "but they will fight for money and they will also fight to show their former masters that they are better warriors. They have no ideals and even less scruples but they are good fighters."

"It pains me to say it but the General is right. They are fierce and they are ruthless. I would be happy to fight alongside them."

"Thank you Brennus."

He shrugged, "Do not thank me Decius, for speaking the truth. It is the way of my people. It is you Romans who lie."

The captain called from the boat. "The tide your majesty!"

"I must go. Well done you have both done all that I asked of you." She rose from her wicker throne and came over to Decius kissing him long and hard on the lips. She said huskily, "Come back to us soon we have missed you between our legs."

"As have I."

She turned and waded through the surf, "Send those barbarians to me."

They waved the guards over and watched as they picked up the throne and placed it in the boat before pushing it off and scrambling on board. The last they heard above the surf was Morwenna's voice carrying like the cry of a lonely gull, "You have but a month! Do not fail me!"

The small fishing settlement of Itunocelum was still a sad place to visit. The murder of so many of its men the previous year and the loss of all its boats had hit the community hard. Some of the more enterprising men had used the mules left by the departing Brigante to begin a new life as traders. This had just made the community seem even emptier with fewer men. The women were strong creatures and, as the nets had not been lost along with the boats, they began, with the remaining old men and boys to begin fishing from the beach. Although this was not as effective as fishing from a boat it did enable them to survive. Already their first boat was nearing completion as the old men showed the younger ones the skills that they would need when they had passed on.

Livius met with Drusus and Marius at the small port partly to see how they had fared but mainly to let them know that the Roman military machine was going to bring security to them. Alana had been the wife of the headman and now, alone, she managed the settlement. "What else is there for me to do? Curl up in a ball and die? It is not our way. My people have clung to this strip of land for generations and we are not going to let that evil witch destroy it. "She waved her arm around and Livius could see the crude palisade which was being erected, "when the cold comes we will have the time to make it even stronger."

"But we are coming old woman. The legion is building a road to the pass and eventually here. Rome has a fleet and soon you will see mighty ships yonder."

She smiled the cynical smile of the old. "When I see your mighty fleet moored where our boats used to be then I will believe you. Until then we fear everyone whether that be the bandits who prey on the travellers or the Irish who come for our children and long after Rome has gone we will still be here. Will you join us for food?" She pointed at the fish on racks drying in the salty air.

Livius shook his head touched by both the generosity of a woman who had little herself but was willing to share and also by the courage and spirit of this indomitable community. "Well Drusus we have another reason to seek the witch."

"She must have gone to Ireland."

"I don't know. She is as slippery as an eel and as cunning as a snake. I would not be surprised if she were hiding somewhere in Brigantia. Send two riders back to the legion with the information about the road." He handed over a wax tablet. "Here is the information in written form but I suspect the prefect would prefer to be told. Then we are off to pastures new."

"South sir?"

"Yes the Prefect wants to know just what lies south of us. There is a small fort at Bremmetenacum which protects the road from Mamucium but there is only a small cohort of auxilia there and they have not explored the land to the coast. I will go to the fort and see the commander. The rest of you can spread out and cover the land as far as the coast. Your maniple, Drusus, can have the land closest to the coast, Marius the middle and I will take the land close to the road." He held out the rough map which he had copied onto the deerskin. "We will meet in a week close to here." He pointed to a spot about twenty miles north of Mamucium. "But as always if you discover something inform the others. The more that know the information the more useful it is. May the Allfather be with you."

The settlement of Belisama was on the Belisama River and had been steadily growing as the lands around became safer. The river provided both water for the settlement and food with its plentiful fish. The soil was rich and the people had grown prosperous by producing more than they needed and taking it to the nearby fort and selling it. Other enterprising farmers had begun to trade with the merchants who used the new Roman road. The headman, Ban, was pleased with the development of his small town. They had no stone buildings but he had visited the Roman fort and was impressed by the strength of such buildings. When he had returned he had ordered the village to build a strong palisade and gate. Some had objected for the Irish had not raided for many years but Ban had heard stories of the Selgovae and Novontae raiding as far south as the land of the lakes; with the new Roman road that land was but a day's travel away. "It is better to be safe than sorry", had been in message. Now that the work was completed his people could see the wisdom of his plan. They had devised a method by which two men from the settlement would guard the gate during the hours of daylight. During the night it was closed and that had produced the benefit of less poultry being taken by the foxes. Ban was seen as a wise and capable headman.

When the Roman column was seen heading towards them from the south they were more intrigued than worried. The Romans from the fort never came west, reserving their limited resources for the patrols on the road which Ban had heard had suffered from increased banditry of late. The two men on the gate sent a boy with a message and, by the time Ban arrived he could see the

135

eighty man column. Having been to the fort he understood a little about the way the Romans organised their army and this did not look like the auxiliaries from the fort for these used the oblong rounded shields of the legion. He was surprised; he did not know that the legion was operating in this region.

The centurion who greeted him smiled in greeting. "Hail. You are the headman?"

"I am and who are you?"

The smile suddenly left the centurion's face and the two guards at the gate were shocked when the centurion hit Ban across the face with the back of his hand knocking the greybeard to the ground. "I am your worst nightmare traitor for I am here to find the traitors who joined with the evil Morwenna in the revolt last year."

Ban wiped the blood from his mouth and, as he tried to rise protested, "We were not part of the revolt."

The centurion placed his foot firmly on the man's chest to prevent him rising. "That is what we thought you would say. When my men discover your weapons we will find otherwise. You two." He pointed at two of his column, one of them a giant with a scarred face, "Hold him here until we have searched this nest of vipers." While Tiny and his companion restrained Ban, Decius led the rest through the gates passing the shocked inhabitants. "Secure and disarm these two. Search every building for weapons and booty."

His men were well practiced in the art of brutality and any minor act of resistance or even a question, was greeted with a savage blow regardless of sex or age. The floors of the huts were ripped up revealing the jars with the meagre and minute monies saved by the villagers. When they searched the headman's roundhouse hut they found his helmet and sword. Decius held them triumphantly aloft. "See the mark of the rebel! Crucify him!"

136

When the women wailed it availed them naught. Decius' men crudely fashioned a cross despite the villagers' protests. Ban's youngest son, a boy of fourteen, tried to release his father. Decius gave a nod and the boy had his throat slit causing a roar and scream of pain from the distraught headman. Tiny found a hammer and waited for the command from Decius. Decius nodded and Ban's ankles and wrists were broken. They tied him to the cross and then hammered it to the gate. "This is the fate of all traitors and your ill gotten gains will be taken as taxes by the Roman Empire. It does not pay to defy Rome."

As the column left, the shocked villagers looked at the devastation left by the vicious legionaries. Ban's eldest son followed them discreetly and returned when he was sure they had moved away. When he returned they cut down the headman and his weeping wife saw to his wounds. "I was not a rebel before," croaked the headman through cracked and bleeding lips, "but the next time I will join and fight for if this is what we get by standing idly by then we would be as well dying with honour and our swords in our hands.

Brennus and his men were waiting in the woods a couple of miles away. "Successful?"

"Aye we crucified the headmen and killed his son. They should listen."

"Did you kill him?"

"No just maimed him. I think you will find ready volunteers just waiting there, they will be eager to kill Romans." This was the third settlement they had raided in the last week and they had refined their methods so that Brennus now had a rebel army of over a hundred angry warriors. They were kept well apart from the deserter army which had raided them and Decius would have to find a way, later on, to integrate the two armies. The region was ripe for rebellion. Brennus no longer went into the villages for he was busy training his army. Gurth was an older warrior who had shown a talent for acting the outraged Brigante and he was the one who now collected the potential rebels.

When Gurth and his three men, looking suitably travel stained and weary tramped into the village they were greeted at first with suspicion. Brennus had learned to affect a saddened look. "Please can you help us we are fleeing from the Romans."

Ban son of Ban strode angrily up to the three men. "Are you the rebels who caused the cursed Romans to do this?" He gestured at the maimed body of his father being bandaged by his loving and tearful wife.

"No we lived across the mountains until the Romans came and destroyed my village. We have walked many days seeking a friendly roof."

Mollified Ban son of Ban said, "You are welcome here. Where are you headed?"

"We have heard of rebels who hide in the woods west of here," shrugging he added, "If they treat us badly when we help them we thought we should join those who fight for what else have we to lose?"

"What else indeed?"

When Gurth left the following day he had twenty warriors with him all of them leaving with Ban's blessing to wreak revenge on those who had so unjustly attacked them.

The Centurion in charge of the fort looked suspiciously at Livius and Rufius as they entered the fort. "Is the Ninth operating down here now?"

"No sir but they will be. They are building a road from Glanibanta to Itunocelum. Our task is to scout the land west of you."

Relieved at their answer he took Livius into the Praetorium. As he went in Livius nodded to Rufius. They had learned over the past months that intelligence could be gathered anywhere, even in a Roman fort. Often the ordinary soldiers knew things which their officers did not. Frequently the information appeared minor but Livius had learned that lots of little pieces of intelligence frequently added up to more significant outcomes.

"Wine?"

"No thank you sir."

"I am glad that you are here for we have had many problems of late."

"The rebellion?"

"No and that is the strange thing. During the rebellion we were largely unaffected. The Brigante here supported Cartimandua and have remained loyal to her ideas." Livius unconsciously let his hand drop to the hilt of the Sword of Cartimandua. In his mind the thought came that there was a continuity which ran through this land and it had all started with the famous Queen, Ulpius of the ala and the sword. "We have had more organised raids along the road. I now have to keep three quarters of the cohort on constant patrol to make sure that traders can ply their trade. A few weeks ago supplies intended for Brocauum and Luguvalium were stolen and the merchants murdered along with their escort."

"You have had bandits before."

"Aye but they were not organised. They were opportunists and they usually only attacked small groups or lone traders. These bandits attack columns with armed guards."

"That is unusual."

"And then we have reports of villages, which have always welcomed us becoming surly and uncooperative. Those who used to bring their goods for trade have stopped and some villages have reported Roman legionaries attacking them." He paused wondering how to ask the next question without causing offence. "It isn't your lot is it?"

Decius shook his head. "We have one cohort in the land of the lakes building a road. The rest are getting ready to go north. The Twentieth Valeria perhaps?"

"They are in Deva and I think they have their hands full with the Ordovices and Silures. The villagers must have mistaken Irish raiders for Romans."

Decius shook his head. "I don't think so. The Roman legionary has a distinctive uniform. And two Irish never wear the same armour or weapons. It seems we have come at a good time."

"Beware the villages. If you are travelling in pairs they may take their revenge on you. Last year I would have been confident that you would have been welcomed by the Brigante, even amidst the rebellion but now...."

"Thank you. This is important information. I think the Ninth may have to come south after all."

When Rufius and Livius compared notes Livius was disturbed by what Rufius told him. "Some of the lads said that when they found the dead traders there were broken bits of mail and broken Roman equipment discarded at the scenes."

"Could it have come from the traders?"

"They reckoned not. They seem to think it was deserters."

"Deserters don't normally wear uniforms or armour. We need to contact the others; I think we need to go in disguise around here. Romans are not welcome."

By the end of the day they had met up with the rest of the maniple and collected Marius' men. Livius reported their finds and Marius also found it worrying.

"There are many deserters, we all know that. Every legion and auxilia has lost soldiers, especially after battles and the rebellion. All it takes is for half a dozen to get together and you have a major problem."

"This sounds more than half a dozen. We need to hide the helmets and mail. If you go in villages go afoot and without

140

anything which marks you as Roman. But we need to get in the villages and gauge the moods. Rufius find Drusus and give him the information I just gave to the others."

"What will you do sir?"

"I will find the Prefect and report this intelligence to him. I should still be able to meet with you as arranged. Be careful there is something going on here which looks bigger than just a few raids."

Metellus rubbed his chin. "It looks remarkably like the work of Morwenna to me. But what do I know?"

"Don't disparage yourself Metellus. You may well be right. Keep your ears open for any witch or druid related intelligence."

Chapter 11

The Prefect was both surprised and pleased when Livius arrived at Glanibanta. The cohort had made good progress on the road and they would soon be able to begin work on the fort. Star looked exhausted to the point of collapse and Livius knew that he would need a spare mount before returning south.

"You are a pleasant surprise Decurion although I suspect that your unexpected arrival means that things are not as they should be."

Once in the Praetorium Livius outlined the problems and unexpected events south of him. "Hm. That does not sound good." He looked shrewdly at the intelligent intelligence officer who had matured rapidly since taking over his new role. "What do you think Livius?"

The use of his first name gave Livius an indication of the Prefect's perception of him and encouraged him to be frank. "I think this is Morwenna's doing. One of my men, Metellus, who has a shrewd brain, agrees with me in this." The Prefect looked at Livius thinking 'as you have.' "He also thinks that this reeks of Morwenna for it is both subtle and insidious. I will know more when my men and I have had the chance to visit the settlements."

"From what you have told me, that could be dangerous. If they do not trust Romans then they may just take their anger and frustration out on your men operating alone as they do."

"We will pretend to be just ordinary Brigante or Trinovante. It is the main reason why I have allowed my men to grow their hair longer and beards," he chuckled, "despite some less than complimentary comments from some of the other officers of the Ninth."

Waving the idea away with a dismissive hand gesture the prefect leaned forward. "I will send for the Batavians to help us build this road a little faster. I think that we can have the road finished in two weeks and then, if I leave the Batavians to build

142

their fort I can bring the cohort south to… What did you say the name of this fort was?"

In answer Livius pointed to the spot on the map. "It is about thirty miles south of here on the road. If you just march down the road you will find it." He hesitated. "If I might suggest something sir?"

"Speak freely Livius, your ideas are rarely frivolous."

"If the Governor were to send some of the fleet around the coast it would increase our intelligence gathering and make a statement about our presence."

"A good suggestion but by the time the message has reached Eboracum and the fleet and then the fleet despatched it could be winter."

"Which may be the time we need it. Besides it would do the people such as the village of Itunocelum good to see the reassuring presence of the fleet. It would put down a marker for our authority. Neither the Irish nor the Brigante have ships. It might give us advance warning of any enemies and it might help with the supplies for there is only one road in the region. You will only have four hundred men and while the legions are doughty warriors they may well be outnumbered with the army facing them similarly armed. They have stolen armour intended for the auxiliaries at Brocauum. This deserter cohort we hear about worries me. We can defeat the Brigante as we have shown before but these may well be Roman legionaries trained by us."

"A dangerous combination indeed. Very well I shall send for the third cohort and base them here as a back up. The Ninth is very thinly stretched and we must head north in the next year if we are to make the Stanegate secure once more. Anyway Livius when will you return south?"

"This afternoon when I have found another mount."

"It is fortunate that you left spares here."

143

"Not fortune sir but planning. The old sergeant from Marcus' Horse brought the string over last month and they are fine horses."

When the Explorates met in the middle of the lonely copse they all had disquieting news for Livius. "It is worse than we thought sir. It seems Roman soldiers have been going into small villages taking what little they have and then killing or wounding a few in every village."

"They even crucified one headman!"

"And all in the name of Rome sir. If we had not grown our hair and beards we would have been torn limb from limb sir."

"As bad as that Metellus?"

"Worse!" said Drusus. "There is an anger and fury amongst the Brigante that I didn't see in the rebellion. They are like a volcano waiting to erupt. Many men have left the villages. I fear there is a rebel army somewhere that was not here before."

"Perfect conditions for Morwenna to make a return. Well the Ninth is coming down and we can't deal with a rebellion but how do we find these deserters?"

"Metellus has an idea sir."

"Well Metellus spit it out."

"It seems to me that they have to have somewhere local to recruit these deserters sir. "

"With you up to now but Britannia is a big province."

"Yes sir but they have to be somewhere close to where we are now and yet far enough away from a legionary fortress to avoid accidental discovery. If they are legionaries I would say Mamucium would be a good place to start as it is an auxiliary fort. I think the fort you visited sir is too isolated. Then there must be some big vicus with a population of men who have deserted from the auxiliary," he tailed off lamely, "well sir that was the idea. Seems a little flimsy as a plan now that I have mentioned it."

"No Metellus, I think you have something. What we need is for one of us to frequent the taverns and see who is recruiting. My maniple will take Mamucium, Drusus and Marius, split the rest between yourselves and find taverns. We only need two men from each of your units to be the bait. The rest can just keep their ears open."

"One thing sir."

"Yes Drusus?"

"You can't be the bait."

Livius' face reddened. "Why not? It is out of character for you Drusus to be insubordinate."

"But he isn't sir. We have spent the last day while waiting for you to discuss this. You are known sir. You are famous. You are the nephew of the Governor. Do you think no-one would recognise you? And if they recognise you then we are all in trouble."

"And the same goes for Rufius."

"Why me? No-one knows me."

"True but you are too young. Deserters are men who have had enough of life in the army. You look like you only started shaving last week."

"No I am afraid it has to be old miserable looking troopers."

"Like me I suppose Drusus?"

"Well Agrippa if we had an award for misery, you would win it every time."

"You are right Drusus, at least about Rufius, Decius and me. So we will give it a week. Metellus, Rufius and Decius your role will be to scout along the coast. Find out if there have been any unusual occurrences. Look for fires and camps where you would not expect to find them. Ask about shipping. When you have combed the coast head inland and do the same. We meet back here in seven days. May the Allfather be with you."

Agrippa had been completely transformed by the time they reached the outskirts of Mamucium. He and Cassius looked as though they had slept in a hedge for a month. They were unkempt with a dirty and stained tunic while sporting a wicked looking non-regulation dagger at their sides. Agrippa also carried a nasty looking cudgel. They waited in some scrubby bushes just outside the vicus while Livius gave them their last instructions. "I will go into the fort first and find out what they know then I will stay at the inn closest to the Porta Praetorium. I would imagine that would be the one least likely to be used by any deserters or potential rebels. You two find any tavern tonight in which to stay and keep your ears open. Tomorrow come to the inn where I will be staying. If I have any information I will try to pass it on to you but If I don't stroke my nose I have nothing to tell you so stay away and repeat the following day. If you have anything for me then scratch your head. I will then give you the sign to talk. Remember we only need an idea of where the deserters, if they exist as a force, might be. There is no need to take risks."

"And I thought our role was one big risk."

"You know what I mean Cassius. I will go first with the horses. You two separate and go in individually."

Livius frowned as he approached the gate of the fort. The sentries were lounging and did not appear to have the usual alert expression he had come to know from the auxiliary cohorts in the north. Prefect Sura would have torn more than a strip off each of them had they been his Batavians. As he approached and looked closer he could see that their armour was rusted in places and their helmets did not gleam as he would have expected. Livius had arrived feeling dirty and dishevelled but already he felt smarter. The two soldiers took one look at him, as he approached the Porta Praetorium, and went back to their conversation. If this was the standard throughout the fort then Mamucium was in trouble.

146

The main avenue in any fort was normally a hive of activity this one seemed to be a drone of apathy and lethargy. He shook his head. Perhaps the Prefect would give him a better insight into this cohort. There was no-one to whom he could give the reins of the three horses and he regretted not stabling them at the tavern. He had hoped that the fort would have looked after them but so far he was not impressed and was loath to leave his horses here. He tied the reins together knowing that Star would not move until commanded.

He climbed the steps and knocked on the door. "Come." When he entered he found the prefect's clerk with a jug of wine in his hand. "Yes?"

"Decurion Sallustius of the Ninth Legion to see the Camp Prefect."

Sniffing the clerk went into the inner office saying, "I'll see if he is free." After what seemed an age, the clerk came out and said, "You can go in now."

Porcius Fortuna was a huge red faced man. Livius had known other auxiliary prefects who liked to drink but each of them had looked fit. Porcius looked like he would struggle to get out of his chair and Livius could not imagine him marching further than the nearest inn. Although the clerk had tried to tidy the office Livius could still see the wine stains on the floor and the amphora peeping guiltily out from under the curtain. The man himself reeked of alcohol both stale and fresh. The stains on his uniform told its own story. The desk itself was devoid of anything other than a vine staff and there were no maps on the walls at all. Livius wondered what the man did to fill the day.

"Prefect Porcius Fortuna at your service. My clerk misheard he thought you said you were a decurion in the Ninth."

"He heard correctly. I am Decurion Princeps."

"But the Ninth don't have cavalry."

"They do and they are called Explorates. " The Prefect looked blank. "We act as scouts."

"Ah and what brings you here. " Suddenly he sat forward his face a picture of panic. "They aren't coming here are they? I mean we have the Twentieth Valeria at Deva already."

"They are coming south Prefect although not as far south as Mamucium. At least not at the moment, it all depends on my report and how things work out." Livius decided on the small lie just to get the walking wine cask before him to cooperate and help him.

"How can we help you?"

"First some questions. Have you heard of any outrages committed against the native Brigante around here?" The blank look on Porcius' face answered the question but the shake of the head and outstretched hands confirmed it. "Do you have trouble with either deserters or men deserting from the cohort?"

He began to wave his arms around and become more defensive, "Every cohort has men who desert. We have no more than the average."

"What would you say was the average?"

"Well I would have to look up…"

"No Prefect you said average. What would you say was the average?"

"Ah you mean in other units as well, oh twenty or thirty a year."

Livius almost gasped at the figure. He had never known more than one or two men desert. In Marcus' Horse it was hard to remember a deserter. He kept his face straight as though this was an average number. "And are there any inns and taverns in the vicus where these men might congregate?"

"Might be. I rarely leave the fort. You'd have to ask my clerk."

"Do you not go on patrols then?"

148

"No I am Camp Prefect. I am kept pretty busy here. Important job running this fort you know. Well if I can be of any further service. Just see my clerk eh?"

Holding his temper in check Livius went to talk to the clerk. It was obvious he had been listening for he said. "I have heard that the inn with the sign of the white horse and the tavern at the holly bush are the most disreputable and I would assume they would be where deserters would go. They are also the furthest from the fort."

"Thank you, you have been most kind." The sarcasm was wasted on the clerk who merely shrugged. Livius would not affect his world and he would go on profiting from a lazy superior.

As he rode through the gate the two sentries paid him no attention at all. This was intelligence which the Prefect would need to know. Mamucium controlled an important road; if it could not be relied upon then the whole of the north was in danger. Next time he would ask to speak to First Spear, which was always a good measure of the quality of a cohort.

He went straight to the first tavern which was within sight of the gate. It had a crude sign of a sheaf of corn and he went in. The owner was a neat little man with a greying beard and moustache. "I wish a room and stabling for three horses."

The man shrewdly weighed up the well built soldier who stood before him. He did not ask why he was not staying in the fort although it was obvious that the thought had crossed his mind, he merely upped his price. "Two denari a night."

The fee was exorbitant but it was vital that he stay here. "Of course and that will include food for me and my horses?"

Although phrased as a question his tone told the innkeeper that it was a statement and he would get no more from this sharp eyed Roman. "Of course sir, the finest in Mamucium. My inn is renowned for the delicacies from Rome. I even supply the Camp Prefect." Livius doubted that but he was not on holiday, he was gathering intelligence and the bed would probably be more comfortable than the hard floor he was used to. Having met the Camp Prefect he was in no doubt that the inn did indeed provide him with food and drink, probably at ridiculously high prices; more intelligence for the Prefect who would, no doubt, have the fort investigated.

Cassius had chosen the white horse. As soon as he saw the tavern keeper, Nautius Naevius, he recognised him as an ex-soldier. There was something about his demeanour and his sharp eye which flicked around the room; this marked him as a military man. He and Agrippa had discussed at great length, when riding to Mamucium the best approach to playing their parts. They had both decided that it would be better if they appeared to desire anonymity and poverty. Livius had given them enough denari so that they could afford to buy food and accommodation but they wanted to appear impoverished. Their hair was long enough to suggest that they had been in the military until recently and they both had enough experience of the rebellion to be able to conjure up a story. They had decided that a story based in truth was better and they would say that they would desert because of the harsh regime of their decurion, Livius Sallustius. Livius himself had gone along with this deception as his brother had been involved with Morwenna and the whole unit felt that the witch was behind this latest trouble.

Cassius sidled up to the landlord and asked, in as quiet a voice as possible, for a small beaker of beer. He made a great act of seeking enough coins to pay for it despite the fact that he had a large number of coins secreted about him. He nursed the beer for as long as possible and when he went for a second he asked if they had any food. The astute Nautius Naevius deliberately suggested a very cheap and plain cabbage soup and black bread using it as a test for Cassius' finances. When Cassius weighed it up and agreed reluctantly, Nautius knew that this was an ex

150

soldier fallen on hard times. If nothing else his soldier's sandals blared it as loudly as a buccina.

The evening dragged on and Cassius waited until he had emptied his beaker and plate before going to the door to relieve himself in the jug placed outside for just that purpose. When he returned to his seat Nautius came over and said, "Another?"

Cassius had obviously missed his calling as an actor in the theatres of Londinium for he looked up at the landlord with a look of panic on his face, as though financially embarrassed. Nautius leaned over and said quietly, "On the house soldier eh?" Cassius played the part beautifully and nodded gratefully. When the landlord returned with two beakers he broached the question which Cassius had wanted. "Fallen on hard times then eh?"

"Yeah. Things have been bad since... well they have been bad."

"Were you a soldier?" Cassius looked around in feigned panic. "Don't worry son. You are among friends here. I am an old soldier meself. Your past ends at the door. We are all comrades together. Which unit were you?"

"Marcus' Horse. They were tough bastards. That Prefect Decius Augustus, he was supposed to be a right evil swine."

"I wouldn't know it was Julius Demetrius who was my Prefect and he was alright. It was that bastard Livius Sallustius I hated." Cassius knew that he had passed the first test with the correction of the landlord. He was glad that they had not concocted a story about another unit. This way they would at least know the facts. He hoped that Agrippa was having similar questions.

"Right, right. It's this wound makes me mix names up. Well listen I know some people who can use useful lads like you. You interested in some work then? Good pay."

"Might be."

"Can't promise anything but how about I let you stay here tonight, a favour old soldier to old soldier eh? No charge and

151

tomorrow you can meet this friend of mine. How does that sound?"

"Well. Why should I trust you and why are you doing this for me?"

Nautius looked around as though he didn't want to be overheard, "Well I owe Marcus' Horse. They saved me and my lads once in a bit of bother up north so let us call it repaying a debt."

"Fair enough. How about another beer then?"

"For one of Marcus' Horse? Anytime."

The next day Cassius got up early. Nautius asked him pointedly where he was going. "I buried something before I came here. From what you said last night I thought I might need it."

"Sword eh? Right well as long as you are back here this afternoon eh?"

"You think I would miss the chance of regular food and pay? I'll be here and thank you. I owe you."

"Don't worry, it's the least I can do."

He soon found where Livius was. When he entered he saw the decurion sitting at a table eating some nuts, olives, fruit and cheese. He scratched his head and was delighted when Livius stroked his nose. Cassius went outside and found the stables. He went to his horse and began to stroke it. The stable boy wandered over, "What you doing then?"

"I used to be in the cavalry. I like horses. Not doing any harm am I?"

The stable boy seemed satisfied. "Well that's alright then but I am just outside so don't think you can just walk off with it."

When Livius walked in they both checked that they were alone. "I take it you have some information?"

"Yes, the tavern proved fruitful. The landlord is an ex-soldier and someone is going to contact me later."

"How did you get out then?"

"I told him I had to retrieve my sword."

"Take it then." Cassius went to the sackcloth which was in the corner of the stable and retrieved his sword.

"Have you heard from Agrippa?"

"Not yet but it is early."

"This may be the last chance I have to talk to you. Where do we go from here?"

Go along with them. When Agrippa contacts me, unless it is a more solid lead than yours I will tell him to forget his trail and join me. We will follow you."

"How?"

We know where you are staying and we know that it will not be until this afternoon. We will watch and follow. To help us you need to leave clues." He looked around for something they could use and then he remembered his meal. "Wait here I will be back." He returned with the olives. "Take these with you. Pretend to eat them. If you come to a fork in the path you take then drop one for left and two for right. Hopefully you should have enough but if they run out then use these nuts, "he handed him some cob nuts, "same code. Remember Cassius we just need where their base is. As soon as you get there escape as soon as you can. Take no chances and get back to the meeting point."

When Agrippa arrived in the tavern Livius stroked his nose. Agrippa looked over and nodded. Livius stood up, ""Why if it isn't my old friend." Agrippa came over to his table. As he did so Livius noticed that his face was bruised. "What happened?"

"Rough tavern. There was a fight and a couple of the locals turned me over."

"You alright?"

He snorted, "I've had worse falling off a horse."

"Any interest?"

"Not really. They seemed suspicious though. I played it like we discussed but they seemed a bit wary. To be honest I think the fight was to see if anyone came to rescue me. Tonight I..."

"Forget tonight. You move in here but I don't think it will be for long. Cassius is being contacted. We watch him. You look suitably rough so you loiter around the inn with the sign of the white horse and I will wait just outside the vicus with our horses. I think we can assume they will come out of the west gate and when they do we follow Cassius."

Cassius was intrigued more than afraid when he returned to the inn. Nautius seemed relieved that he had returned and wandered over. He slipped him a denarius. "Here is your signing on pay. You got your sword then?"

Cassius was in no doubt that the innkeeper had seen him enter with the sword for nothing escaped his notice but he played along slapping the hilt of the gladius. "Yeah." He leered a conspiratorial grin. "Feel dressed now."

"Know what you mean. A soldier always feels naked without his weapon. You wait there and the contact will be along to pick you and the others up later on."

"Others?"

"Well you don't think you are the only one who has left the eagle do you?"

Cassius wondered if Agrippa would be amongst the 'others'. He hoped so. It was one thing operating behind enemy lines and hiding but he was walking into the wasps' nest, alone. He was reassured by the decurion's comments; all he needed was the location of the camp. He was confident that he would be able to escape. He assumed that they would be careful on the road but once at the camp they would think that he was committed to the cause, whatever the cause was.

When Centurion walked in with the three shabby looking ex-soldiers Cassius saw the nod he gave to Nautius and then the flick

154

of Nautius' head towards him. The man walked over to Cassius and leaned in close. "You the one who served in Marcus' Horse?" Cassius nodded. "Get your things."

Cassius small pack was next to him and he rose waving his thanks to the innkeeper as he left. When they emerged into the light Cassius was pleased to see Agrippa tossing dice with a one armed beggar. Although Agrippa did not look in Cassius' direction he knew that he had been seen and he felt safer. They did not leave the vicus as Cassius had expected but instead went to another inn with a holly bush outside. Centurion gestured for them to wait outside. None of the other men appeared to know each other and none spoke so Cassius followed their lead. It suited Cassius for it afforded him the opportunity to look around and spot Agrippa some hundred paces away lurking in a doorway. This time the leader emerged with five men.

"Right we are finished here now. You call me Centurion. I don't give a rat's arse what your names are so don't bother telling me. We have twenty miles to go today and this isn't the legion. You drop out," he paused dramatically, "and I slit your throat. Regard this as both an initiation test and a test of your fitness. Now move."

Cassius put himself at the back, confident that he could keep up but aware that he needed to be able to leave a trail should they deviate from the road. Centurion set off at an easy lope, the line of men spread out over thirty paces. Cassius could see that they were heading north west from the sun and the moss growing on the north side of the trees. He could tell that the man next to him was struggling as, after the first mile on the well worn track, he began to slow up. Cassius looked at him. He was older than even Agrippa and looked to be carrying a wound of some kind or an old injury. "You had better keep up, I have a feeling that big bastard meant what he said."

155

The man turned to Cassius, his eyes sunken with pain. "I'll be alright it's just a sword wound I have in my leg. Makes me a bit lame. I'll be alright once it loosens up.."

"Right well I'll stay with you makes you stand out a little less."

A grateful yet surprised look erupted on the older man's face. "Thanks. Why?"

"Let's just say I saw enough comrades left with wounds like you have and this is my chance to repay them." Cassius hated the lie but he needed to stay at the back for the track they were following was not a Roman road but an older path way and he didn't know if it would be straight or not. He was desperate to look around and see where his friends were but he had to assume that they had seen them leave and were watching. The problem was that the land through which they were travelling was largely devoid of cover.

He heard Centurion's voice boom out and saw him looking over his shoulder at them. "You two ladies at the back keep up or else…" He let the threat hang in the air.

"Yes Centurion, just getting our first wind." Cassius gritted his teeth and murmured to his companion. "I think we are going to get sick of that bastard sooner rather than later."

The man grinned showing great gaps in his teeth. "What do you mean later? I am fed up of him already. By the way my name is Mocius, Twentieth Valeria."

"Cassius, Marcus' Horse."

"How in Mithras' name did we end up here, deserters?"

Cassius shook his head. "The Parcae I suspect." He looked again at the man. Mithras was the god and the cult of many legionaries. In many ways it was a secret society. Cassius wondered why the others of the sect had not aided him as they normally did. It mattered not but it spoke volumes about the man.

He was a soldier first and when he had said he would make it Cassius now knew that to be true.

Mocius nodded. "They are bitches and that is the truth."

Chapter 12

Agrippa soon found Livius waiting with the horses. "They picked men up from the inn I visited. The ones who roughed me up are with Cassius."

Livius wondered if that were significant. "Well they have a fair number there."

"Yeah I counted ten including Cassius. The big one leading them he looks like he has seen service."

"Didn't he look familiar to you?"

"How do you mean sir?"

"I think I saw him on one of the boats that left Itunocelum last year."

Agrippa closed his eyes to picture the scene. "You could be right but the dirty cloak he is wearing covers much of him up." He gestured at the straggling column disappear along the track. "North west but no cover."

"I know." He scanned the horizon. The path went into a hollow and a low ridge ran north south, away from the path. "If we cross that ridge we can make better time than those on foot and, hopefully, we will find a better vantage point if we cut west further up."

"It's a risk."

"If we lose them then we backtrack along the track until we find sign. Cassius will be letting us know if they turn off that track." They headed their horses north east and dropped over the ridge. There was another track way heading north and Livius could see that, some way in the distance it joined the Roman road. "Well we have a track for part of the way. We will ride for a couple of miles." He held his hand up at the weak sun. "If we keep the sun at our backs then we should get some distance between us and them."

After two hours the column stopped and Centurion passed around a water bottle. "If you ladies didn't bring any food then tough titty. I am not your mother."

Cassius had the olives and nuts but he had to keep those to mark the trail. He had secreted some of the bread Nautius had provided at breakfast and he took some out. He offered half to Mocius who took it gratefully. As they chewed Cassius scanned the track behind them. There was no sign of horsemen and no cover. He could see a ridge away to the east and to the west the land fell away to low lying damp ground. Cassius hoped that Livius knew what he was doing for he sensed that they were getting close to the camp. The rest was only for a few moments and they started again. Cassius felt the stiffness in his legs as soon as they started to run. He was a fit soldier but being fit for riding and fit for running were two different things.

Mocius saw his pained expression and he grinned. "It is good to see a horseman struggling. The times we watched lads like you galloping off while we were trudging through mud and rocks. How we cursed you."

"Well you have your revenge now. Give me a horse any day."

The land began to climb again, away from the soft spongy turf, and Cassius could feel his calves tightening. With a sickening feeling in his stomach he saw the Centurion's left hand come out as they approached a fork in the path. They took the path which veered sharply west. It was time for his first olive. He had the olive in his hand already having placed it there at the halt. He dropped back slightly so that he was running just behind Mocius. As soon as they reached the trampled area he pretended to half stumble and then dropped the precious fruit to the ground.

"You alright?"

"Yeah just a bit of cramp. Cleared it now." He was well and truly in the Allfather's hand now. He glanced up to see the wood which started some four hundred paces up the other fork and cursed. Had the wood been next to the road then his companions would have been able to watch over him. He was on his own now unless they could find the olive.

"Good shout sir!"

"Thanks Agrippa." Livius had got ahead of the column and they had waited in the woods until the column with Cassius had appeared. The two men watched from the eaves of the wood as the deserters headed west. "It looks as though Cassius is able to leave sign. I saw him drop something."

"If we ride over there we should be able to see how easy it is to spot."

"We will just wait until they get further ahead. I don't want to make our friends jumpy." When they did leave the safety of the woods they walked their horses down to the parting of the ways. Livius' sharp eyes easily picked out the olive.

"The track sir or another inspired guess?"

Livius looked back along the tack and then ahead. "We have come what five, six miles?"

"About that."

"I can't see them doing more than fifteen to eighteen miles so we will follow slowly. We know that we can see sign and so far there is nowhere for an ambush."

Livius could see that they were skirting the edge of an upland area, not a steep slope but one which led, eventually, to the road and then the high divide. This was new country to Livius and he knew that his Explorates would have to become familiar with it if they were to be able to give the right intelligence. "Have you noticed Agrippa how few rivers there are?"

"Yes sir. In the east they cross the whole land. We have not seen many at all apart from that little one to the north and the one near Mamucium."

"The Seteia?"

"I'll take your word for it. Well they are the only two. Is that important sir?"

"To the legions? Yes. It means they haven't got natural points to block an invasion. That little river in the north, the Belisama, why a child could wade that which means that if Morwenna comes over she can go anywhere. There are no barriers. Glanibanta and the new fort will, effectively stop anyone going north or south but down here well they could cross the divide and raid the rich lands near Eboracum at any time. I think she is coming." Agrippa looked at the younger man and thanked, not for the first time, the Allfather for not giving him the ambition to be anything other than a trooper. He could just do his job and not worry, as his decurion did, about the bigger picture.

Centurion halted them one more time and gave them more water. They had not deviated from the path but their run had almost exhausted them. "You have done alright for a bunch of unfit rabble and we have finished with running. We are nearly at the camp and we will now walk. Rest over. Let's go."

As Cassius stood up he let fall four olives. Although not a fork he wanted to warn his friends, if they were still following, that they were approaching danger.

Agrippa was on point and he waved over Livius. "Sir four olives but there is no fork in the path."

"There has to be a reason but I can't think what it could be. Search around and see if they left any sign." A few minutes searching revealed that they had indeed continued along the path. "Let's just take it steady then. Perhaps he was warning us."

"Could have been dropped accidentally?"

"Agrippa do you think Cassius would have done that?"

"Not really."

"Then onwards."

Metellus and his companions approached the dune filled area with apprehension. They had seen increasing tracks both of horses and men and yet they had not seen a sign of civilisation neither civilian nor military. Metellus halted them. "Someone has been here recently and there were a lot of them. Look around. See what you can find."

"Metellus, droppings, from horses."

"Well done Rufius. Nice to know you are still the shit master. That rules out the Brigante over here and makes me think cavalry. Is it ours?"

Rufius knelt down to examine the spoor. "Don't think so this is just grass fed." Roman cavalry, certainly Marcus' Horse and the Exploratores liked to supplement grass with grain. It gave their horses an edge in terms of stamina and strength.

"Well that is a worrying thought. " He looked over at the pine forest which grew out of the straggly grass flecked dunes. "The tracks head over there. Let's follow. But boys, let us be careful. Especially you Decius."

The young man bridled a little. "Why me?"

"Let us just say, that, as the only trooper wounded so far in this maniple, that you are sometimes a little impetuous, one might even say headstrong. Remember the cave and the almost fatal incident?"

"One little…"

"Seriously Decius, in our line of work one mistake can mean your death so do me a favour and think before you gallop eh?"

It was the smell of wood smoke which made them halt. Metellus waved them back towards the edge of the woods. Once they were in the dunes he dismounted. "Wood smoke suggests a camp. I think we have found something. Decius you need to go back to the meeting point and wait for the others. This is valuable information."

Decius stuck his chest out belligerently. "Why don't we wait until we have found something a little more important than what could be charcoal burners?"

"He's right Metellus. This is just the kind of place charcoal burners would come or it could be hunters we don't know. It would be a mistake to send a message back and find that we were at the wrong place."

In his heart Metellus knew that he was right and that this was the deserter's camp but he could also see their argument. They had to be certain. "Right. Let's find somewhere to hide the horses and then we will investigate that smoke."

Centurion halted them at the edge of the wood. The sandy soil showed that many feet both human and animal had passed through before them. "Right we are close now. You need to follow me in single file and follow exactly where I go. We have put a few traps around in case anybody sticks their nose in here."

Cassius was glad that he had only dropped a few of his valuable fruits and nuts. He would need them all now. He held them in his hand as he followed Mocius through the pine forest. Once again he placed a handful at the spot where they entered the pine trees.

Almost immediately they turned left and only went forwards for ten paces before jinking right. Cassius began to worry that he would run out of fruit. After another three sharp turns they found themselves on a broad track which Cassius could see led to a clearing. As he stepped out in the light the sight almost took his breath away. There was a camp albeit without a palisade. There was a Praetorium and stables and a watch tower which just peeped above the surrounding pines. He had found the camp and he just hoped that Livius was close behind.

Like Metellus, two miles away on the other side of the wood, Agrippa and Livius smelled the wood smoke when they reached the small pile of fruit. "Looks like this is where they went in then sir?"

"Why the small pile?"

"Eh?"

"Why not one or two? You wait here with the horses I will go in on foot." Agrippa could not understand his superior's caution but he respected him enough to stay silent. Livius walked gingerly and when he saw the next pile of fruit, only three pieces this time, he paused. There was no discernible path; the floor uniformly even. He knelt down and he could just see the faint imprint of a footprint leading left. He took out his dagger and scored three lines in the bark of the tree to his right, the resin oozing slowly out in the cool of the evening. This time he crawled on hands and knees; when he found the next fruit he became more confident and, again marked the tree with three lines. He turned right, confident that this was the correct path. After two steps he began to doubt himself and dropped to the ground to examine the footprints. As he did so the dead fall was triggered and the branch, with nails embedded in it, flew over his body to where his head would have been and thudded into the tree. Realising he had come the wrong way he backtracked. He heard the loudly whispered, "Sir! Sir" You alright?"

"Stay there Agrippa I am fine." He backtracked to where he had marked the tree and looked around, he found the footprints and saw that he had not gone far enough right. He stood and retraced his footsteps to Agrippa.

"What happened sir? I heard a crash."

"This is the camp alright. They have deadfalls and the path twists. I was lucky the trap missed my head by an uncia. We'll camp back up the path a ways and watch for people coming and going. Cassius has only just arrived and if he does escape it will be in the night. I am hoping that he has the route in his head and will come out here."

164

On the other side of the wood the three troopers had also discovered the traps, fortunately it was the smallest one, Decius , who had triggered one and it had only stunned him. Metellus and Rufius helped him back to the horses while they returned to the path. Like Livius they had marked the trail with bark marks but Metellus had the advantage of the sharpest eyes and the best tracker in Rufius who was able to find the main, trampled route easily. Rufius waved Metellus to the ground and they crawled. Rufius held his hand up again and they waited in silence. When their ears became attuned to the sound of the woods they heard the unnatural noise of talk, just a low murmur and then the clang of metal on metal. Rufius signalled for Metellus to remain where he was while he crawled forward, disappearing from view. Metellus had to wait in silence, listening for the cry of discovery. He suddenly started as a hand appeared from behind him to tap him on the shoulder. Even as he dragged out his pugeo he saw, to his relief that it was Rufius who led him to the edge of the wood.

"You nearly made me jump out of my skin back there. Where in Hades did you learn to move so quietly?"

"Hunting when I was a kid. If I was noisy we didn't eat."

"Well?"

"That is it alright. A full camp with barracks and stables." His face suddenly became serious and worried at the same time. "If I didn't know better I would have said it was one of our camps."

"Why?"

"Everyone was wearing Roman armour, helmets. Gladii, everything."

They had reached Decius and Metellus checked the wound which was superficial. "How are you feeling?"

"Stupid."

"Don't worry about it. One of us was bound to have tripped those traps; the Allfather was watching over us for he made sure it struck you, the smallest of us. Had it struck either of us it would not have been the branch which connected but the nails and I do not think we would have survived."

"Well. Is it the right place?"

Grinning Metellus said, "It is. Now this is what we will do. Decius you find the Prefect. Head back to Glanibanta and stay on the road. That is the route he will be taking. Tell him it is a huge camp. How big Rufius?"

"Almost a cohort and fully armed."

"Got that?" Decius nodded realising the import of the message. "Tell him we think that boats have brought others ashore so there may be a second camp or even an army here." He paused before continuing. "Tell him I think that the Queen may be back causing more mischief."

Rufius looked at him. "Sticking your neck out a little aren't you?"

"Just doing what we are supposed to be doing gathering intelligence and making intelligent guesses. If I am wrong they can laugh at me. But if I am right… We will go back to the meeting place." The three of them wasted no time in goodbyes but, fearful of discovery rode swiftly away.

Cassius and Mocius found themselves at the centre of the camp on an area which had been cleared to form what was in effect a parade ground. Cassius was impressed by how military it looked. The man, who had brought them, Centurion, had obviously held that office in a previous life. What intrigued Cassius was the reason for his desertion. It was rare for someone of that rank to do so. That would be an interesting story.

The object of Cassius' speculation Centurion just barked, "Wait here!" and he disappeared into the Praetorium. Most of the other soldiers they could see ignored them making Cassius think that this was not an uncommon event. He quickly took in the layout. He needed to know where the tower was and the barracks if he was to slip out later on. He could easily remember the route out. He had already decided to wait until dark and then head to the point where he had left the pile of olives. He would expect the decurion to be there if he had succeeded in following and if not then Cassius would have to make his own way north to the meeting point. He almost smiled to himself. It looked like the assignment, which had once seemed impossible, was going to be a success.

When Centurion came out of the Praetorium he was accompanied by the biggest legionary Cassius had ever seen; a huge scarred warrior but what took his breath away was not the size of the man but what was revealed when they parted and he saw their leader for the man was the double of Livius, his decurion. He quickly hid the shocked expression from his face; it could not be Livius and, as he peered more closely he could clearly see the differences: the hair was too short and there was something about the sneering smile and the cold dead eyes that marked him as different. He also noticed the way he walked; there was arrogance about this man that marked him as different from the decurion.

When he spoke the voice too could have been that of Livius. "Thank you gentlemen for joining our little enterprise. I am Decius Lucullus Sallustius and my men call me General. You will address me as such. Centurion you have met and you will meet my friend here I can assure you." Tiny gave a suitable lopsided and rather frightening grin. "You have left the Roman army with its rules, regulations and er poverty." The men all laughed for the smile on their new leader's face told them that he had made a joke. "You have joined an army which looks out for itself. We are a private enterprise army. We raid where we want and we take what we want. Soon we will raid even further and be joining another army to fight the Romans. The same Romans who I don't doubt flogged all of you many times." The nods were reassuring for Decius. It confirmed their implicit acceptance of his putative rebellion. You will be given a uniform, similar to the ones you wore when in the service of Rome and you will be assigned to a century as with Rome. There the training ends. Tomorrow you begin to earn your first salary." He nodded to Tiny who disappeared into the Praetorium. "We do not have many rules however one of them is that you do not leave. We will not call it desertion we will call it, termination of contract. Your contract can only be terminated when you die. Here," Tiny dragged a man who had obviously been beaten badly, "we have someone who only joined yesterday and tried to leave us last night." Tiny pulled back the head and Cassius realised, with a sinking heart that it was Seius, one of Drusus' men. The eyes were almost closed and Cassius prayed that he would not open them and give away his secret. "You will now see what the punishment is for desertion."

Centurion nodded to two legionaries who brought out a sharpened stake cut from a young pine tree. It was as long a man's body. They brought it to the centre of the parade ground where Cassius noticed, for the first time, a hole which was surrounded by stained soil and sand. The men planted the stake in the hole so that it protruded with the spike uppermost, and suddenly Cassius had a sickening vision of what the punishment was to be.

Seius could not see what was coming and he looked exhausted as he was dragged by Tiny to the stake. "This is the punishment for desertion!" Tiny lifted the trooper up as though he was a piece of wood and then placed him slowly onto the sharpened point so that the spike began to enter his lower body. He did it gently at first so that Seius did not know what was coming, however as the point drove deeper upwards he uttered a scream, a scream so loud that Livius and Agrippa heard it, on the edge of the wood and shuddered. Tiny then let go of the prisoner and Seius' own body

168

weight drove him down onto the staked which ripped up into his body. His feet flailed around which merely aggravated the effect of the stake. It went further into his body and Cassius watched in horror as the man's bowels opened and joined the blood which was seeping from his body. After what seemed an age but must have only been moments Seius' head slumped forward as death and the Allfather mercifully claimed him.

"Now that you have seen the punishment, go and claim your uniform and the rewards of fighting in this army."

As they trudged slowly away each man's eyes were drawn to the horror that squatted on the parade ground. Cassius would have to rethink his escape attempt. He had more to tell Livius than he had expected. He had found his brother; all of the Exploratores knew the story and knew the anger which burned inside their leader. There was now an even greater reason for him to escape. The problem was how for it was now obvious to him that they watched for those who wished to leave the camp.

Later that night after they had tried on and adjusted their armour and made sure the other equipment, including swords and daggers were in good shape Mocius and Cassius strolled around the camp. They were mindful of the stares that they drew when they approached the perimeter but both men made sure they did not incur the wrath of Centurion or any of the other tough looking officers. They both found their eyes oddly drawn to the monstrosity that had been Seius.

"Horrible way to go."

"You are right Mocius. Not that I was thinking of running but that would certainly stop me."

"Really?"

"A man would be stupid to run."

Mocius bent down to pick up a stone which he casually tossed in the air. He caught it and stared hard at Cassius. "Then why were you leaving a trail when we came into the woods?"

Cassius felt a cold chill race through his body. "What do you mean? I wasn't leaving a trail."

"You weren't dropping olives and nuts?"

"What makes you think I was?"

"The fact that I watched you and I saw you do it were fairly big clues. Listen Cassius, you were considerate and kind today and I won't forget that. Whatever you did and for whatever reason your secret is safe with me. Just be careful. I would hate to watch you die like that."

"Don't worry Mocius you won't." Even as he was warned by his new friend Cassius was planning his desertion. After they had been given their uniform and food Centurion had told them of their first patrol. They were going on a raid the following day and, marked as a cavalryman, he had been assigned the role of scout. Once out in the open he would defy anyone to catch him. On foot he was a fish out of water, on a horse and he was like a centaur. He just hoped that Mocius would not suffer repercussions for his actions.

Chapter 13

As dawn approached Livius and Agrippa watched the trail for any sign that Cassius had made good his escape. "I am still not happy about that scream we heard last night."

"Me neither Agrippa but there is little else we can do. We'll have to wait here until someone emerges. The good news is that if no-one comes out then there will be no more raids for a while and if it is someone other than Cassius we just follow them."

They settled down to a cold breakfast and watched the early morning mist slowly burn off. They could smell the camp even though it was some miles away. The smoke from the breakfast fires and the stink of unwashed men wafted through the pine trees and assaulted their senses. Agrippa suddenly dropped his hard tack and started along the ridge and the hedgerow which ran along it. "Saw some movement sir. Up there."

Although Livius had not seen it he trusted the judgement of the ever reliable Agrippa. "Well spotted. Let us move back into the trees and see who it is. It may be more recruits joining." Whoever it was they were moving carefully and trying to stay concealed. Had Agrippa not caught the slight movement in the hedgerow they could easily have escaped their notice but now that Agrippa knew where they were he was locked onto them like a hound on a scent. Both men slipped their swords from their scabbards and jabbed them point first into the ground. They strung their bows and notched an arrow ready to defend them if attacked. "I count four."

"Me too sir. Can't see any uniform though."

"Which means they could be rebels, they could be more deserters, or..." he peered into the hedgerow more carefully, "or it could be Marius and his maniple? Signal them."

Agrippa dropped his bow and putting his hands together gave the bird call which was their signal. The four man patrol stopped and then one of them returned the call. Livius stepped out of the tree line and waved briefly before rushing back before he could be observed from the foggy woods which contained the camp.

"Good to see you sir. I take it that like us you had a success?"

"Yes Cassius is in their camp which is somewhere in those woods. And you?"

"Seius managed to get chosen but we lost him about five miles back a couple of nights ago. We tried to pick up his trail but none of us have the skills of Rufius and we only found it today. It crossed the land and ended just below the ridge."

"Yes that is the way they brought Cassius in which is good news because it suggests that this is the main entrance. Do not go near it though; there are traps everywhere. Now that we have doubled our numbers send two of your lads left and you and Ovidius go right just in case this is not the main entrance. We know now that we are looking for Cassius and Seius."

They did not have long to wait but Livius had been wrong because this was not the main entrance. He heard the whistle signal from Ovidius, who waved to show that a column of men was leaving the camp about a mile away and were heading north east. Livius turned to Agrippa. "A good job Marius turned up we might have missed them." They waited until Marius waved to them and they knew that it was safe to move. Agrippa signalled the other two scouts and within a few heartbeats the six men were gathered together; finding shelter amongst the elder bushes and hawthorns which erupted across the ridge.

"That is a large force sir. We counted ten riders and over a hundred infantry. They are all wearing our armour. No wonder the Brigante think it was us who inflicted the atrocities. I thought for a moment that it was us!"

"Right, here is what I want you to do. Ovidius, you ride to the Prefect and tell him what we have found. Tell him this confirms the earlier vague message I sent. Marius, you ride to the meeting point and wait for the others to arrive. Let them know what we

172

have found and then wait for us there. Stay hidden and ride south first to avoid being seen. "The two riders galloped off keeping low in the saddle to maintain a low profile and silhouette.

"Metellus and Rufius, you two cut around and ride parallel and to the south, we will do the same to the north. We'll have to keep our eyes open for Seius and Cassius. If they are with this lot then they may well use this as the chance to escape."

Cassius was in the second pair of riders which made escape impossible at that moment but he was a patient man. He had found the rider next to him, Salvius, to be a friendly chatty trooper and he was pleased that they were together for he was a mine of information. Cassius had always been a good listener and he was born to be an Explorate. Most people just like to hear themselves; not so Cassius, he preferred others to do the talking.

"This is a much better life than with the Gallic Horse. I mean I know you lads in Marcus' Horse had all the glory but the Gallic Horse just pissed around on patrol. This is better. More action and there will be a lot more to come believe me."

"Really?"

"Oh yes. We had this Brigante with us, Brennus he was called. Anyway he was one of that Brigante Queen's bodyguards. He fought alongside us at first then one night this boat came in with a bunch of bastard Irish and the Queen. The next thing is Brennus is away with the Brigante lads building a Brigante camp and a Brigante army; bigger than ours now. Apparently the Queen is coming over soon."

"How do you know that?"

Salvius showed doubt on his face, "Well I don't know for certain but some of the lads heard Centurion talking to the General about liaising, whatever that means, with the Queen and Brennus. Makes sense anyway. The General is always going on about the future and the freedom and the end of Roman rule."

"Do you actually think we can overthrow the Romans?"

"Well the Emperors don't give a fuck about this province do they? They are always taking away the decent legions and leaving it under strength. Look at us. Less than four hundred men and yet we have paralysed this part of the country and no-one has bothered to do owt about it. I reckon this General and the Queen might just succeed. Those savages further south still haven't been defeated. If this lot joined with them well... we could be on a right result here. We are in at the start. If it comes off we'll be the officers above those who come later."

Although Salvius was full of hot air Cassius had to admit that what he had said had made sense. "Well that is what I wanted to hear. One day on the job and already well on the way to a fortune and becoming an officer."

"That's the spirit. You stick with me mate and we'll do alright."

Centurion, who looked too big and uncomfortable on his horse, halted them about a mile from the sleepy little village that nestled in the lee of the hill. Cassius could see a water mill which suggested that it was prosperous. Salvius leaned over and whispered. "There will be a ton of gold here believe me."

Centurion flashed a savage look at Salvius before addressing them all. "Cavalry, I want you to circle the settlement and stop any bugger leaving. Infantry we go in a column of four. The story is like the others we have used, they are hiding Brigante rebels. Kill a couple but preferably just wound them, it is better that way."

From his vantage point on the ridge Livius saw them halt. The tendrils of smoke had already told him that there was a settlement nearby. "Well Agrippa this may be our chance. Have you seen Cassius or Seius yet?"

"No but if they bought the story about Marcus' Horse then they should be with those cavalry lads."

174

"I agree. We'll follow them. It's a gamble but with only two of us we haven't much choice have we?"

As Cassius and the other nine galloped off, the two Explorates followed desperately trying to identify their two comrades. The problem they had was that they had to stay behind and above the riders which meant they could not see their faces. Marius and his trooper would undoubtedly be doing the same. The thought flashed through Livius' mind that, if he had been with Marcus' Horse he would have been racing down to fight at five to one odds to save the settlement but now as an Explorate he would have to watch whatever depredations were heaped upon the unsuspecting community. His new role would take some getting used to.

Cassius was the right hand of the pair and he could see that they would swing left once they had passed the settlement and crossed the small river. He edged his horse right so that he was clear of the man in front. Once clear of the river he would kick right before they noticed. He hoped that they would be too busy fulfilling their orders to worry about one deserter. As they splashed through the stream he heard the officer at the front shout, "Draw swords!" he made pretence of trying to draw but he wanted both hands free for his reins.

As soon as he reached dry land he kicked the horse hard and pulled on the reins racing up the gentle slope. He heard the shouts from behind but he kept his head down to maximise the speed of the horse.

"You two get after that deserter and bring me his head!" The roar from the angry Nuada carried clearly to Cassius.

Cassius glanced under his arm and saw that Salvius and another trooper were forty paces behind in hot pursuit. At least he had better odds than Seius for he had a fighting chance, a weapon and a horse. He risked another glance and saw that the two men still had their swords drawn. He kicked left and aimed his racing steed at a rocky part of the hillside. Sure enough when they tried to match his manoeuvre their mounts stumbled and he began to extend his lead. Once he reached the top of the ridge he paused briefly to let his horse regain some wind. The two troopers were still fifty paces back but in the distance he could see the smoke and hear the faint cries as the villagers were attacked. "Come on then boy; let's see if we can end this."

He kicked the horse on and it opened its legs enjoying its freedom. Suddenly disaster struck as its hoof caught in a hare hole and it tumbled forward throwing Cassius to the ground. Instinct took over and he covered his head, relaxed and rolled. As soon as he stopped he leapt to his feet drew his sword and turned to face his pursuers. The looks on their faces told Cassius that they would enjoy butchering him and he prepared to sell his life dearly. They slowed their horses down and spread out giving Cassius even less chance.

"Another coward, a deserter, I will enjoy this."

"Don't count my gold until I am dead Salvius."

"Oh you will be sunshine, you will…" the rest of the comment was stopped by the arrow which erupted from his chest. He looked down in surprise at the barbed arrow head protruding from his chest before falling dead from his horse. His companion looked around for his attacker only to be struck in the neck by another arrow.

Cassius watched with relief and an ever increasing grin as Livius and Agrippa rode up. "Am I glad to see you sir."

"What's the matter Cassius did you upset your new mates? Or didn't you fancy them?"

"Let's just say Agrippa that they wanted to do things to me that I would not have enjoyed." He looked around for his horse which was lying in an untidy heap, its neck broken and its breathing laboured. Cassius sighed and taking his sword knelt next to the horse. He stroked its head, "Thank you for saving my life. May you ride with the Allfather." He gently cut its throat and its pain ended.

Agrippa brought up one of the horses of the dead men while Livius collected the other. "I'll keep this in case we find Seius."

Mounting his horse Cassius said sadly. "Seius won't need a horse in this life. He was caught escaping and they planted him on a stake."

"That will go hard with Marius when we tell him. Let us find him if we can and then seek out the others. While we ride give me your report."

"It is far worse than we either thought or imagined. They have a cohort of well trained and armed soldiers and, believe me, they are incredibly well trained. There is a Brigante army training too."

"Where?"

He shook his head. "That I do not know but it must be close by the camp I was in but worst of all, I have just discovered that Morwenna is returning with an Irish army. The rebellion is on once again."

"I believe you are right Cassius. I hope the messengers I sent to the Prefect prompted him to move south or it may be too late."

They rode in silence for a while and then Cassius blurted out, "There are things about this new role that I did not expect decurion. The hardest thing I had to do in my life was watch poor Seius die. All I wanted to do was to free him."

"I know Cassius and if you had freed him then what?"

He looked at Livius perplexed. "Then we would have fled."

"And would you have escaped the four hundred men hungry for your blood?" The silence spoke volumes. "The answer, which you know, is no and you would have died and we would not know either of the Brigante army nor the Irish army and many more men would have died. It is sad that Seius died but his death enabled you to prevent further death and, you are correct, our role has changed and it is a hard role but, Cassius, it is a vital role."

177

When they reached the meeting point the whole of the Explorates were there. "For us it was a fruitless exercise," Drusus spread his hands in apology. "We tried but no one wanted a deserter.

Marius was excited. "We managed, like you decurion, to plant Seius in the rebel camp."

Cassius walked forward and grasped Marius' arm. "I have some news which will be hard for you to take. He was captured and.... butchered."

For Marius it was the first of his men that he had lost. Seius had been amongst the first recruits from Marcus' Horse and a close friend of Drusus. Cassius took him to one side and told him the whole story of the dreadful death of the young Seius. Cassius waited with Marius as he cried the tears of frustration and, when he was composed, led him back to the others.

The Explorates understood Marius' grief and they all dealt with it the same way. They ignored it. They would all say prayers for their friend and they would all remember their comrade but none would speak of it. It brought their own end too close to think about, it made them think about mortality and for a soldier that was never a good thing..

"We found where the ships came ashore. I can confirm what Cassius said, the Queen has been here and she will return. This is a rebellion."

Livius nodded. "You have all done well, Metellus. Far better than anyone could have dreamed and our losses were lighter than they might have been. The Prefect should know of the situation which means we can now try to find the Brigante camp and then the bitch Morwenna."

Although the raid had been successful Decius sat at his desk, incandescent with rage. Centurion, Tiny and Nuada all quaked before him. "How in Hades did a spy manage to get into our camp?"

"We don't know that he was a spy."

"Nuada, are you an imbecile? He runs off and two of our men are slain by Roman arrows." He held up his hand. "I worked for Rome and I know Roman fucking arrows when I see them. What I am asking is how did he get through?"

Centurion knew the leader the best and he stepped forward. "You and Morwenna asked us to get deserters. We did. You asked us to get them into action as soon as possible. We did."

"So you are saying this is my fault?"

"In a nutshell? Yes. For we did not bother to check the men and to find out if their stories were true. In the end it did not cost us much but now Rome knows what we are about and we need to strike quickly."

Nuada and Tiny shrank back from the inevitable onslaught. Decius looked at the desk. "You are right. Thank you Centurion. No more recruits. We work with what we have and, Nuada, send a rider to Brennus warn him that his camp may have been infiltrated."

Nuada left, pleased to be away from the intense heat of the office. "Now the Queen is on her way with her whole army; over fifteen hundred warriors. With the one thousand Brigante and our four hundred we only need fear the Ninth and they are on the northern border. The Queen will be here by the end of the month. We have two weeks to disrupt even more and our first target is the fort at Mamucium."

"Mamucium! Are you mad? Attack a fort without siege equipment?" Centurion thought that his superior had finally lost his senses.

"You have been to Mamucium. How would you describe the fort Centurion?"

"Alright I admit that their security is lax."

179

"Lax? The vestal fucking virgins from Rome could walk in there! The point is, if we take it then that will make the Twentieth Valeria get twitchy, hide themselves in Deva and it will secure our southern flank. When the Brigantes take Bremmetenacum then the Queen can march up to Glanibanta and take it easily." The silence told Decius that he had won his argument. "But," he held his finger up to emphasise the point, "there are Roman spies out there. Keep your eyes open for them. He looked at Centurion, "The spy; who did he come in with?"

"No-one."

"Friendly with anyone?"

"He walked next to the runty looking soldier; the one I thought was lame."

"Fetch him and we will see what he knows."

Mocius looked apprehensively at the three men before him. He had served in the Roman army for long enough to know that you avoided officers at all costs. Now that he was in this copy of a Roman army he felt the same way. The smile which Decius gave him when he walked in was not reassuring. It was the smile of a cat greeting a mouse. "Now then…?"

"Mocius … sir er General."

"Relax Mocius; this is not a trial we just want to know as much as we can about this Cassius who ran off today."

A chill ran down Mocius' spine. "I barely knew him. I only spoke to him that first day when we came from Mamucium."

"Well then there is nothing to fear is there? What did you learn of him?"

Mocius was in a dilemma. Did they know about the trail which Cassius had laid? Even if they did they could not know that he knew of it. He determined to keep silent on that issue but tell the truth about the rest. "He said he had served in Marcus' Horse and he left because of…," he paused uncertain of the effect of his next statement, "your brother Livius. Cassius said that he was a cruel

180

bastard. Sorry sir. His words not mine." Decius held his hand up. "When he told the optio he had been in the cavalry he was whisked off to the horses and I didn't see him any more."

"Well thank you for your honesty Mocius you may rejoin your unit." He stared hard at the man who was obviously frightened. "You have a future in this army and I will not forget your loyalty. You will soon be an officer." When Mocius had left Decius turned to Centurion. "Make sure he is in the front rank when we fight the Romans at Mamucium. He is a loose end I would like to be rid of."

"Was he right about your brother?"

Decius laughed, "My brother a bastard? He was as soft as they come. No that was just confirmation that my brother sent him in as a spy." He thought for a moment, "And, probably, the other one we executed; the one who tried to run. That means that Marcus' Horse is out there."

"But the word was that they were disbanded."

"Smoke and mirrors Centurion; I have no doubt that there is no ala called Marcus' Horse out there but that doesn't mean that the men and officers from the ala aren't out there. We will have to be on our guard. The Queen will be interested in this news for she hates Marcus' Horse with a passion which you would not believe."

"Do you know why?"

Decius nodded. "They crucified her mother. If she got her hands on my brother I dread to think what his fate would be."

Centurion nodded. "She is one woman I would not get the wrong side of."

The ten troopers who met at the rendezvous were in a sombre mood. Cassius had told them of the manner of Seius' death and it had had a sobering effect. It was one thing to die in battle but to

181

be tortured to death was another matter. Cassius' and Metellus' news of the size of the army had also disturbed them.

"One thing is for certain they will be on their guard now which means no more infiltration of their camps."

"If we knew where their camps were."

"We know where one is Drusus. Marius I want you to take your maniple and keep watch on the Roman deserter's camp. You know where that is. Let me know if and when they move. Drusus you need to ride to the coast and watch for ships and the Queen. My maniple will try to find the Brigante camp." Metellus cleared his throat and coughed. Livius smiled. "Well out with it Metellus either you are coming down with something or you have an idea."

The others laughed as Metellus reddened. "It seems to me sir that the best place to enlist rebels would be in the villages that your bro.., that the deserters have pillaged."

"All of you do not step around my feelings so carefully. I know from Cassius that my brother is a traitor but I already knew that. He betrayed my uncle and he betrayed Rome. At least we know who the enemy is and I will recognise him, believe me. Carry on Metellus. You were saying."

"The village yesterday; there will be warriors who will join the rebels to gain revenge on Rome."

"And?"

"And we follow them. They will know how to reach the hidden camp even if we do not."

"That is such a simple idea that it might work. We will use this dell as our base. One rider from each maniple should ride back here each night and camp here. The three can share information and I will be kept informed. When our riders return from the Prefect they too will come here. We can also hobble our spare horses here for it will keep them fresh and from what I have seen this is a remote spot well away from accidental visitors. One more thing, from what Cassius has told us these are not the kind of soldiers who will treat you well. If you are captured you will die painfully. Avoid capture at all costs. Discretion rather than heroics; a dead Explorate can give no one the valuable information in his head."

Chapter 14

With Rufius on point they soon picked up the trail of the Roman and the Brigante raiders. "Sir."

"Good lad. I take it you have found their trail."

Rufius pointed to the ground and nodded. "They both followed the same trail up to here and then the Romans went that way. Back to their camp. You can see the imprints from the hobnails. They also have some horses. The Brigante went that way. Their prints are lighter; they don't have armour or caligae."

They looked at the direction the trail headed. In the distance they could see the land dropping away to the sea and the Belisama estuary twenty miles away. The undulating land was covered in extensive woods with many hollows and dips affording both cover and the opportunity for an ambush. Decius pointed. "My guess is that it will lead to one of those woods."

Cassius looked troubled. "If the camp is like the one I was in there will be a watchtower which is at tree top height. We won't be able to see it but they will have a clear view of any nosey intruders. They are clever builders."

"Like us?"

"Like us Agrippa."

"Another dilemma eh? I think we go back to the pairs of riders. Agrippa you and Cassius head west towards the sea. Rufius and Metellus you cut around north east and head for the estuary. I will keep along the trail. I am hoping that they will have had recruits from other parts of this land and you may be able to pick up their trail. Take a straight line from here and we will meet at the nearest point on the estuary. We can compare notes."

Cassius leaned over. "You have the most dangerous route sir. Please be careful, these people play for keeps."

"I know Cassius and if I do not meet you at the estuary then assume I have been taken. Back track and look for," he reached into his bag and took out a leather glove. They normally used them in the winter and it would not be missed, "this. If I am caught I will drop it at the point I am taken. Rufius would you recognise Star's hoof prints?"

Dropping to the ground Rufius lifted up the right rear hoof and with his knife scored a cross in it. "I will now sir."

"Good. Take care and see you all tonight."

Once alone Livius felt strangely calm. He knew he had taken the most challenging and hazardous task but in all the time with the ala he had never seen Decius Flavius, Marcus Maximunius or Julius Demetrius let one of the troopers go where they would not. This was a new and dangerous game and he knew he would have to experience the same dangers as Seius and Cassius if he was to perform his duties as well as possible. He also needed to understand what it was like to be alone and behind enemy lines; only in that way could he make the Explorates fulfil the potential he knew they had.

Within two miles he knew that he was nearing the right wood. More tracks crossed from the north joining those he was following. The wood where the camp had to be was less than two miles away and, mindful of his instructions to his men, he turned Star to miss the woods to the east. When he met the others later he would compare notes and they could use the cover of darkness to investigate the camp. A watch tower could only help the enemy during the hours of daylight and the Explorates would use night's cloak to their advantage. The wood was extensive and he could see why they had chosen it as their base. It was at least five miles across and when he arrived at the other side he was surprised to hear gulls and to see the estuary just a mile away. He now fully understood why they had situated it here. They were less than ten miles from the Roman camp and close enough to the estuary for the Queen to join her army in the shortest possible time whenever she arrived. He was now convinced that she was somewhere across the sea, probably, Ireland. Livius could only hope that the vagaries of the sea and the long crossing from Ireland might cause the witch problems but he had a feeling that the Parcae, for their own sinister reason, favoured the priestess.

He heard, as he approached the estuary, the distinctive whistle which told him his men were nearby. He let Star have his head and the intelligent beast headed towards the copse close by the water where he had scented the other horses. A neigh from below told Livius that he was close and he peered to see them. "An excellent hiding place. I was looking for you and still couldn't see you. Well anything to report?"

"That wood there. There are tracks leading into it from the north, south and east."

Livius nodded. "That was my assessment. Eat, get some rest and we will go into the woods tonight."

Surprisingly they all fell asleep quickly relying on the horses to warn them of approaching danger. When they awoke they blackened their faces and the backs of their hands. "Agrippa when we get there you remain with the horses. We may need to get away quickly and I don't want to have to look for them. Rufius, Metellus tells me you have found the knack to avoiding the traps they like to leave for us so you can lead. Cassius bring up the rear; you mark the route with your knife in case we get separated. Hand signals and no voices once we are in the wood. We all know how sounds travel at night. Agrippa, if you see or hear any trouble then you whistle. Let's go."

It was a cloudy night and whatever moon there was remained mercifully hidden. Agrippa sat astride his horse with the reins of the other mounts firmly in his hand. The darkened Explorates seemed to be swallowed up by the night, instantly. Rufius dropped to all fours once he had found the footprints and he began to crawl carefully along the leafy floor. The others followed suit leaving four or five paces between each of them. Rufius would occasionally stop and raise his hand for stillness

186

and he would listen for the sounds which would warn them of danger. What none of them wanted was for a trap to be triggered; although they might avoid injury, at night the sound would travel large distances. Rufius pointed upwards at one point and Livius saw the deadfall about his head. He repeated the signal for Metellus.

After what seemed an age they saw a lightening of the sky which told them they were approaching a clearing. Rufius held his hand up again and once again they had silence except that they could hear the faint noises from men and horses. They had found the Brigante camp. Rufius signalled Livius to remain where he was and then he disappeared. To Livius the scout seemed to be away for an age. When he eventually returned he pointed to Livius and then left, Livius nodded. He pointed to Metellus and right. He too nodded. He looked at Cassius pointed to his own eyes and the spot he occupied. When Cassius nodded he slipped away again.

Cassius found that he was oddly nervous as he waited there in the darkness. The last time he had been alone was when he was in the deserter's camp. Although a cool night he could feel the sweat on the back of his neck. Seius' death still preyed on his mind and he had not managed to convey the full horror to his comrades but he could remember the tortured look on the boy's face as he had died the most horrible death imaginable. All he wanted to do was run from the wood but he knew he had to wait, patiently, for the return of his comrades. The first to arrive inevitably was Rufius whose white grinning smile seemed to glow in the gloom. Livius was next and then they waited for Metellus. Perhaps his concentration wavered for a moment but the loud crack of the decaying branch echoed and reverberated in the quiet. Suddenly they heard a challenge from the camp. Livius stood , pointed to Cassius and mouthed, 'Run!'

187

Cassius needed no urging and, watching for his marks on the trees, ran as quickly as he could the others close on his heels. Behind them they heard the uproar as warriors raced through the pine trees eager to capture these spies. Far quicker than they had imagined they reached Agrippa who had heard the noises and had his bow, with an arrow already notched in his hand. The four men quickly mounted; not a moment too soon as a huge Brigante erupted from the woods a few paces behind Metellus. The arrow fired from twenty paces struck him in the throat and threw him back into the man who was close on his heels. The five men kicked their horses and headed south west towards the beach. Their pursuers stood no chance of catching them for they were on foot but the five men knew that there would be riders in the camp who would already be in pursuit.

Livius lay as low in the saddle, close to Star's neck, as he could. There was little point looking back and, mindful of Cassius' fall when being pursued he wanted no spills. Spying a hollow he led his men down the small drop so that they disappeared from sight. As soon as he was in the hollow he turned Star to head north west. The men who were on foot would have told the riders which direction they had taken. Livius intended to head back to the estuary and wait there for Drusus to arrive. If he did not come in the next two days he would return to the meeting place but he wanted to remain close to the camp and the sea for he felt that the Queen was coming and he wanted to be in the best position to gather that most vital of information which the Prefect would need if he was to stop the rebellion before it caught hold.

The Brigante rider waited patiently outside the crude hut which served as the office for Decius Lucullus Sallustius. He found it strange to be amongst these Romans who were not Romans and yet dressed and acted as though they were. His scalp itched. One of Brennus' men, he had been with Morwenna since Aodh had

188

left and he respected the ideas and methods they were now using but it did feel unnatural. It was not the warrior's way and the cunning and guile felt foreign to this old fashioned Brigante. Decius, as usual, was flanked by Tiny and Centurion. "Yes?" Blunt and to the point Decius hated time being wasted on pleasantries.

"Brennus said to tell you that Roman spies have scouted our camp."

"Did you capture or kill any?"

"No they had horses waiting and they escaped. We have men looking for them now."

"Go back and tell Brennus that the time for deception is at an end. We will bring our men to join his at his camp and await the Queen. She will be here soon." The warrior vaulted his horse and galloped off. Decius turned to Centurion. We have to assume that they will take their information to the fort."

"Which fort?"

"Probably Bremmetenacum why?"

"I agree for it is the closest garrison and then they will send riders south to Mamucium and north to Glanibanta."

"And?"

"If we were to go straight to Mamucium we could capture it and they would be unaware of any disturbance in the province. If they know of the rising then it will be so much harder."

"You are right. Take the men towards Mamucium. I will go with Tiny and bring Brennus' men to help us."

"And the Queen?"

"We will leave some men at the camp and, when we have destroyed Mamucium we can jointly assault Bremmetenacum with the Queen before the Ninth can reach us from Luguvalium."

Decius and Tiny reached the Brigante camp shortly after the warrior who had delivered Decius' message. Brennus had regrown his beard and his hair was longer. He looked and felt more Brigante than he had when fighting as a Roman "Where are your men?"

"Change of plan. We'll take Mamucium now before the Queen arrives. If they know of your camp and mine the Romans are sure to attack here. They will not expect us to attack their fort. Leave some men here in case the Queen arrives and, when Mamucium is no more we will take Bremmetenacum."

The idea of fighting Romans again appealed to the barbarian and his men too were keen. This would be a chance to show the deserters how Brigante warriors fought. "Very well."Turning to his lieutenant he said, "Leave ten warriors here, and arm the rest. We march. The Brigante go to war!" The roar which greeted the order told Brennus that his men were ready, very ready and the death of their first warrior the previous night had made them even more eager to fight.

Livius heard the roar. "Something is up. Let's go a little closer." The maniple was supremely confident that their horses, well trained by Sergeant Cato and looked after like the fine weapons they were, would easily outrun any nags the Brigante had acquired. They headed due east, first keeping the wood to their right. Rufius' sharp eyes soon spotted the barbarian army heading south eastwards.

"So they are on the march. Agrippa ride to Bremmetenacum and tell the Prefect of the danger. Metellus and Rufius ride to Mamucium and warn the garrison there." He chose Metellus for his intelligence and his ability to think on his feet. "The Prefect there is a lazy man you will have to be persuasive. Cassius and I will trail the army."

"What of the men at the meeting place? They may well be there and the extra men might help."

"Right. Cassius you ride to the meeting place. If any of our riders are there send one to find the Ninth and report the enemy army's route. Any others return with you. I will be following these. They should not be hard to follow."

"There are over a thousand sir."

"Well done Rufius. Right boys let's ride. The war comes."

Metellus and Rufius knew that they had the longest ride ahead of them and Metellus was regretting not having a spare horse. He hoped that they would reach the fort ahead of the barbarians and that the Prefect would have some backbone about him. From what Livius had said he was not confident but it was only a barbarian horde, with no siege equipment. If they could take a fort like Mamucium with just foot soldiers then the whole province was in greater danger than the Governor realised.

They had been riding for an hour and just emerged from behind a long hedgerow when Livius suddenly reined Blackie in and pointed south. There they could see the deserter army heading in the same direction they were. The advantage lay with the deserter army for they were on a well trodden track whereas the two troopers were riding over rocky, shrubby terrain. To Metellus' horror the cavalry attached to the army suddenly wheeled and began galloping in their direction. Without a word they both turned their mounts and headed east towards the road. They had been taking the most direct route, now they needed to escape their pursuers and then take the road. Even as they were riding Metellus' mind was working overtime. The Camp Prefect would not see an army of deserters, he would see what he expected to see, a Roman cohort coming to spend the night in his fort. The gates would be opened and the garrison slaughtered. If they could evade pursuit they might be able to warn him but even then they would find themselves surrounded by two armies one of which knew how to take such forts for they had built them.

"Rufius if I slow you down you just kick on. One of us must get to the fort. "

"I am not leaving you!"

"Yes you will! You are lighter and you can travel faster. I am expendable. If I can I will take them away from you. Now go! I can see you reining in Blackie, let her go, give the horse her head!" Rufius nodded and then kicked on his horse, Blackie leapt forward as though she were an arrow released from a bow. Metellus could see the road some way ahead and he veered his horse left to narrow the gap and, perhaps split the pursuers. Glancing back over his shoulder he saw that only four of them were chasing after Rufius, the rest were following him as the closer target. Metellus leaned over his horse's head, stroked its ear and said, "Well old girl we'll see what you have got eh? Let's show these traitors that a trooper and horse from Marcus' Horse can still outrun anything they have." Whether it was his words or the stroking it mattered not for the beast found a sudden burst of energy and Metellus almost shouted for joy when he saw the road less than a mile away. He decided to head north for then that would take them away from Rufius. The heavier armour and weapons of the pursuing cavalry began to take its toll and soon Metellus could see them falling further and further behind. Finally, as he reached the road, he saw them stop. He headed north until they were out of sight and then turned his horse and headed south, at a steadier pace to help his mount regain her wind.

He found himself breathing almost as hard as his horse. The urgency was gone. Rufius would easily reach the fort before he did and he slowed Badger down even more as he conserved both their energies. He didn't know if he would come across the four who were pursuing Rufius. Glancing to the west he saw a smudge which appeared to be moving. The deserter army had made good time and Metellus hoped that Rufius had reached the fort for it was less than an hour away. By the time they both had their wind they had covered another five miles. Metellus made the classic mistake of relaxing too soon but fortunately Badger scented Blackie before Metellus saw his comrade's mount.

As soon as Badger nodded her head up and down Metellus' senses became alert and attuned to danger. "You smell something eh? Let's just see what there is up the road then." Within a few heartbeats Metellus was horrified to see Blackie standing forlornly at the side of the road and as he drew closer Metellus could see a lump on the ground near to the horse's hooves. Metellus kicked hard and was soon at Blackie's side. Leaping to the ground he saw the arrow sticking out of Rufius' shoulder. He eased the boy around and heard, to his relief, his laboured breathing. He was alive!

"That you Metellus? Sorry about this one of them managed to hit me with an arrow. Held on as long as..." Then he passed out.

"You did well, son. Now let's get this out." As he examined it he could see that the arrow had not gone far into the boy's body as the leather armour had absorbed most of the impact. The head was not barbed and had only penetrated in a couple of uncia. Making sure that Rufius was unconscious he took out his medical kit. It was scrupulously clean although if had had time Metellus would have lit a fire and heated the scalpel but he had no time for that. He had to work swiftly while Rufius was out for he would have to cut it out. He eased the sharp point into the side of the head relieved that it was pale surface blood which seeped out. He worked the blade down until he felt no resistance, pushing in with the blade and pulling gently on the shaft he began to pull the arrow out but it refused to move and he felt Rufius moan a little. He pulled the scalpel out and repeated his action on the other side. This time, as he pulled, he felt it slowly move until with a pop it slipped out. Metellus pushed on the shoulder to let a little more blood out. It came out clear and he took out the wad of cloth and poured some wine on it jamming it on to the wound. He bandaged it as tightly as he could and then, turning over Rufius' inert body forced some wine down his throat.

"What I should do my friend is to make a camp and give you hot food but time presses and men may die if we do not move." He lifted the body and draped it over Blackie's saddle. "Well Blackie you will have to look after him now." He took a length of short rope from his saddle bag and tied Rufius' hands and feet together. Taking another length he passed it under the saddle and around his body. "That's all I can do I am afraid."

Taking Blackie's reins he mounted Badger and they headed south down the road. Although they travelled faster than was good for Rufius, Metellus knew that they were barely keeping pace with the army of traitors which was heading in the same direction. It would be a close run thing.

Porcius had heard disturbing reports of barbarians rampaging through the countryside. Fewer travellers had headed down the road and those who had spoke of bands of warriors raiding and killing. He had taken the unusual step of actually telling his First Spear to double the guards and question everyone who came to the fort. This was not the posting that Porcius wanted. He preferred the easier life he had had before. As soon as it was close to twilight he ordered the gate closed and he and First Spear stood in the tower atop the Porta Praetorium.

"I don't like the atmosphere in the vicus First Spear. They are normally welcoming and friendly but they seem very sullen and look to be avoiding us more than usual."

First Spear did not like this posting either. "I agree. I would be happier if we had some reinforcements. This lot," he waved a dismissive hand at the men on the walls, "have not had to fight for a long time." In truth neither he nor the Camp Prefect had seen a weapon raised in anger since Agricola had left when they had both been starting their careers in the auxilia.

The guard on the topmost level of the tower suddenly shouted, "Riders approaching."

"Can you identify them?"

"They are not in uniform."

"Barbarians! To arms!" The buccina sounded and they both heard the sound of men running to the ramparts.

Metellus drew up next to the ditch which surrounded the fort. He shouted up. "I am from the Explorates and I bring news."

"Give me the news then."

"I have a wounded man with me."

"Sounds like a barbarian trick and I don't know you!"

Cursing the man's caution Metellus shouted up. "There is an army coming down the road to attack the fort. They are dressed as Romans but they are deserters and there is a Brigante army close behind. Now open the gate and let us in. This trooper needs medical attention."

"An army of deserters dressed as Romans! Do you take me for a fool? Archers! Shoot them down."

Fortunately for the two Explorates the sentries were neither efficient nor prepared and did not have their weapons aimed. Metellus wheeled his horse around and tugged Blackie back into the gloom and darkness before the archers could aim their weapons. "Well Badger we have done all we could. We'll head north and then make camp. The fate of the fort is now in the hands of the Allfather but the fool may have doomed his cohort and the vicus to a brutal and unnecessary death."

Decius rode up the fort at the head of his twenty horsemen. "Hail the fort. Decurion Gaius Augustus of the Third Pannonian Horse. We seek shelter for the night."

The Camp Prefect looked at his First Spear. "Thank the gods we have reinforcements." He leaned over to order the gate to be opened.

First Spear grabbed his arm. "Are you mad? Did not the rider say there were men dressed as Romans?"

"Fool! It was a trick of the barbarians. This is obviously a Roman listen to his voice. He sounds and looks Roman."

"He may do but the rider said deserters and they would be Roman. Besides he said they were Pannonians. Yes?"

"Yes. And?"

"In which case why are these auxiliary cavalry wearing gladii and the Lorica Segmenta armour of the legionary?"

"These are foolish and cowardly words First Spear. Who knows why they are wearing Lorica Segmenta." Even as he chastised his comrade doubt began to creep into his mind. Now that he looked down he could see that they did not look right, they didn't look, well Roman.

"Hurry man. My men are cold and hungry. Would you deny us shelter?"

"Where have you come from?"

"Bremmetenacum."

"And how is Camp Prefect Lividius at the moment? Is he still unwell?"

"No he is fully recovered I am pleased to say."

"The Camp Prefect is not Lividius, I made the name up. Shoot them!"

First Spear turned to the archers. "Fire!"

Decius sense of self preservation took over and he wheeled his mount just before the archers fired. Five of his men were too slow and tumbled to the ground. Roaring his anger Decius shouted into the darkness, "Attack!"

Centurion and the rest of the deserter army were crouching close to the other walls of the fort and, with a shout, leapt at the walls. They had avoided the lillia and had ladders to help them scale the palisade. All attention had been on the front gate and First Spear had been correct, their lack of action had made them slow to react. The first sentries fell to arrows shot from the dark and in the hiatus which followed Centurion and Tiny's men found a foothold in the fort and one wall was quickly taken. The strength of the fort was in holding an enemy at a distance. Allowing the deserters to close with the walls had taken away their one advantage. That was the beginning of the end for the garrison.

Tiny took his chosen legionaries down the stairs to the Porta Praetorium where they hacked and slashed their way through overweight auxiliaries who were out of their depth. As soon as they reached the gate they opened it, allowing Decius and his cavalry to charge in followed by the baying barbarians of Brennus. Porcius watched in dumb horror as a spear took out the only fighting soldier who could have organised a defence, First Spear. Self preservation took over and the portly Porcius grabbed the men nearest him, "The Fort is lost we must leave and tell Deva!"

The ten men around him realised this would be their only chance and they ran down the stairs towards the rear gate. Porcius allowed them to run for the gate while he ran for the stables where he knew there were horses. Others had had the same idea but fortunately for the Camp Prefect he managed to haul his carcass onto the back of one of them. The ten men he had sent ahead, now reduced to eight managed to open the Porta Decumana and five of them fled down the road, south. Porcius and the other six horsemen were the last to manage to escape the massacre of Mamucium, galloping away for the security and safety of Deva.

Behind him his command was ruthlessly butchered by Decius, angry that his simple plan had been thwarted. Long after they had killed the inhabitants of the fort, they and their barbarian allies wreaked havoc on the vicus and even erstwhile allies such as Nautius were butchered. Many fled north towards

Bremmetenacum while others ran to the woods to hide until the nightmare was over.

As Livius peered from the road at the slaughter he wondered what had happened to Metellus and Livius but he knew he had no time to think of such things. The rebellion had started and his Explorates had to head north and find, hopefully, the Ninth Hispana which he hoped had already reached Bremmetenacum. If not that fort too would suffer the fate of Mamucium because it would not be two armies attacking, it would soon be three when the Red Witch returned to Britannia with her Irish army. Livius had been too late, he had failed. He grasped the hilt of the Sword of Cartimandua. Had he let down Ulpius, Marcus and Gaius? All those who had wielded the sword so successfully and he, wearing it in his first campaign, had been a miserable unmitigated disaster.

Part Three
The Rebellion
Chapter 15

Prefect Fulvius greeted the weary Livius when he rode through the gate. The decurion was delighted to see the Second Cohort of the Ninth grimly improving the defences of Bremmetenacum and it raised his spirits. "Good to see you Livius. From your expression I gather you have not brought me good news."

Livius shook his head and almost fell from the saddle. "No sir. I failed. Mamucium has fallen and two armies are heading north; a deserter army led by my brother and a Brigante army. In addition I believe that Morwenna is bringing an army of Irish to these shores. The rebellion has begun."

The Prefect put a paternal arm around Livius' shoulder. "You did not fail. Your man Metellus reached the fort and warned the camp Prefect but his words were ignored and your intelligence means that I arrived here to reinforce this fort. The Third Cohort is on its way south. I think that, if we have the right information then we can still beat her and her traitorous allies."

A smile of relief spread over Livius' face. "My men are they safe?"

"Yes decurion. One of your men was wounded. I have sent out some of your men to find the Queen but the rest are here awaiting your orders. Rest today and we will discuss our plans at dinner."

Livius found Rufius in the sick bay. Although looking pale he tried to rise when his superior entered. "No Rufius lie back. Where is the wound?"

"An arrow in the shoulder. Metellus removed it. It is healing well and I should be up and about in a couple of days."

Livius shook his head. "No you will be up and about when they," he waved at the capsarii who were busy organising the

199

sickbay in anticipation of a war, "say it is time. Our job is hard enough when we are fit. When we are wounded it is impossible. You will not know what went on at the fort then will you?"

"No sir, I was strapped to Blackie like an extra saddle cloth."

"Well you rest now and I will find the others."

"Drusus and Marius are out with their maniples scouting for the Queen."

"Good. You rest."

The fort was, by contrast with Mamucium and the lethargic Prefect Porcius Fortuna, a hive of activity. Prefect Fulvius had begun strengthening the defences as soon as he had arrived and the ditches were being deepened and sown with the deadly lillia. Inside armourers were sharpening weapons while First Spear Lartius drilled legionaries and auxilia together. Metellus, Decius, Cassius and Agrippa were in the overcrowded stables grooming their mounts.

"Good to see you sir."

"And you Metellus. You did well."

"Not well enough. I was just telling the lads that."

Livius shook his head. "Tell me how Rufius became wounded."

"Bad luck really sir. An arrow hit him in the shoulder. The leather saved him but the loss of blood meant he came off his horse."

"Lucky for him you are the best capsarius in Britannia."

Metellus shrugged. "If we had got to the fort in daylight we may have been able to persuade the Prefect to resist and…"

"It would not have made any difference Metellus. I arrived at the fort as it was overwhelmed. Porcius Fortuna could not have defended the fort for he was not a fighting man. The Parcae were watching over you and Rufius. Had you been admitted to the fort your bones would be lying now in the debris."

"It is destroyed then sir."

"Yes Agrippa and the vicus too. They were both burning fiercely when I left."

"Did any escape?"

"I saw some figures fleeing south and they were not pursued. I assume that the twentieth will know what is going on."

"Will they come to join us then sir?"

"Afraid not Decius. The Twentieth has to control the wild lands south and west, including Mona. The best that we can hope is that they send a cohort to rebuild Mamucium but I doubt even that. I suspect that the best we can hope is that they fortify the bridge over the Seteia and hold there."

"Things look bad sir."

"Yes Cassius but the Prefect is a good commander and the Ninth are the best we have. I don't think my brother will best them. But we could do with an ala of cavalry to give us the edge."

"You mean like Marcus' Horse."

"Just like Marcus' Horse."

Morwenna had only waited until she had given birth before embarking with her new army. Maban was wet nursing the boy as she also had given birth to a boy. The new born baby's body now rested in the holy grove on Manavia allowing the acolyte to use her milk for the new heir to Britain, the child of Morwenna and Decius. The boats which brought the army up the Belisama had been of all shapes, sizes and comfort. It had been the part of the rebellion which had concerned Morwenna the most. If the Classis Britannica had discovered them on the short crossing from Manavia then it would have been easily destroyed. As she watched the warriors disembark she felt more confident. Tadgh, beside her, was resplendent in his new armour at the head of the Brigante and druids who formed the Queen's bodyguard. The Irish were commanded by Ernan, a young Irish prince whose lands had been stolen by an uncle with more allies than the youthful heir. He had a desperate passion to return to his lands and reclaim his birthright. Morwenna had seen in him someone who could be bent to her purpose and she had promised that, when her kingdom was reclaimed she would help to fund his war in Ireland. She knew it would make him fight fiercely for her.

She had a good army; a thousand wild Irish warriors, her four hundred bodyguards, a thousand Brigante under Brennus and the deserters, six hundred in total under Decius. She knew that soon others would flock to her banner and this time they had the weapons and the gold to ensure that their rebellion succeeded.

Tadgh organised the camp on the shores of the estuary as they waited for contact to be made by Brennus or Decius. The niggling doubt in Tadgh's meticulously military mind was their lack of horses. It slowed them down and made them blind. He hoped that his men had managed to acquire horses or they would have to blunder blindly through the land seeking an enemy who had both the eyes and ears to find them first.

Marius was alone when he saw the small fleet edge gingerly into the estuary. He wavered wondering whether he should inform the Prefect immediately or wait to make sure it was the rebel army. In his own mind he knew it was the enemy but he had to make sure that Morwenna was there. She would be the difference between success and failure for the rebels. Despite the hatred felt for her, he also knew that her warriors would fight far harder for her than any man. He had seen it before and he had heard the stories of her mother who had the same power over men. He felt safe in the copse; someone would have to stumble over him to find him. His cloak was dark and he had a mount whose colour varied from black to light brown and blended into any undergrowth like a bush with a tail.

The boats kept on arriving, disgorging warriors. Marius could see that someone knew his business for the first warriors formed an armed perimeter and scouts were sent out even further to ensure they avoided detection. The Irish warriors looked every bit as fierce as Marius had expected. He had never seen any but heard the stories of their incredible valour fighting to the last man if honour decreed it. Few had armour but many had helms and shields. Their axes were long two handed affairs and many had swords longer even, than a spatha. Worryingly Marius also saw druids, armed druids at that, amongst the well armed and armoured Brigante warriors. Druids were dangerous for they inspired fear in their foes, as Caesar's legions had found out and courage in their own ranks as they fought believing the gods were amongst them.

Finally he saw Morwenna who disembarked from the boat which had arrived first. As she stepped ashore he could see that it had been planned for the whole army turned and whooped a roar which caused the flocks of gulls and sea birds to take to the air. It was a symbolic gesture designed for effect. Marius was about to leave when a movement to his left arrested his departure. A column of men was wending and snaking its way from the camp in the woods. Marius did not dare risk running for he saw that they had horses, not many, but enough to chase him down. He waited patiently; better to leave safely and take his information than to be hasty and die unnecessarily.

Once the two groups had met they set off in one mighty horde for the camp in the woods. Marius knew where that was but he did not think they would remain there for long. As soon as the last warrior was out of sight he rode swiftly from his hiding place and headed for the prefect with the news, Morwenna was back.

"How many men did she have with her?"
"At least a cohort."
"And we know where they are?"

"Yes sir," Marius looked over to Livius, "they all went to the Brigante camp."

"They may not stay there sir and I think they will link up with the other two armies."

"I think you are right decurion. Now we await your other scouts."

"With your permission sir I would like to take all my men out for a reconnaissance. Without information we are blind."

"You are right. There is no point in us moving to this camp if they are heading for Mamucium."

"I don't think so. If they were going to use that as a base they would not have destroyed it."

"Even so we have no idea where they will go."

"I hope they come here."

"Quite so First Spear but I can't see them accommodating us that easily. This is a good base and we can move in any direction quite easily but without cavalry we will have to move slowly and carefully."

"The Emperor must need them more in the east sir."

"Yes decurion but without them we may lose this particular part of the west. Take your men out but return quickly for even a negative patrol will give us information. It will eliminate where they aren't."

The eighteen Explorates were gathered outside the fort's recently strengthened walls; the bolt throwers peeping over the ramparts like the teeth of a wolf.

"I want us to spread out like the spokes in a wheel. We will travel from south, round to the west and then north. Drusus you will take the road and your men to the east of you. Marius you will head due west and your men spread out to the south of you. I will head south east and my men will fill the gaps to yours. Go as far as you can in one day. If you discover anything do not look for another Explorate but head back here and tell the Prefect then find me or Drusus. If you have found nothing by the first day then return on the second day here."

"What if they are further away?"

Livius shook his head. "We can travel further and faster, Drusus, than the behemoth which is Morwenna's army. One day's riding should take us beyond where they could be. I am hoping that we find them half a day from here for then the Prefect can attack them and nip this rebellion in the bud. But make sure you take enough supplies for a week for you and your mounts. If you cannot return because you are following then we will know and we will send other Explorates to follow."

The Queen was also holding court with Tadgh, Brennus, Decius, Centurion and Ernan. "We need to strike quickly and raise the people's hopes. If we can defeat a Roman army they may see light at the end of the tunnel."

"We destroyed the men at Mamucium."

"Yes Decius but there were no survivors amongst the people to tell the tale."

Tadgh coughed. "We need more horses majesty. If we had horses then we could cover a larger area and we could scout as the Romans do."

"I have thirty horses."

"Not enough Decius but it gives me an idea. There are many horse farms in the land between Morbium and Eboracum. If you were to send your men there they could acquire more horses and bring them to us."

Tadgh nodded. "They would not expect that. What of the main army? We cannot sit here waiting. That is what the Romans would want. They would easily find us and destroy us."

"No we will not wait here. As Decius has destroyed Mamucium we will head south on the road and then across the

205

country to Eboracum. When we have the horses we can meet in the fertile and unprotected heart of the land of the Brigantes."

All of them nodded for the plan was both bold and sound. They would leave the auxiliaries guarding the road north while the men of the Twentieth Valeria would be hiding behind the stone walls of Deva. "Decius. Who will lead the horsemen east?"

"Centurion."

"Centurion, take your men to the fort first. Make them think you are scouting it and then head north. Take the road east later." All the men nodded for the plan was a sound one which had no risk for Centurion. He had sufficient men to be independent and there were no cavalry close by who could threaten his rustlers. "Bring your horses south west towards Eboracum. We will be there."

It fell to Agrippa to spot the cavalry heading towards the fort and he wasted no time mentally debating what he should do. He followed at a discreet distance. The armoured men were much heavier than he and his lithe mount. He was confident that he could outrun any beast that the deserters could field. He could see that they were heading for Bremmetenacum and he kept looking over his shoulder for the rest of the army following. Once he was certain which direction they were taking he looped back and back tracked to look for the rest of the army. They were nowhere insight. He quickly regained the trail and found the column which was still heading, resolutely east. Even when he could see the fort, looming up in the skyline the column did not deviate from their route. He could hear the buccina braying its alarm call as the auxiliaries and the legionaries raced to the ramparts.

Suddenly the cavalry halted and raced north eastwards to the road bypassing the fort. Agrippa took a quick decision, a decision which had an effect far beyond the moment. He rode to the fort. He deigned to enter but shouted up to the centurion on the ramparts. "Tell the Prefect there are no men following this column. I think it is a ruse to make us follow them. Tell my decurion I will follow the cavalry." He wheeled his horse and headed to the east of the road. The last thing he wanted was to be ambushed by those he was trailing. They would follow the road and, if they turned off he would see their trail and their tracks.

It fell to Metellus to find the main army. As he later reflected, a man would have had to be blind and drunk to miss the swathe they cut through the land. He settled in to following at a discreet distance. He could see that there were only a couple of horsemen with the force which meant he could be half a mile away and still safe. He had been following for an hour when he was joined by Cassius. "Well we have found them and they are heading south east."

"The fort?"

"Could be. When we know we will send a rider back to the Prefect." An hour later and Livius joined them.

"One of our easier assignments eh Cassius?"

"Yes sir."

The huge army was moving far quicker than a Roman army for they were not keeping ranks nor worrying about stragglers. The Explorates had no problem following but Livius knew that a Roman army attempting to pursue would struggle. "Metellus, ride back to the fort. Tell the Prefect that the main army is moving south west and heading for the road." He paused, knowing that his judgement would affect the Prefect's decision. "I think they are heading for Mamucium."

"Sir." Although Metellus agreed with his superior's assessment he was pleased that it was not his call.

Cassius felt much better now that the decurion was with him. He trusted Livius' judgement more than any other man he had known. "Well sir what do you think they are doing?"

"Not what I expected Cassius but then again Morwenna has always been unpredictable. Two things spring to mind. Deva or Mamucium."

"Deva?"

"No I am not confident about that call. Her people live to the east not the south but I do think the army heading in their direction will make the legion there a little worried and might stop them coming out to fight the army. My bet would be Mamucium but we will find out when we meet Drusus and his scouts. Until then we follow."

The snaking column that was the army soon arrived at the deserted and fire ridden settlement that had been Mamucium. The scavengers had already begun to feast on the dead and decaying bodies. Flocks of ravens, crows, magpies and chuffs took to the air as the first soldiers marched in. Foxes fled to the safety of the hedgerows to await the passing of this enormous army. "We camp here tonight."

Her leaders looked at Morwenna almost daring to question her orders. "But majesty," ventured Tadgh, "we could move on a little and be away from the rotting corpses."

"Are you afraid of the smell of death Tadgh? If so then I fear you will not enjoy this campaign for it will be one filled with the rank and rich smell of the dead, the Roman dead." Her body banged the pommels of their swords on their shields in noisy approbation. She held up her hand. "I want the Roman scouts following us to send a message that we are here and that we look like we are going to stay. Tomorrow we will make it look as though we are rebuilding the fort while the bulk of the army heads east. I want a small force to spend a couple of days pretending to rebuild and force the Roman's hand. Once they are committed to the road we can keep ahead of them."

Drusus saw the signs of an army rebuilding and establishing a base. He sent one of his men as a messenger back to the fort. "Tell the Prefect they are refortifying Mamucium." Although the decurion made the best assessment, his decision would cause hardship and death for many around the Vale of Eboracum. Livius might have considered his decision but the Explorates did not have the luxury of hindsight. Unlike the alae they had to make instant decisions and judgements. Even as the messenger headed north, Morwenna's plan was succeeding.

When Livius finally met up with Drusus, just outside the ruins of Mamucium he had more information and intelligence than Drusus had had at his disposal Marius had joined them having found nothing to the west but the detritus of empty camps and the dead bodies of murdered villagers.

Livius was less than happy with Drusus' reading of the situation but he kept his thoughts to himself. "Drusus you keep your maniple here and watch the building of the fort. Keep both the Prefect and myself on the progress. Marius, bring your men and join me. I will head along the road to the east. I think the witch has bewitched us again. Drusus, send one of your men to say that I am following Morwenna east. Tell the Prefect I believe she is heading for Brigante homeland. She appears to be heading for Stanwyck, the ancient capital of the land of the Brigante."

Morwenna pushed her army along ruthlessly. Despite the increasingly unpleasant late autumnal weather she did not allow any of her leaders and men to ease off and maintained a gruelling and killing pace. "If I, who gave birth in the last ten days, can still campaign, why not warriors who say they are tough? When I stop, you stop."

The warriors' honour made them push on even when their bodies cried to stop. It was a desolate place through which to travel filled with deep valleys, empty moor land and snow topped hills. The divide of mountains was devoid of people and they were invisible but for the tiny group of Explorates who dogged their trail.

Marius pulled Livius to one side. "Sir. I beg you. We have no supplies and our mounts are exhausted, we must rest."

Livius sighed, his haggard face showing the effects of the constant pursuit. "Marius. I would stop now if it were any one other than Morwenna leading this army but both of us know of what she is capable and she is, I believe, heading towards the land we love and more importantly the people that we cherish. If we must, we will eat our horses but I know that her people must be suffering as much as we. I am also concerned for Agrippa has not joined us. He must be following a contact and I believe that the Queen has some plan which even Metellus cannot fathom." He leaned over to Marius. "Trust me Marius."

Marius became upset. "Sir I never question your judgement but I know that the fate of the province hangs in the balance here."

Livius shook his head sadly. "Believe me Marius I know that."

Far behind them the Prefect was marching south to Mamucium with a cohort of the Ninth. He had had the foresight to send the other cohort back to Glanibanta to finish the road building. Two centuries of the Batavians gave him his only light infantry and he hoped that it would be enough. How he longed for a turmae or two of cavalry to screen his men. At least he was marching down a Roman road and he would not be ambushed. He was just five miles from Mamucium when Drusus' scout found him. "Sir. Decurion Drusus' compliments and the Brigante have abandoned the fort and are heading north east, following Morwenna. My maniple is following."

"Damn she has fooled us." He considered his options and did not like any of them. "Return to your officer and tell him to continue to follow the Brigante and tell him that your other men in the north are still following the cavalry."

As the rider saluted and galloped away First Spear looked at Prefect Fulvius. "And what will we do?"

"Finish off the rebuilding. Leave the two centuries of auxiliaries there and then follow the Queen."

"She will have a head start."

"I know. I just hope that the Explorates do not lose her." He stroked his chin. "I just wonder where she is going. Eboracum? Lindum? Ratae? Until we get a message from Livius we will just have to follow."

Chapter 16

Marcus and Cato viewed the mares; all of them were heavy with foal. It had been a good summer. "When Livius next visits we will have some fine animals to sell to him." Marcus felt his old wounds now that winter was creeping closer. The damp weather made him stiff and his whole body seemed to ache. He had not been hunting with Gaelwyn and Gaius for months now and he missed the old comradeship but it had been a good summer for the lush grass had brought the horse's coats to a sleekly lustre and he had enjoyed just talking horses with his old friend Cato.

"I was thinking that we could get the slaves to build a birthing barn for the mares. It would not take much building and it would give some shelter, especially if we have an autumn and a winter like last year."

Marcus grinned at Cato who had never changed in all the years he had known him. He always thought of the horses first. He would have built an inn for them if he could with beds and servants but Marcus could see that a birthing barn was soundly thought out. "Excellent idea. I will ride to Gaius and borrow a few of his slaves. You get Atticus to start work on the foundations."

"We have some timbers all ready and I think we have enough stones prepared."

As he rode away Marcus realised that Cato must have been planning this all summer, collecting the wood and the stone, preparing the ground. He smiled to himself. No wonder he had had the slaves clear the long grass from the rear of the stables. Still it was a good project and the two of them never shied away from hard work. Gaelwyn would moan and complain but he knew the old Brigante, now a true greybeard, would relish the challenge. Gaius and his boys would drop everything just to join in with Uncle Marcus. Sergeant Cato had done it again.

Centurion and his men had slipped into the land around Morbium with ease. They were careful to avoid the fort and the area patrolled by Rome. Fortunately, that just meant avoiding roads and, once they had dropped down from the land close to Brocauum, the terrain had been easy to navigate. Centurion however had a crick in the back of his neck, a nervous feeling. He was certain he was being followed but, despite setting up ambushes and backtracking he had not see anything but he knew there was someone following. Nuada had laughed it off blaming the infiltration of their camp by the Roman spy. "Besides it is but one man, what can one man do?"

Centurion had cast him a contemptuous look, "One man can alert the fort to our presence. But until we see him we continue with our raid." They were in the bend of the Dunum Fluvius many miles east of Morbium. As far as Centurion knew the nearest Romans were at Morbium, and Derventio. The fort at Derventio was over thirty miles away; their only problem would be the Batavians at Morbium. The herd of horses grazing in the field bounded by the river would make an excellent start to their horse herd.

"Will the Queen have reached Eboracum yet?"

"No Nuada it will take her more days yet for she has to traverse the rocky divide which runs through this land but we need to start the herd and this one is sizable." It was indeed the largest herd they had seen.

The owner, Questus, was a Brigante who had seen the success of other horse breeders and realised that it was a fast and easy way to maximise his profit. He sold his mounts unbroken and young. Now that it was at the end of the breeding and birthing season he was already preparing to take fifty or sixty down to Eboracum where he hoped they would be bought for the auxilia. It had been a blow when Marcus' Horse had been disbanded but a few beakers of wine bought for the Roman responsible for

213

acquiring horses had revealed that a new ala was being formed over the winter. He would take fifty down first and then a second fifty when the weather changed again.

He and his chief slave, his farm manager, were checking which horses they would take when they saw the column of Roman soldiers rise from the river like spectres. "I did not know there were cavalry nearby."

"Nor me master but these look to be mounted legionaries."

Questus rubbed his hands together. "We may be able to offload the horses now and save us a long journey to Eboracum. The Allfather is smiling on me today." The farm manager was not so sure. The legionaries had a lean and hungry look about them, like wolves about to descend on sheep. When half of the column suddenly wheeled away to head for the farm he became even more worried but Questus seemed unconcerned. He stepped forward with his hands out in greeting. The greeting was returned in the form of a volley of arrows which took the two men down instantly as the screams and cries from the farm told of Nuada's own attack.

Agrippa had watched it all with growing horror from the far side of the river. He was gaunt and thin. He had had to forage for both himself and his horse which was showing the effect of the pursuit. He had managed to track from far enough back to avoid all of Centurion's traps but he wished he had had Rufius with him for that boy would have been able to follow at an even safer distance. He saw the raiders slaughter the farm's inhabitants. It was the most remote farm they had passed, tucked away as it was in a loop of the river. No-one would discover the raid for some time. Now, however, he knew what they were about. They were hunting horses. That also made his job easier. A herd this size would be easy to follow. Even as he watched he saw the deserters capturing the lead horses, the stallions who could be led so that the herd would follow. He took a decision. He would head for

Gaius' farm. Gaius could send a message to Morbium and Agrippa could get another mount and some supplies. Besides he wanted someone else to know what was going on in case anything happened to him. This was why the decurion liked them in pairs. He grimaced ruefully. He should have sought help at the fort instead of just shouting a message.

When he rode through the gate of Gaius' farm he was disappointed to find it almost deserted. He was about to ride to the fort himself when Ailis emerged from the building. "Yes can I help you? Why it is one of Livius' men is it not? Agrippa?"

"It is my lady. I seek your husband."

She could see from his condition that he was both tired and hungry." Come in and take food." Agrippa began to shake his head. Ailis took hold of the reins and said firmly, "The men have gone to Marcus' farm which is not far away. You will eat and you can tell me of the trouble you have found then we will go together."

Her glaring eyes and firm voice told him that she would not brook a refusal and the smells emanating from the kitchen had him salivating already. "I will not refuse kind lady for I have been living from the land. I will just let my horse graze over there."

"Put your mount in the stable. There is grain there and when we leave you can have another mount for that poor beast is out on his legs. Come into the kitchen."

Agrippa wolfed down the food, a fine stew and freshly baked bread. Between mouthfuls he told her of Morwenna's return and the war which had started. Ailis had shaken her head, her eyes angry at the remembrance of the wicked witch's last mischief. She also remembered the way she had been treated by the witch's mother- they were an evil brood. "We have heard nought of this war."

215

"You wouldn't for I am following the first who have left her army. "He waved his spoon eastwards. "They have slaughtered the people who had horses in the bend of the Dunum."

"Questus? He had a fine herd."

"Had is the right word for they have been taken by the deserters who masquerade as Romans and I fear they are heading for Morwenna." He wiped his mouth. "And now my lady…"

"Here," she gave him another loaf and a bag with dried venison. "We will find my husband and one of the boys can take your message to Morbium. Gaius will know what to do."

The happy mood at Marcus' farmstead was shattered by the sudden arrival of Ailis and Agrippa. The fact that Ailis was riding was a clear indication of trouble. Cato recognised Agrippa straight away. "Agrippa? There is trouble?"

"Morwenna!" The one word struck fear into all of them. Agrippa did not dismount but spoke quickly and urgently. "Livius' brother Decius has armed deserters and they have joined Morwenna as a Roman army. She is raiding towards Mamucium but a column of men has stolen a herd of horses. I assume they will be taking them to her. I will follow them and hope that one of the other Explorates can find me. Could you get a message to Morbium?"

Gaius nodded, "Aye." He turned to his eldest son. "Decius Gaius, ride to the fort and tell the Prefect what Agrippa has said." He handed him his ring. "Here is my seal but he knows you anyway." As the boy eagerly mounted his horse and galloped away Gaius looked at Ailis. "I think, Agrippa that you need some help I will…"

Ailis grabbed hold of his hand. "No you will not. You are an old man." She glared at the four older men. "You are all older men. Look at Agrippa he is a much younger man and even he is exhausted. You would not last a day and you would slow him up. And if it came to a fight Gaius… I do not want lose you."

Gaius could see the wisdom of her words. "But Agrippa needs help."

Young Marcus looked at Decius and they both nodded. "We can go father." Ailis looked in horror at her son and adopted son.

Decius Macro's eyes pleaded with Ailis. "You said we could join the Explorates."

"Next year."

"But if we do not help Agrippa then the raiders and the rebels may destroy our farm. At least let us help him. We could bring messages back to the farm."

Gaius took his wife's body under his arm. "They will be safe."

Gaelwyn grunted. "They are the best trackers I have ever trained and they can hide better than even I."

Agrippa was torn. He knew he needed help but could he take the boys from their mother? "If you do allow them to come they must obey all my orders." He glared at the eager young faces. "Especially when I tell them to run and return to their mother." Ailis' thanks were in her eyes as she nodded to Agrippa.

Realising they had won the boys raced to their horses. Marcus shouted. "You need your bows and you need food!"

Over their shoulders they chorused. "Yes Uncle Marcus we know."

As they trotted eastwards Agrippa looked at the two boys. Although born in the same year Decius Macro already looked a head taller than Marcus Gaius. In truth they both looked only a little younger than Rufius. They both worked hard and had well muscled, lean bodies. They wore their hair in the Roman style and their leather tunics showed that they were preparing to be warriors as were the short swords and daggers which hung from their baldrics.

"The men we are following are ruthless. They may dress as Romans but they are savage barbarians." He paused as he deliberated; should he tell them of Seius' end? "Perhaps this is a

217

good thing. You wish to join the Explorates for you think it is exciting, well one of our number, a trooper only a little older than you was captured by these Romans and he was impaled upon a stake. He did not die a noble and honourable death he suffered and died alone. Perhaps when you return to your farm you may decide that this is not the life for you and I would not blame you. So just do as I say and we will have you back with your mother once I find out where the enemy are going to."

The two young men grinned at each other. No matter what Agrippa said this was the adventure of a lifetime and was the life they had both dreamed of. Marcus Gaius' brother, Decius would be happy running the farm but these two knew that they were warriors however to placate Agrippa they both nodded their assent.

They soon found the trail which headed due south. The bodies of the owner and his slave were still lying in the field and Agrippa took the boys so that they could see that this was not a game. "It looks like they swam the herd across the river. " The steep bank on the other side was heavily churned up by hundreds of hooves.

"Well at least the trail is easy to follow."

Agrippa shook his head. "We are not trailing just horses. There are men ahead who will try to ambush and kill us. They are cunning and crafty. We have to be invisible."

As they swam their horses through the water Decius Macro asked, "How many Explorates are there?"

"The Ninth has thirty but the decurion only has fifteen with him. We normally work in pairs but we had some casualties and some of the Explorates are wounded." He noticed the look they exchanged. "It is not a game. Your fathers joined the cavalry when a little older than you and they learned quickly that war is not for the faint hearted and being a man on a horse just gives you more opportunity to hurt yourself."

Suddenly Marcus Gaius shouted, "I can see them."

Agrippa immediately lay across his horse's head and peered in the direction the young man was pointing. "Get down as I do!" He cursed himself for his carelessness. The raiders were heading through the low vale which led, eventually, to Eboracum and the woods and copses prevented the three riders from seeing long distances. Were it not for Marcus Gaius' keen sight they would have stumbled upon the deserters and it would not have gone well for them. He turned his horse and led the two boys back the way they had come.

"Are we giving up?" Marcus Gaius sounded disappointed.

"No son. We have to be circumspect. We can see that they are heading south by east." He pointed due south. They have to cross the river which runs through Eboracum and there is but one place available. Due south of us." He rubbed his chin as he tried to work out what the raiders were doing. "I cannot believe they are heading for Eboracum for there will be patrols around that fortress which means they will have to turn west eventually. We can head even further west for we can travel faster than they. In the Explorates we learn to anticipate. Now enough questions. We ride."

They kicked their horses on and took the higher ground to the west. Agrippa was pleased that it afforded them a better view of the land and, although the herd had disappeared from sight, he knew that he could find it again once it neared the river.

"Are you sure there were three of them?"

"Yes Centurion. I saw three horses and they looked to have riders on them. They had no helmets and I think they are scouts."

Centurion was not unduly concerned that they were being followed. He was more worried in case their pursuers chose to inform the garrison at Eboracum before they had delivered their mounts to the Queen. Centurion knew that the Queen would still be bringing her horde across the top of the hills; he would not expect to see her for at least three days. He had hoped to corral the horses and send a rider to the Queen so that she could head for them rather than the other way around. He was acutely aware of how few men he had and how vulnerable he would be to an attack. He could not afford to be dogged by these pursuers. "Nuada," the cruel looking warrior jerked his mount's head around and rode next to Centurion. "There are three men following us. They look to be lightly armed scouts. Take five men and ambush them. I want them dead."

Relishing the thought of trapping someone and killing men less well armed than they, he grinned. "Consider them dead already."

Agrippa let Decius Macro lead for a while. He had sharp eyes and ears which Agrippa knew from past experience could make the difference between life and death. He was considering sending one of the boys back to Morbium for he was now almost certain that the horse thieves were heading south west away from Eboracum. The problem was in that word 'almost'. He couldn't quite work out where they were going. Had he been with Cassius or Metellus then they would have talked it through and some ideas would have come. Agrippa was frustrated because he was on his own and so much rested on his shoulders. He had no idea where Morwenna was nor where the rest of the Explorates were. Perhaps they were already on their way to Morbium; it was the uncertainty which galled him. He decided that he would send one of the boys back; that way if there were any news at Morbium he would get it quickly. He kicked his horse on to come level with Decius Macro.

Nuada cursed as his arrow thudded not into the boy who had been on point but the side of the older warrior. "Get them!" This would be easy for as soon as he had seen the age of the two boys, they were almost children, he knew that they would be easily despatched. As he urged his horse forward he was shocked to see the trooper on his left fall clutching the feathers which protruded from his neck. Before he could react a second arrow hit the the warrior to his right and then he found himself flying through the air as his horse took a hastily fired arrow in the neck making it rear.

Agrippa could feel his life blood slipping away. The arrow had been fired from such a close range that it had pierced his armour. He was dying but he had to live long enough to save the boys. He would never be able to face Gaius and Macro in the afterlife if he had failed to prevent their deaths. He kicked his horse up the hill towards the hedgerow and weakly yelled, "Ride!" He saw them both fire another arrow each before following him. It took all his concentration to hold on to the reins and retain consciousness and he did not see Marcus Gaius turn in the saddle and fire an arrow at the deserter who was but thirty paces away. At that range he could not miss even on a speeding mount and the man was plucked from his horse making the last two men who were following to have to veer left and right to avoid tripping over him. The action gave the boys and Agrippa the time they needed to extend their lead and disappear from sight. The two men reluctantly kept going but, having seen three of their comrades killed and their leader unhorsed they were not keen to follow these boys who appeared to be easy targets but had proved to be deadly.

Agrippa held on for as long as he could but after a mile he slumped from his saddle and crashed to the ground. Decius Macro took charge. "Marcus, see to him I will see if they are still close by."

Agrippa's eyes opened and he saw the boy leaning over him. "Leave me and..."

"Quiet Agrippa."

Decius returned. "They have stopped following we are safe."

They both looked at the arrow and then each other. Gaelwyn had told them of arrow wounds and how they could be removed but neither had paid much attention at the time. They had a dilemma and neither was certain what to do. When they had been attacked their instinct had taken over and they had fired their bows almost automatically as Gaelwyn had taught them. The men had just been big animals and easier to kill than the foxes and hares they had hunted.

Agrippa opened his eyes. "I am done for. I will be with the Allfather soon. You must return to Morbium. The horse thieves must be heading for Morwenna. Tell him of the direction they were taking and…" The last effort had sapped his strength and with a gasp he died.

The two boys looked at each other. "What do we do? Bury him?"

"No Marcus, we take him home. Your father will know what to do and we can pass our message on."

"You are right." They manhandled the Explorate onto his horse and they tied him on. Marcus led the beast by its reins while Decius scouted a safe path. He headed up the low ridge to afford them a better view of the land below them and he saw the three surviving riders looking for their trail. They were heading south; he held out his hand and pointed, north.

When Centurion was told of the disastrous ambush he was coldly and quietly angry especially when told that two of them had been boys. "But we did for the scout."

"You fool! Did you find his body?"

"No but we found where he fell and from the blood he cannot be alive."

"No but the fact that you cannot find his body and the two boys escaped means that the Romans will soon know where we are. We will have to risk discovery and get to the Queen as soon as possible. Try to redeem yourself. Find the Queen and bring her to me." He leaned over and added menacingly, "Fail me again and you will need to hide in a very deep dark hole for I will rip your heart out with my bare hands. Now go."

It was night time when the two weary boys rode up to the barred gate of the farm. Gaius' guards recognised them and, as he opened the gate, awoke the house with his shout. Ailis rushed out and when she saw the boys embraced them, tears coursing down her cheeks. Gaius noticed the body. "Decius Gaius help me with Agrippa. Close the gate and Ailis take the boys in."

Marcus Gaius fought free. "We must get to Morbium. Agrippa sent us with a message."

Gaius was in no mood to argue. "You can tell me and I will deliver the message!" He softened a little. "You are both tired and from your quivers I can see that you have fought today. Take it from an old soldier that you need to rest. Let this old soldier complete your mission eh?"

The boys nodded as shock finally made them realise how close they had come to death. Gaelwyn helped Gaius and his son to take the body of Agrippa and, reverently lay the warrior on the ground. Gaius looked at him and closed the dead eyes which stared up at the sky. "Well old friend you brought my sons back to me. Tomorrow we will bury you and send you to the Allfather with our thanks and you can tell Macro of his son who today took his first steps to becoming a warrior."

Gaius set off for Morbium even though it was a pitch black night. Agrippa had given his life that the message might get through and Gaius could at least be slightly inconvenienced. The optio at the gate was young and somewhat reluctant to wake his superior. When Gaius mentioned raiders and rebellion he soon changed his mind. Gaius was left to cool his heels while the centurion was wakened. He saw a glow appear behind the door and then it opened. A red faced optio was looking at his caligae as though they were the most important thing he possessed.

"Sorry about that Gaius; he is new to the fort. He will recognise you next time. What brings you out so late?" As they walked to the Praetorium Gaius related the news of the horse raid and Agrippa's death. He nodded, "Interesting that. You are not the first messenger with ill tidings tonight and Agrippa was not the only Explorate who arrived. A rider came in today with news from Prefect Fulvius of the Ninth. Morwenna has returned with an Irish army and raised some Brigante to join an army of deserters. Can that be true that men who once followed the eagle now fight against it?"

"I have not seen it myself but both of my sons were attacked by Roman cavalry."

"Are they safe?"

"Aye they are resourceful little buggers. They managed to kill three of their enemies and a horse." He added proudly.

"I will wake…"

He got no further as Rufius entered the office, "I am always a light sleeper and when I heard the horse I thought it might have been another Explorate."

"I am afraid our visitor has bad news for you."

"Yes Agrippa died today at the hands of the traitors who dress as Romans."

"I know he will have died well and we will have our revenge. Where was he when he died?"

"South of here pursuing the traitors who had stolen a horse herd."

"That is what Decurion Livius feared that they would acquire horses and be able to range further."

"Where is the Queen?"

"Travelling east from Mamucium." Both the Centurion and Gaius started at that news. "If I can pick up their trail I might be able to do something."

"My sons know where they went."

"If they could describe it to me I might be able to..."

Gaius shook his head laughing wryly. "They would take you for they wish to be Explorates and if it had not been for them then Agrippa would have died in vain for we would not know the news. It is their mother who will be the one we need to persuade."

"There is no point returning now, Gaius. Stay the night and leave first thing."

"Aye for they will have barred the gate and she will be like a she-bear tomorrow. I would not like to face a she-bear who has been deprived of sleep."

When Gaius and Rufius rode into the farm the next morning Gaius had been rehearsing what he would say all the way from the fort. He realised that he had been rudely silent and the young Explorate next to him excluded. "Excuse me Livius my thoughts were elsewhere."

"You don't need to apologise sir. It must be a hard decision you are making to trust your sons to a stranger."

Gaius shook his head vigorously. "You are not a stranger for you were... you are Marcus' Horse. I would trust not only my sons but my wife to any who served in Marcus' Horse for they are all like brothers to me. Tell me what Prefect Fulvius has planned?"

"He is bringing the second cohort to Morbium. With the information you have added he will head down to Eboracum to reinforce it. There is but half a cohort of legionaries there and half a cohort of auxiliaries. The rest are preparing to head north."

"Yes this rebellion has come at a difficult time." He saw the smoke from the farm. "Let me break the news to my wife."

Rufius grinned, "Sir my father taught me well that a man does not interfere with a mother, especially a she-bear."

Decius Macro and Marcus Gaius were waiting by the gate and he could see that they had their horses already packed. He frowned as he saw a third horse already packed. Gaelwyn was standing close by fussing with their saddlebags and he could see, even from a distance that Ailis was upset. Ailis was so strong in many ways; she had endured slavery twice, once as a young woman and the second time as a mother with her children taken as well. She had endured both stoically, far more bravely than Gaius and yet now she was crumbling.

Gaius dismounted and embraced his wife who had wiped away her tears before he had entered the farm. They hugged each other far longer than they needed and Gaius realised that Ailis thought he too was going away. That was who the extra horse was for. He whispered in her ear. "I am not going anywhere. I am staying and Rufius only needs the boys to show where they last saw the herd. They will be back before supper time."

She stepped away her eyes wide with joy. "Thank you." She turned to Rufius. "I will bring you some supplies Rufius, you look like you haven't been fed for a week."

Gaelwyn shuffled over his arthritic knee playing up in the damp weather. "Well Gaelwyn you sneaky old Brigante. How did you persuade her?"

"She didn't take much persuading. She could see that more than her happiness depended on the boys helping and after that…"

Gaius wandered over to the two boys. "Just show Rufius where you last saw them and then return. We want you back tonight. "The two boys looked crestfallen. Gaius could see that they were prepared for a campaign. They both wore leather jerkins. Short swords hung from leather baldrics and they had their hunting spears as well as their bows and arrows. Gesturing at their equipment. "Did you think you were going to war?"

Marcus Gaius said lamely, "We thought we might hunt…"

"Hunt Brigante eh?" Just then Ailis came out with the supplies for Rufius.

"Thank you lady. Well boys the sun is burning daylight let's be away. Say goodbye to your parents."

"Bye!" They quickly hugged their mother and waved cheerfully at Gaius and Gaelwyn. They were eager to be away.

Gaius came up to Rufius, "Look after them Rufius." In answer Rufius saluted across his chest and the look on his face was more than an answer. He nodded. "May the Allfather be with you."

Chapter 17

Livius was becoming disenchanted with the game of cat and mouse he was playing with the Brigante scouts. As they had reached the high part of the moors it became harder to follow them without being seen. They had almost fallen foul of ambushes from hidden dells and all his Explorates bore minor wounds from falls, stones or arrows. The Brigante boys were proving excellent shots with their slings and had injured both Explorates and mounts.

It had been Metellus who had devised the strategy which made life easier for them. "We know they are staying on the road sir why don't we leap frog them by sending a pair ahead on the road each day so that we are ahead of them and they can report to us when we arrive at an agreed point. Each day another two would leave so that we had a line of sentries, constantly changing. If the witch deviates from the route then they will know and they can backtrack to find where they left the road."

"Good idea. We will run with that. Drusus, what did Prefect Fulvius say he was doing?"

"Well sir he didn't see the point of just following the Queen, going further away from the barbarians in the north. He decided to turn around and head north. That way he could approach Eboracum from the north. He said the roads were better and he could bring down more cohorts if he needed them."

"A risky strategy that. There is no legion at Lindum anymore. If she heads south there is nothing in her way."

"Except sir he said that that they are not Brigante down there, they are Coritani and they seem quite happy for Rome to be here."

"Yes but she could still cause chaos. I am arguing against myself here. It is our job to follow her no matter where she goes and it is now shorter to ride to Eboracum than Bremmetenacum. Right Metellus, as it is your idea you and Cassius take the first patrol. Drusus take your men north of the road and Marius take yours South. I will continue to follow and then leapfrog Metellus tomorrow with Decius."

All of the Explorates were heartily sick of the weather they had to endure: they had relentless winds which whistled across the wild and empty moors, sudden snow flurries and insidiously dense rain which insinuated itself through however many layers they had managed to put on. The grazing, what there was, was poor and their horses were suffering as they had run out of grain. At night there was no shelter and they had to camp far enough away from the road to avoid and ambush or night attack by the army they were following. Livius had to hope that the enemy was suffering as much as they were.

Morwenna did not view the journey as a hardship. She had endured worse when she lived in the cave. In fact she had bloomed and blossomed out in the fresh air. The frailty of motherhood had passed and she now looked not as a girl queen but a woman majestically approaching the best years of her life. She had enough horsemen now to raid the surrounding areas keeping their meagre supplies augmented. They had also had their numbers swollen by new recruits. Many were disenchanted Brigantes but others were deserters who had heard of the lucrative incentives being offered and they travelled from all parts of the frontier to, once more earn money for doing that for which they were trained. The wagons with the extra weapons purchased by the precious gold meant that they were better armed than one might have expected.

If anyone was unhappy it was Decius. This was not the life style he had envisaged for himself. He was certainly rich but where could he spend the money? Where could he surround himself with the trappings of a rich man? Certainly not here on this forsaken and desolate moor with rain slashing down like knives and, already, the tops flecked with the snow which grew day by day. His only consolation was that they could now see ahead into the rich populated valleys south of Eboracum. This was the rich hinterland which would swell both their coffers and their army.

Tadgh and Brennus were relishing their new roles as leaders of an increasingly large and polyglot army. They had already begun to boast of how they would deal with the Ninth when they met them in battle. Tiny and his leader had listened to their fantasies and kept silent for when they did voice an opinion the Brigante became both belligerent and violent. Although Decius was certain that Tiny could easily despatch any of the boastful warriors he did not want to risk an injury to the man who might save his life in the future. Privately they talked long into the night about how they would fight the Ninth. "General, the Ninth are fine warriors. They are well disciplined. They can withstand missiles for they go into testudo. When you attack they throw their javelins and then their pila and when you get in close you have no target to strike for they are armoured and their wicked blades can easily find holes, especially when their opponents don't wear armour. The Brigante are talking out of their arses."

"I have never seen them fight Tiny but what you say is confirmed by my father. Why when they fought the Iceni they destroyed an army of over eighty thousand warriors. I fear that we are too few and far too undisciplined."

Tiny nodded. "We are growing but it is not enough and if they bring their ballistae and scorpions then all will be lost. If we had more deserters we might stand a chance for the men all know of the tactics of the legion and can copy them." It was one of the longest speeches Decius had ever heard Tiny make and it made its content all the more telling.

"Listen Tiny we need to find some trustworthy men amongst our army. Not the rabble we had before but men who will fight when needed and be able to protect our gold effectively."

Tiny's eyes darted to the far side of the camp where the small wagon with their weapons and gold stood. "I have four such men who sleep with the wagon."

"We need more and we need to be able to move and leave quickly if needs be."

"It can be done."

"And Tiny, not a word to the Queen."

The next day they dropped down from the high moors to the relative shelter of the valley bottom and the temperature leapt making Decius feel almost warm. Ahead they could see the vale which lay close to Eboracum. They were less than two days from that rich plum which was just ripe for the picking. With just a cohort inside its walls it would soon fall. When Decius saw Nuada ride in the next day his spirits rose. He had missed the comforting bulk that was Centurion and Nuada's arrival meant that his lieutenant was not far away. The Queen saw Nuada heading straight for Decius and she sent Tadgh to intercept him. His eyes narrowed in anger but Decius could not afford a confrontation at that moment. "Come on Tiny let us see what news Nuada has brought."

Much to Tadgh's annoyance Nuada waited until Decius and Tiny arrived before breaking his news. "Centurion is less than half a day away, "he pointed due north away from the road, "in that direction and he has a hundred horses." He omitted the news of the scouts and his failure. Perhaps Centurion would have forgotten it by the time they met.

Decius' eyes lit up. A hundred horses; it would give him his cavalry and enable him to slip away with his precious gold. Now that he was on the eastern side of the country an idea to take a boat re-emerged as a viable proposition. "Excellent news is it not your majesty? Now that we have horses we can range far further and eliminate these scouts who are dogging us."

Tadgh snorted, "We have not seen them for the past two days. I think they have given up."

"It makes no difference now for we are within half a day of the newly acquired horses and we are within a day's ride of Eboracum," he looked pointedly at the Queen, "if that is still your intention?"

"Eboracum is important but it is only part of a grander plan I have. It is important because the last time we came here we nearly captured it but failed because of Marcus' Horse. Well we know that ala no long exists and we have left most of the Ninth behind us. Eboracum is a symbol of Rome's power. We need to destroy it to give the people encouragement."

Decius smiled inside. She had said people as though she cared for them which of course she didn't. They were a means to an end; the end of Roman rule and the damned religion which ruled her life. However he could play act with the best of them. "Well tell us how do we destroy it?"

"The same way we destroyed Mamucium; by deception. You take the horses and pretend to be a new ala of cavalry. When they open the gates your men take them and we capture it."

"Good plan but once again it is my men who take the risks while the blowhard Brigante come along and reap the rewards." His insult was planned for he needed the Brigante to take the risks rather than his men.

Tadgh's hand went to his sword as did Decius but the four huge Irishmen who flanked the Queen stepped between the two men; easy grins on their faces leaving the two men under no illusion as to what would be the outcome of a fight between the two of them. "Both of you, this is not a cockfight! I will use any of your Brigante or your deserters to achieve my ends. the Brigante will be with you pretending to be prisoners. It will assuage the fear of the garrison and put them at their ease. They will think that you are a successful General."

Decius had to admit that it was a sound plan and stood a good chance of success. Tadgh would die at his hands but not until he knew that he could escape with his treasure. "Very well. Now let us ride to Centurion. Those horses need to be schooled as quickly as possible. Come along Tiny let us see these horses and their quality." Trotting away Decius turned to Nuada. "When we reach Centurion I have a task for you."

Nuada looked over at his leader intrigued by the statement. His failure to catch the scouts might be forgotten if he could ingratiate himself with Decius, perhaps he could even supplant Centurion as the number two? "Whatever you wish General."

As they left Morwenna called over Brennus. "Send two men into the vicus at Eboracum. I want to know the strength of the force which awaits us. One man can stay in the vicus. If he could get into the fort and get some additional information then that might help us. Let us take a trick from the Roman spies and use our own."

Brennus grinned. "I have two men who are perfect for it."

When he disappeared to find his spies Morwenna called over Tadgh. "You are my General not that popinjay. Do not let him goad you again. When Aodh left you to guard me he did so because he trusted you. You let down his memory and my protection when you indulge these acts of bravado."

Shamefaced Tadgh trudged away but he swore that he would watch Decius and, when the opportunity arose, he would have his revenge.

It fell to Livius to discover that the army had left the road and changed direction. He quickly sent for the other two maniples and, when Drusus and Marius had arrived discussed their strategy. "We need to send a message to Morbium in case Prefect

233

Fulvius is there and of course another message to the garrison at Eboracum." He looked at his two decurions. "At least we don't need to worry about Lindum now. Drusus, take a man and head to Morbium tell the Prefect of this change then rejoin us here; hopefully you will have information about Prefect Fulvius. Marius, take a man to Eboracum and stress to the Prefect that this woman has been here before and almost succeeded. When you have passed your message on, head back to rejoin us. I will keep your other trooper and try to discover what they intend."

Marius looked over at Livius. "Tell me you aren't going to try to get into the camp." Livius was silent. "If Marcus, Julius or Gaius were here sir they would tell you that it would be suicide to go in to the camp. They are looking for us and both Morwenna and Decius know you."

"I know all that but at the moment we are just reacting to what they do. We need to anticipate. But I agree, at the moment it would be suicide but I still need the intelligence."

Marius turned to Cassius, "Make sure he doesn't go Cassius." Cassius nodded, he would not let his friend go to his death.

When Decius found Centurion he was delighted with the mounts. "The Queen is coming. We can head in her direction slowly." He gathered his inner circle together. "I fear that the Queen may have over reached herself and in that event I do not want to either end up on a cross or as a galley slave. "Nuada and Tiny, I want you to go back to the wagon. When the army moves off hang towards the rear of the column. Feign some damage and, when the army is out of sight head due east to the river. Nuada you and the guards wait with the gold. Tiny you return as though you have been scouting south towards Lindum. That way I will know where the wagons are when we steal a ship. If things go badly then Tiny will fetch you back into the fold once more. If things go well then we will join you Nuada, with a ship and we can sail away to safety."

"Why wait by the river? Why not head into Eboracum?"

Decius could hear from Centurion's tone that he was not questioning or challenging merely clarifying. "South of Eboracum the river is wide enough for quite large ships we will take a ship from the quays at Eboracum and head for Gaul or Hispana."

"Which was the original plan."

"True but now we have better men, better equipment and as much gold as we had before. Our brief alliance has proved successful."

Centurion looked shrewdly at Decius. "You are planning to leave come what may."

"Let us just say that even if we win I may end up with a Brigante blade in my back and I would like to plan for all eventualities."

"So we keep a low profile in any battle?"

"We take the best horses and, if we are away from the main army then how will any one know if we fight or not. These Brigantes don't know a horse's arse from its head. We and those we choose will be the cavalry so choose our loyal men. Now off you go Tiny and Nuada. We may soon be free of this land."

Rufius liked the two boys who were but a few years younger than he. They had decided to call Decius Macro just Macro as he had grown tired of giving a mouthful of names when he wanted the boy to do something and the boy seemed to grow uncia with pride at being called by his father's name. Marcus Gaius would just be Gaius. As Rufius explained, "We have to do things quickly in the Explorates and shouting a list of names can cost a man his life. Also do not wear your bow about your body. It stretches and does the bowstring no good and you waste time unslinging it. Keep it across your saddle cloth."

The two boys did all that Rufius said. Keen to learn from someone they were rapidly looking up to. Gaelwyn had told them that he was the best tracker he had ever seen and that was praise indeed. "We picked up the trail here Rufius and followed them there."

"I can see the tracks. You two keep going as you did before. I will scout around and catch up with you. Have your bows ready for our enemies may have decided to wait and ambush us."

They watched as Rufius quickly disappeared down a gully. Now apprehensive they kept watch on both sides for an ambush. Their horses neighed as they trotted along the heather littered hillside. Suddenly Rufius appeared in front of them and both of them had an arrow notched in a heartbeat.

"Well done but boys your horses told you I was there. Listen to your mount for he is as much a warrior as you are. I found their trail and saw the hoof prints of the ones who laid the ambush. Follow me and you will see your handiwork." Both boys were annoyed with their lax behaviour which Rufius had seemed to criticise.

Half a mile up the trail they saw the two men they had first slain and, a little further on the dead horse. Already the scavengers had pecked out the eyes of the dead and other creatures had invested the bodies. "The men we fight are not honourable or they would have buried their comrades. We have no time but we will pause to say a few words. Allfather take these treacherous men and decide if they are worthy enough to join the warriors in the hereafter. Look over us and these warriors." He looked at the boys. "It does not do to offend the Allfather."

Macro said, "It was a little further up where Agrippa died." They soon found the bloodied patch of grass.

"Let us find which way the herd went and then you can return home."

"But Rufius," they both began.

He held his hand up. "I promised your parents."

They rode down a dell and began to work their way up a steep slope. The hoof prints showed quite clearly the direction the herd had taken. Suddenly Rufius' horse's ears pricked up and, in an instant, he had an arrow notched and his hand held up to halt the two boys. He slid off his horse and gestured for them to keep watch. He bellied up to the ridge and after a moment or two slithered down and remounted his horse. "Well boys we not only have the herd, we have the whole Brigante army. I will be riding back to the farm with you."

The three riders turned their horses around and headed back down the trail. Rufius kept them in the lowest parts of the shallow valley, avoiding the skyline. The track led through scrubby hawthorn, elder and blackthorn which masked and hid them from view. Part of Rufius wanted to stay and scout but he had been the only one to see the army and he needed to report as soon as possible to a superior. Morbium was only half a day's ride away and the army he had seen had been so large that it would be easy to find again. Even one of the boys could find it.

He had been impressed with the boys; they had not panicked or become over excited and had followed his orders to the letter. Their reactions had been so sharp it was like looking at himself. They would make good Explorates and he would tell Livius as soon as he saw him.

Livius had found the Brigante army again. He sat with Cassius and Decius watching the huge horde snake its way northwards. Although huge it was moving quite quickly and Livius could sense urgency about the way it was hurrying. They had to know there were no enemies close by, there had to be another reason for their speed.

"Sir?"

"Yes Cassius, they are no longer heading to Eboracum. That suggests a meeting or they have sighted our forces."

"Could the Prefect have reached here in such a short space of time?"

"Possibly. They were travelling on roads and when they put their minds to it legionaries can eat up the ground but I don't think it is the Prefect. They are not preparing for a battle. Look, the Brigantes are not wearing their helmets or carrying their battle standards but I would like to know who they are meeting. Decius, you continue to follow them. As soon as you come across either Eboracum or any of our forces join them. If they suddenly head for Eboracum or south then find me, quickly."

"And where will you be sir?"

"Cassius and I will head north west and skirt around them. There is higher ground there and we can make good time."

Riding along the ridge they could see how vast the army now was its numbers swollen in recent days by rebels and deserters heading from the south. They were easily identified by their lack of weaponry. When the battle was imminent they would be armed and organised. Morwenna could be clearly seen on the pure white mount and surrounded by the six huge Irishmen who looked to be uncomfortable sitting on their horses. They might be fearsome warriors but on a horse they would be no challenge even for a lightly armed Explorate.

"Sir!"

Cassius' sharp eyes had pickled something out in the distance and, shading his eyes from the light Livius peered in the direction of Cassius' pointed finger. "Horses. That is why they have changed direction. That is a big herd."

Cassius suddenly looked worried. "Sir that herd has come from the north. The Prefect and Gaius…"

With a sinking heart Livius knew that Cassius could be right. The best horses were just south of Morbium and that was but half a day's ride from where they were. "We cannot worry about that yet Cassius. Let us circle the herd and then decide what the information means." In his mind Livius had a couple of options and, having Cassius with him allowed him to pursue both. He could send a rider to Morbium to inform the prefect of the situation, although he was confident that the Batavian would know and, at the same time contact and warn Eboracum.

Casca was the deserter guarding the northern end of the herd. He had really sharp eyes and, as he scanned the tree line, a movement caught his eye. He kept his head still not making the mistake of looking around for what he though he had seen. If there was something out there it would move again and he knew where he was looking. A few heartbeats later and he saw it, this time much clearer. It was at least one horse and a rider. He risked a glance over his shoulder. Centurion was close by and another twenty riders. He turned back to his prey and quickly located it. He then saw a second horse. These could be the scouts who had killed his good friend Massilius. "Sir! I have something." He kept his eyes fixed, not daring to move and lose them.

He felt a horse rumble up next to him. "What is it Casca?" Centurion liked Casca who was a hard working and uncomplaining soldier. He was the kind who would have been a chosen man when Centurion had fought for Rome. More importantly he had good eyes and it was obvious that he had seen something. He was like a dog on point with an unwavering stare.

"Saw at least two riders sir. There, about half a mile away. No uniforms so it could be those scouts we ran into the other day."

"Well done." Now that Centurion had more men these insects which had dogged and annoyed them for so long would be squashed. He turned in the saddle. You six men come with Casca and me. You," he gestured at the nearest guard, "tell the General we have gone to catch some scouts."

Centurion smiled a cruel, grim smile; that fool Nuada had allowed them to escape the last time and it could have resulted in disaster. The fact that they were heading away from the army meant they were heading somewhere to report, probably Morbium and the last thing they needed was for a cohort of auxiliaries to be loose on their left flank when they attacked Eboracum. He would easily catch and kill these spies but not before he had extracted information. He was intrigued about them as a force. They were not like the alae he had fought alongside for so many years and yet they were organised and they, he had to admit, were very effective.

He gestured for Casca and two men to head east and cut off the scouts while he and the others headed west up the slope. He could see from the movements of the birds and the bushes that the scouts were moving slowly so as not to attract attention. That suited him for they could move faster and now they were in the perfect position for a pincer movement. They were his for the taking.

Rufius had sharp ears as had his horse and when Blackie's ears pricked up so did Rufius'. He leaned forward to stroke its head. "Well done!" He hissed to Marcus riding in front of him and held his hand for halt. Marcus repeated and Rufius was pleased to see instant obedience and no questions. He was also pleased to see the bows appear instantly in their hands with an arrow notched. The grins told him they were not afraid.

Now that Rufius was still he could hear and see better. A quick glance to his right identified at least two soldiers and another to the left spotted one high up on the ridge. He was under no illusions; they had been spotted and would have to move soon. The two boys were watching Rufius intently waiting for instructions. He pointed to his right and then at his bow. He mimed riding and shooting. When they nodded he knew they understood. He was gambling that, if they charged whoever was on their right they might be lucky and hit a couple and make their escape. He did not know how many there were and, if it were a large column they would be cut down but he was confident that the three of them could react quicker than the deserters and he had already seen what good riders they were. It was a gamble but then wasn't life?

He kicked his horse hard right and Blackie responded leaping out. The two boys followed closely. Casca and the two men with him were taken by surprise. None of them was armed with a missile weapon but they all drew their swords. Casca's companions both fell to the ground one pierced by two arrows from the boys and the other by Rufius'. Casca turned his horse to face Rufius but the scout jinked his horse around and was beyond the startled soldier in a couple of strides. By the time Casca had turned his horse the three scouts were racing east. Behind Rufius heard the roar of rage as Centurion and his men hurtled through the hedgerow in pursuit.

The three lightly armed boys began to draw away from Casca. Rufius was confident that they would outrun their pursuers. They would head east for a while and then return to their northern route. They rode down a small, shallow valley and up on to a ridge. As they reached the top Rufius realised to his dismay that the Brigante army had been moving steadily in that direction and as they crested the ridge they could see, less than half a mile away, the outriders of the Brigante army. They were trapped. They would have to outrun their pursuers who could now cut them off. "Right boys. Head left and keep your eyes on the men on your left." Rufius loosened his sword. Soon he might need it.

Chapter 18

Livius saw the pursuit of the three men just as he saw Drusus and his man Lepidus. "Cassius follow those deserters while I attract Drusus' attention. Cassius kicked his mount on and Livius gave the Explorate whistle. Drusus raised his arm in acknowledgement and they galloped over.

"Someone is in trouble down there. I can't see who it is but if those deserters are following them then they must be friends of ours."

"Yes sir."

"Sir, the one at the back is Rufius."

"You are right Lepidus. I don't think the three on this side have seen us. Let us hope that we can reach them in time."

Livius could see the gap between Rufius and his two companions and the three Roman deserters who were pursuing them narrowing moment by moment. The warrior behind them was urging his mount on supremely confident that he would soon be in range and would be able to use his spatha to strike them. To his amazement Livius saw the figure in front of Rufius turn in his saddle and loose an arrow at the eager pursuer. Although the arrow missed the man it forced him to swerve to one side and bought them time. "Good lad! It is Decius Macro." He shouted to Drusus, "It is Macro's son and that must be Gaius' son."

The three men were now even more frantic to stop the deserters catching them. Cassius was within bow range and he began shooting arrows, more in hope than expectation but it made Centurion and his companions look around. At first they only saw Cassius but Livius saw that they had been seen. Although they only slowed up for a moment Rufius and his two companions managed to stretch their lead a little. Centurion could see that he was outnumbered but what worried him most was the fact that so many scouts had appeared at the same time. Did it presage the Ninth? "Leave them. We will return to the main column." As he rode back the warrior stared at the scouts etching their faces into his memory. Lightly armed scouts were something he would have to mention to Decius. Even as the thought came into his head he laughed. He and Decius would not be with the army long enough to form another unit. They would be taking their gold and living the life of luxury. The men formed a column behind him and they kept glancing over their shoulders. They had seen enough of the scout's ability with arrows to worry that they might be attacked but it soon became clear that pursuit was not on their minds.

Rufius had a grin from ear to ear when Livius rode up. "Am I glad to see you sir, a few more minutes and we would have all been with the Allfather."

Livius shook his head, "With young Decius Macro shooting like that I think you might have evened the odds. Good shooting Decius Macro."

"Er just Macro sir."

"Just like your father eh? Well your father would have been proud of that shot but I think Ailis would have had kittens if she had seen you out of the saddle like that. What news Rufius?"

"The boys and I were trailing the horse herd; it was stolen a few days ago." His face became serious as he remembered the other news. "And Agrippa died. He was with the boys here."

"He died well?"

Marcus Gaius nodded the memory still fresh. "He took an arrow intended for Macro here. We took him back to the farm."

Cassius shook his head in amazement. Young boys and they still have the ability to save a comrade's body and honour the dead. "It must run in the blood Cassius. And you Drusus. What news?"

"I was on my way to find you. Prefect Fulvius is over there," he pointed towards Derventio, "with the Second cohort and a cohort of Batavians from Morbium. He is trying to get between the Queen and Eboracum. The Tribune is force marching to help with the First Cohort. They are half a day away."

"Good. You said find me. Was there a reason?"

"Yes sir he needs all the Explorates so that we can share the information we have."

Livius could see the wisdom in the Prefect's thinking. They had been out of touch for some time and even he did not know all that his men knew. "Very well. Decius round up the rest. I suspect Marius will be south of here and probably the others too so you will need to take a wide sweep and then come up Ermine Way it will bring you to Eboracum. If we are not there keep heading north."

After Decius had ridden off, Livius took the small group east, keeping a keen eye to the south and the Brigante army. Rufius rode next to Livius. "Er sir, the boys?"

"What about them?"

"Well I took them with me so that we could find the horse herd easily and I told their parents that I would return them as soon as…"

"But Rufius…"

Rufius turned around and snapped," What did I say about following orders?" He turned back to Livius giving him a wink. "Should we send them back?"

Livius tried hard to keep a straight face when he turned to see the tormented boys behind, both dreading the order to return home. "I am not sure that it will be safe for them to do so. They are safer with us and, when we reach the Prefect they can always look after the horses."

If Livius thought that such a demeaning role would be beneath the boys he was wrong for they both gave a whoop of delight. "I think they quite like that idea sir."

A day's ride to the south Nuada and the wagon were approaching a bend in the river. If they went any further they would meet the road, Ermine Street and that might bring them into contact with Romans. Nuada found a small wood with willows overhanging the river. He ordered his men to make a camp and they prepared to wait. When it was dark he would send a man back to Decius with details of their location. He still did not know how Decius would get a ship but he appeared to be quite resourceful and for Nuada his change in circumstance was definitely a change for the better.

They found Prefect Fulvius just building his camp. Livius wondered why he had not just stayed at the fort at Cataractonium, just ten miles north but he knew that the legionary would have had a good reason. The Prefect was genuinely pleased to see Livius. "I am glad that you and your men made it." He held him at arm's length and frowned. "But the journey has taken it out of you and your men. You look like wraiths." He seemed to notice the boys for the first time. "And who are these?"

"This is Gaius Aurelius' second son Marcus Gaius Aurelius and this is Decius Macro Culleo son of the famous Decurion from Marcus' Horse."

"You should both be proud of your fathers, yours was a great warrior and yours is an inspiration to all in the province. And now decurion your report."

"The Queen and her army are about ten miles away. It has grown since she landed. There are five thousand Brigante although some of them are not warriors. She has a bodyguard of druids and the Irish. There are a thousand of those and the deserter army is now as large as the First Cohort and they have horses."

"That is the one thing we do not have. The men you have and the other ten Explorates I brought me with me are the only eyes and ears we have. Still they will have to do. Your men and these new recruits," Macro and Marcus Gaius beamed with delight at the thought, "can get food and rest but I need you for a talk about our strategy. Come to my tent."

Centurion was red faced and angry when he rode into the camp. He had been thwarted again but this time he could not blame Nuada. Casca had done as well as he could but his men only had swords and archers would make mincemeat of them. As he slowed down, once in the huge sprawling camp he looked at the army from the point of view of an opponent. The men were tough; there was no argument about that: the Irish, Tadgh's Brigante and his deserters, man for man he would stack them against anybody. The rest? They were just gladii fodder. The problem was the whole war hinged on the ability of the fake Romans to manage to get into the fortress using a ruse; a ruse which had not worked at Mamucium. Centurion knew that were it not for incompetent leadership they would still be outside the walls and you couldn't count on two incompetent leaders in such a short space of time. If they did not manage to trick their way in then they would have to batter their way in and that meant facing the ballistae and scorpions as well as the archers. Morwenna's army would be slaughtered before it reached the walls. Centurion had to admire his superior, Decius had it all planned out. He knew that if they didn't carry the fort then they would lose and his plans were to leave. Centurion was also certain that they would have to leave and he would not be risking his life for the witch. Perhaps instead of Gaul they could go to Africa. It was said that it was always warm and one of his old optios had told him of the beautiful women who inhabited that land and lived to pleasure men. His days of fighting would soon be over and with the gold they had stolen, and that included a large portion of the gold intended for the druids, he would live life as a rich potentate.

"Centurion how did it go?"

He shook his head. "Those damned scouts again. They have bows and they can run faster." He quickly looked around to make sure they were out of earshot. "The wagon? Nuada has taken it?"

"Aye. He will tell us tonight where it is and then we just need a boat."

"That will be easier said than done."

"Don't forget old friend that we have to go to Eboracum with the Brigante as part of the plan to trick them. I am hoping that we see one either going up or coming back from the port. Unless it is Classis Britannica it will have no soldiers aboard and we will easily be able to over power them."

"Has she said when the attack will take place?"

"No. Tadgh has Brigante scouts out; the ones who know the area but I believe that it will have to be tomorrow. The longer she delays the more chance we have of being caught in a trap. The Twentieth are only at Deva and despite what she says I still think they could attack and the Ninth are at Luguvalium. If they both left when we attacked Mamucium then they could be here in a matter of days. No it is either tomorrow or we desert."

"I have been thinking about that. If we make sure the men loyal to us have the horses we have been using that leaves the half trained ones for them. I can't see them being able to train and control them."

"Good plan. One way or another tomorrow night or the following morning we will be afloat and free."

It was dusk when the Brigante scouts returned. Their faces told their story. "There is a cohort of legionaries and some auxiliaries just ten miles away."

"Let us fall on them and destroy them."

"Brennus! We have not come this far to jump into the fire. Let us weigh up the opposition. Do they look as though they are moving towards Eboracum?"

"They are camped for the night."

"Good then that gives us our answer. Send for General Decius." Tadgh snorted. "Don't do that Tadgh it is petulant and makes you sound like a wild boar. Decius is the key to our plans. We can destroy the Roman army and take Eboracum tomorrow if we plan our strategy well." Tadgh shrugged his shoulders. He was a warrior and understood fighting toe to toe with an enemy, not this deceit and sleight of hand.

Decius arrived flanked as usual by Tiny and Centurion. Tadgh and Brennus did not like it but there was little they could do about it. "You sent for me?"

"Yes tomorrow is the day, our day. You will take Brennus and fifty warriors to Eboracum as though they are prisoners. You will leave in the middle of the night so that you arrive before dawn."

Decius frowned. Tiny and Centurion exchanged looks as they saw the wicked smile on the faces of the two Brigante leaders. The Irish prince was in his usual position, sat with a jug. For him this was about gaining riches and a kingdom. He left the strategy to others, he was a warrior. "That was not the original plan. Why the change?"

"You see Tadgh. The General is a man who thinks. He doesn't lose his temper when things go wrong. There is a Roman army ten miles away and my warriors think we can defeat it."

"How many?"

"A cohort of the Ninth and a few auxiliaries."

"You could but if so why go ahead with the Eboracum deception?"

"If I defeat the army it may well be that Eboracum is forewarned and we cannot take it. If we just go ahead with the deception then the Roman army may move and prevent us from succeeding. We need both at the same time."

Decius' mind saw a way to work this to his advantage and ensure that he would be able to get a boat and flee without any pursuit. "You will need all your other Brigante to defeat the Romans. If I give half of my men to support you then perhaps we could take Eboracum with the fifty warriors under Brennus and just two hundred of mine."

Even Tadgh and Brennus looked surprised. "That is supremely confident General. Why?"

He smiled. "Perhaps the fact that my spy returned yesterday and told me that Eboracum is only held by four centuries and they are a mixture of auxiliaries and legionaries who have either been wounded or waiting for their pension. They could still withstand an assault, especially with the Roman army so close but once inside it would be child's play and Brennus and his men could then let you know we had taken it."

Morwenna's face lit up and she embraced Decius. "I had wondered about your enthusiasm as we crawled across the moors but now I see that you are the leader we all hoped for. Well Tadgh, Brennus, can you see a problem with that?"

Neither could and they both stood and embraced Decius. "We never doubted you or your men. Tomorrow will be a great day." Ernan just raised his beaker and belched.

Later when Tiny and Centurion walked the horse lines with their leader Centurion asked the question which had burned in his mind since the meeting in Morwenna's tent. "Does this mean we are staying with the Queen in Britannia?" He could not keep the disappointment out of his voice.

Decius laughed. "No. Do you not see it is the perfect opportunity to escape? When we enter the fortress, Brennus will take his men to help the Queen to fight the Ninth. She will lose by the way; this rabble cannot defeat a cohort of the Ninth. We will go to the river and choose the ship we want. You know our men Centurion. they will rape and pillage while we slip away and pick up Nuada and the gold. It is the perfect plan. No-one will look for us for they will assume we died."

Even the normally taciturn and silent Tiny was moved to words. "Good plan!"

Livius met with his Explorates. The Prefect still had four of them watching the Brigante and Marius had still to return. He had spent a long time with Prefect Fulvius discussing the plan for the battle which they both knew was not far away. "We have an interesting role to play in the coming battle. The Prefect and I do not know if the Brigante will attack Eboracum or us. Until the First Cohort arrive we will be outnumbered somewhat. If they attack Eboracum then the legion and the auxiliaries will attack them."

Metellus spoke up, "Sir, I am flattered that the prefect is taking us into his confidence but I don't see how we fit into this particular scenario."

"As ever Metellus your sharp mind has got to the nub of it. The point is we will be involved for the Prefect wishes us to make the Brigante attack us."

"I am most definitely intrigued sir. How will the fifteen of us…?"

"The nineteen Metellus, four are on duty."

"Fine. The nineteen of us then. How will we do anything that will affect the thousands of warriors who are out there?"

In answer Decius pulled out the Sword of Cartimandua. "With this."

Gaius Marcus couldn't contain himself. "It's father's sword." When everyone laughed he sat down blushing. Rufius tousled his hair and Macro grabbed him around the shoulders.

"Yes Marcus Gaius Aurelius your father's sword but not just the sword. He went to the rear of the tent and pulled off the blanket which had been placed there. He revealed a pile of auxiliary shields and the swallow tailed standard of Marcus' Horse.

They all looked in amazement at the standard and the shields. Most could not comprehend what it meant. Metellus, of course, grasped it quickly. "You wish us to dress as Marcus' Horse."

"You have it Metellus. Tomorrow Marcus' Horse will ride again and we will ride to the Brigante."

Rufius looked confused. If it were a track or trail he was following then he had no peer but this was too subtle for him. "But why sir."

"We are seriously outnumbered here but we do have the First and Third cohorts coming to our aid. They should be here by noon. We need to precipitate an attack and then use the auxiliary archers and artillery to thin their ranks. The Prefect has five scorpions and they will also cause many casualties but the plan only works if they attack in a rage not in ordered lines. The First and Third are coming from the north west and should be able to roll up their flanks. But we need the Brigante to stop the deserters coming to grips with us. They are trained as we are. If they chose to fight as we do tomorrow with the Irish and the Brigante in support then, quite simply we would lose. They have too many men but the Brigante are the biggest contingent and the most undisciplined."

Young Macro spoke up. "But why would the sight of the sword and the standard upset them so much?"

Livius looked sadly at Macro who had never known his father and did not know that the Queen who faced them was his mother, and would never know that terrible secret. "Marcus' Horse captured and crucified the Queen's mother Fainch and destroyed the Brigante in the last rebellion. She and her warriors would risk

251

everything to finally destroy those who destroyed all that they held dear."

"And of course," added Metellus, "there is the sword. The Sword of Cartimandua is the symbol of Brigante honour and every warrior who faces us believes that it should be wielded by a Brigante and not a Roman soldier."

"So tomorrow we dress as auxiliaries once more."

"Sir we don't have armour."

"I know. We shall wear our cloaks and we will carry spears again. Our task is to make them charge us, while we will throw one volley of javelins and then lead them to the killing ground. It is dangerous men and I know that not all of you fought in Marcus' Horse but I also know that you will not shirk from your duty." Every man stood taller and nodded his agreement.

As they all went to touch the standard again and select their shield, the two boys went up to Livius. "Can we ride tomorrow in Marcus' Horse?"

Livius shook his head. "No. Firstly we have no uniform or helmets to fit you but mainly because your mother would skin us all alive."

"But we want to help."

"And you shall… I want you two mounted behind the auxiliaries with your bows. Rufius tells me you are excellent archers. While the auxiliaries will loose volleys, I want you two to target the leaders. Without their leaders they will be lost. Can you do that for me boys?"

They both chorused, "Yes Sir!"

Cassius gently took Livius' arm and took him to one side. "Of course you do know that there is someone else interested in you and that sword."

"You mean my brother?"

"Exactly. If he sees you on the battle field and he brings his horsemen then the whole plan could fail for his cavalry would keep pace with us and see the trap the prefect has planned."

"I know but I am hoping that my brother has not changed."

"How so?"

"He always had a deep sense of self preservation."

"You mean he is a coward?"

"Not a coward but someone who weighs things up in his mind first. He might send someone else after me but he would not want to face me in front of his men in case he failed and lost their loyalty."

"Unlike you sir who, I am sad to say, would never run. Even though your whole command would wish it."

"We cannot change what we are Cassius. The Allfather made me one way and Decius another. Marcus, Gaius, Gaelwyn and Macro they all added to the Allfather's work and I am what I am."

Chapter 19

General Decius Lucullus Sallustius was many miles away from the battlefield as his brother was dressing for the day. He had had his armour with him and he wanted to make sure he looked the part. Decius, by contrast, was worrying over the smallest detail which might cause a problem with his complicated plan. He and Centurion had persuaded Brennus that he and his warriors should hold the rope bonds to make it look as though they were prisoners whilst that all wore their swords over their shoulders hidden by a cloak. One of Decius' officers led them and it did look like a triumphal parade. By arriving early in the morning they hoped to catch sleepy guards who would see, in the half light, what they expected to see, victorious Romans with captured rebels. They had their story already worked out. They were from Deva and they had pursued these assailants from Mamucium over the divide. It seemed plausible when they had concocted the story but as the sky began to lighten Decius found more and more flaws in it.

"It is a good plan General and the story is a good one. Our fate is in the hands of the Allfather but I have a good feeling about this and remember General, we have the witch with us and surely she must bring dark powers to our side?"

"You are right Centurion, I am worrying over things which have yet to happen. I just hope nothing untoward has happened to Nuada and the gold or all this will have been for nothing."

"Don't worry he will be waiting. He would not dare to cross me and Tiny would follow him to the ends of the earth if he did betray us." That made Decius feel better; Tiny was his most loyal soldier.

The column was moving quietly up Ermine Street towards the fortress. The vicus was still asleep but they could see the glow from the lanterns on the Porta Decumana. The gate had been chosen because it was some way from the threat which the garrison must know was out there. Brennus at the front was eager to get to the fort. He truly believed in the Queen as a witch and knew that, with her powers they would easily fall upon the garrison and they would be as wolves feasting on sheep. Had they thought about it the silence of the column was unnatural but the sentries and optio on duty did not seem to notice. All that they saw was a small column of Roman cavalry with a handful of pathetic looking rebels.

"Halt!"

"Decurion Modius on detachment from the Twentieth Valeria with Brigante prisoners."

Decius was close enough to see the conversation between the sentry and the optio. "It is a little late to be bringing in prisoners is it not?"

"We caught them late last night and, as we knew how close you were we decided not to build a camp but push on." The man played his part well and gave an easy laugh, "We're early really. Come on brother we have been riding all night. Do the Twentieth a favour and if you are ever over …"

"We are the Third Tungrian but we can be as generous as our legionary colleagues. Open the gate."

Decius almost shouted with joy. The plan had worked. All they need to do now was to get the whole force inside and then the slaughter could begin. He nodded to Centurion who began to hold back when the troopers went forward. The ten men they had chosen were all at the rear, hanging back. The column moved in and when Decius reached the gate he yelled, "Now!"

The Brigante were like wild animals released from a cage and they raced into the barracks hacking and slashing at the sleeping bodies. The deserters raced up the walls to kill the Tungrians who had not even had time to draw their swords. The optio died with a puzzled expression and his body hurled to the ground next to the butchered sentries who had unbarred the gate. Decius turned to the Irish warrior who was sitting uncomfortably on a horse which was far too small for him. "Tell the Queen the fortress is ours and she can begin her attack." As the eager warrior galloped off he turned to his lieutenant, "Find us a ship Centurion before the mariners hear the commotion and set sail without us."

Brennus and his men set about their task ruthlessly, massacring all that they found in the first two barracks. The auxiliaries stood no chance against Brigante who had faced the killing machine that was the Roman army on a battlefield. This was not a battle field, this was a slaughterhouse. Brennus kept his head for he was mindful of his second task; he was to take his men and attack the Roman left flank for he assumed that the battle would have commenced. He yelled to his men, "Brigante! To me!" All of the 'captives' had been chosen personally by Brennus for their personal allegiance to him and he nodded with satisfaction as they gathered in the parade ground. He looked around for Decius but could see neither him nor the bulk of the horsemen. He assumed he was at the Porta Praetorium and he led his men off at an easy lope.

The deserters quickly finished the job of butchering sleeping Romans and then fired the barracks. It would take time to burn but that did not worry them for, having stripped the dead soldiers of their valuables, they now launched themselves into the vicus where the pickings would be that much greater, especially amongst the merchants who had built their houses so close to the protective walls of the fortress. Others who ran voraciously from the fort had enough treasure and sought only one thing, women. Having campaigned and fought across Britannia they were desperate for women and the females of Eboracum were going to have a rude awakening when the rapacious raiders entered their homes.

Decius and his disciplined detachment were making their way down the quayside examining boats. They did not want a bireme for that required an oared crew nor were they seeking a boat which was too small. Eventually they lighted upon a two masted ship known as a cladivata. They could see a name, a little faded, painted on the rounded stern, **The Dubris**. It was about fifty paces long and could easily accommodate both Decius' men and the gold. Even better from their point of view there was a watch aboard, evidenced by the orange glow from the light beneath the canvas awning close to the rudder. Centurion tapped Tiny on the shoulder when they were less than a hundred paces from the vessel. Tiny and the five men detailed for the task slipped from their horses and ran down the cobbled quayside covered with sand to the boat. They slipped over the side of the wooden ship and surrounded the four men of the watch. The watch keepers were used to pirates and thieves, the cudgels and knives they kept at their side was testament to that but armoured Roman soldiers were another matter.

The second mate thought at first they were from the fortress, "What is wrong we have paid our mooring taxes tell the..."

Tiny grinned his evil toothless lopsided grin, "Forget the taxes you now have new owners."

"Who?"

Centurion and Decius had followed Tiny and Decius hissed, "Us! Now cast off and get this tub underway."

"Where to? The tide..."

Decius slipped his gladius under the chin of the first mate. "Do not try to be clever with me! The tide does not affect the river here and we wish to go downstream. Now will you give the order or shall I promote someone else whilst lightening the load by one fool?"

Realising that the soldier knew more than most about sailing, he turned to his men. "Cast off aft. Raise the foresail."

"That's better." As the four men raced to their work Decius watched the flames take hold of the fort and heard the screams from the vicus. Soon his men would realise he had fled. Some would desert once more, a few might actually rejoin Morwenna and a few, possibly, might emulate their General and steal a ship to leave Britannia. Decius did not care. Soon his gold would be aboard and he would be sailing south. He had reflected on Centurion's idea about Africa and, although it seemed a long way away, that in itself was a good thing for the Imperial memory was long and for him to have escaped twice would necessitate a hunt of some kind. If he found sanctuary in Africa it would give him the chance to build up a power base; working with Morwenna had shown him that he and Centurion had a flair for raising and organising an army. The Kingdom of King Decius, he liked the sound of that.

Morwenna and her army were also awake soon after midnight. The scouts had reported the small Roman camp and were watching from a safe distance. Her army would march the ten miles and arrive soon after dawn. By then the attack on Eboracum should be well under way making it safe for her to begin her attack. Ernan, Tadgh and even Decius had been agreed about the timing of the attack; they wanted it to take place just when the Romans were breaking camp. The sudden appearance of Morwenna's huge army would throw even the disciplined Roman force into uncertainty and possibly confusion. She had no doubt that she outnumbered the force which faced her by ten to one and she was equally confident that she would defeat it. If Brennus and Decius could capture Eboracum then she had won. The whole of the land of the Brigante could be controlled from Eboracum. The Romans had built the lynch pin of the north with its port and its roads; by capturing it she would control the region and she knew that many others would flock to her banner. Trinovante, Iceni, Atrebate, Silures; all would flock to the only place in Britannia outside of Roman control and then they would regain the whole of Britannia for her son, the child of the Trinovante and Brigante. The Romans would send other armies to attack her but the steady stream of soldiers leaving Britannia to fight in Trajan's eastern wars meant that there were only three legions left in the whole of Britannia; the Ninth was the only one which could strike at her and here she was destroying one, possibly two cohorts at one fell swoop. Once Lulach and those north of the Stanegate realised that the frontier was crumbling they would flood towards Coriosopitum and Luguvalium, eliminating the rest of the Ninth. She smiled, the Mother was indeed with her, this morning's work would see her victorious.

She mounted her white horse her druidic and Irish bodyguards surrounding her like a phalanx of steel. Tadgh raised his sword and the army moved like an enormous snake towards the Romans who still appeared to be abed, still asleep and still unaware that death was hunting them.

The Roman camp was anything but abed. Every man was already dressed and had been fed for some time. Prefect Fulvius knew the value of an army which had a full stomach and the cooks had made cauldrons of hot food the previous night and it was still warm in the cold early hours. They had deliberately camped early so that the men could get some rest before their early awakening. Every century was collecting the caltrops and lillia which would litter the ground before them. The auxiliaries were packing their quivers as full as possible of arrows for they were the rain which would dampen the Queen's parade.

As each century was equipped they left by the Porta Decumana to take up their positions on the low ridge which overlooked the camp. Livius' Explorates had established that there were no enemy scouts there and the lethal bolt throwers were already in position. The centuries lined the ridge below them.

The Prefect and Livius stood with First Spear watching the silent centuries calmly take their positions on the gentle ridge below the scorpions. "This is the hard part eh First Spear? The waiting?"

First Spear shook his head at the idiocy of the prefect's comment. "With due respect Prefect the worst part is when you are nose to nose with a tattooed hairy arsed barbarian who is trying to disembowel you. The lads down there will take this every day of the week and twice on their day off."

"Quite." The Prefect, who had never fought in a shield wall, was perplexed.

"I think what the prefect means is this is the worst time for us waiting to see have we made the correct decision and plans."

"Exactly decurion. Quite the point I intended to make."

"Ah well that could be true. If they don't bother attacking us and just take Eboracum then we have lost. The fortress controls the main road north."

"That was my worry but I want to destroy this army sooner rather than later and we will have to destroy it First Spear."

"Even if she does capture Eboracum sir, and from what you said about the depleted garrison I think you may be right, it doesn't matter. We can just get the engineers to build some ballistae and pound the walls down. The barbarians do not have the mentality to fight behind barriers. They think it is womanish to fight behind a shield or a wall. They like to get at you man to man."

"So you are saying First Spear, that I could be right?"

Winking at Livius he replied, "What I am saying sir is I hope you are right or my lads' guts will be spread over this field and Rome will have lost."

Livius pointed at the fort, now largely deserted apart from the smoke from the camp kitchen, giving the illusion that it was still occupied. "They will either waste time attacking the fort or be channelled across your front."

"Hopefully the latter but that largely depends upon you and your men Decurion Sallustius." The Prefect became serious. "I realise I am putting a large burden on your shoulders but if you can enrage them and draw them into our arrows before they are ready then I believe we will succeed."

"I can I am sure but that means that you will have to hold for a long morning until the reinforcements arrive."

"I know but it is like the Queen's world, all magic. We make them think they can win against our small numbers and crush them at just the right moment."

First Spear coughed. "And speaking of time decurion...."

"Yes I know. It is time to go."

First Spear clasped Livius' arm firmly, "May the Allfather watch over you and your men."

The rest of the Explorates were waiting looking far more military than normal. They all wore the helmets with the red horsehair crest and had their red cloaks over their shoulders. Their shields had been burnished and each man held three javelins. Proudest of all was Cassius holding the swallow tailed standard of Marcus' Horse. He looked at the men before him and felt pride fill his throat. There were but nineteen in total; Decius, Drusus, Marius and the others would have helped swelling their numbers to twenty four but they could still make a show. If Morwenna and the Brigante thought that Marcus' Horse had reformed they would do all in their power to destroy them but the real attraction and the real bait was in the scabbard hanging from his side. The two boys had spent all night polishing the razor sharp blade and burnishing the metal on the scabbard. It now gleamed and sparkled in the early sun just rising behind them.

"Men we are, for one day only, Marcus' Horse again. But understand me we are not here to fight. We are here to make them

261

charge us. Ovidius and Rufius, yours will be the hardest of roles for you will be the last pair and the pair closest to the enemy are you prepared?"

Rufius nodded holding up his bow. "As you ordered we have no javelins just bows."

"Good. You are the best two shots we have," he heard a snort and realised that Macro and Marcus Gaius were close by, "the best two shots we have who are soldiers I should say." The men laughed for they had all become fond of the two boys who had endeared themselves to the Explorates with their energy and enthusiasm not to say their courage as recounted by Rufius. "It may be that you can emulate young Macro and fire backwards from the saddle." he became serious. "Remember the field before the ridge is sown with caltrops. We will need to ride parallel to the front and only wheel on my command. It will expose us to their archers."

Cassius snorted in derision. "I have seen their archers and they couldn't hit a barn door."

"Yes Cassius but all they need is a lucky hit on a horse and that could spell disaster. Daylight is here. Let us ride."

He was gratified to hear a roar of Marcus' Horse, not only from his men but the auxiliaries and legionaries who watched them ride proudly off into the west.

Morwenna saw the Irish warrior galloping in his face filled with excitement and she knew the news he brought. "We attack now."

Ernan looked at her in amazement but Tadgh and the Druids knew of her power. "But he may be bringing news that they have failed."

"Ernan, he is bringing the news we seek. Tadgh, forward."

The rider slewed his horse around, almost falling in the process. "Message from the General, we have Eboracum. Brennus will be following soon."

Ernan was not convinced and leaned forward. "You saw the fort fall?"

"I saw the gates opened and the Brigantes butchering the garrison if that is what you mean."

The army moved forward on a wide front. Tadgh and the elite warriors were in the centre while the recent recruits were on the right. The remainder of the deserters made up a cohort on the left of the line. Morwenna was tucked behind Tadgh with her druidic and Irish bodyguards around her like a box. They had a front of five hundred men and it was over ten warriors deep. Tadgh wanted the momentum of a huge block of men to roll over the Roman line. The scouts had reported that the Roman camp was in a shallow valley between two ridges which would give his men the momentum of a downhill charge. He just hoped that they had not moved out in the hours of darkness and he prayed, as the sun began to peep over the skyline, that they would see the legionaries labouring to dismantle their fort; then he knew that they would win.

Tadgh had impressed upon his men the need to keep a solid line. He had fought against the Romans before and admired their cohesion. Orders had been given that any man who was ahead of Tadgh would be sent to the rear of the line. None of them wished to risk that and the line was far more ordered than one might have expected.

The deserters on the right all had shields and helmets but they had a variety of other weapons from spears and javelins to gladii and spatha. They looked formidable but they were leaderless and they were the weaker element of the deserter army. Mocius was now one of the officers having shown bravery at Mamucium despite being thrust into the front line of the attack. He looked around and realised that he was the last of the first volunteers, the rest were either dead or with Decius. If it gave him any concern he did not show it for he was enjoying being a soldier again, albeit a private soldier.

The Brigante in the middle deigned to wear armour but many had shields and their weaponry ranged from axes and spears to swords. On the right the ordinary Brigante had spears or improvised weapons such as a wood axe or a scythe. Tadgh had placed them there because he knew that they were the weakest element of the army but he also knew that Brennus would be arriving from that direction to bolster them. As they emerged over the ridge he saw that the camp was still there, the Romans were abed. The Queen had been right and they had caught them napping. A roar began to erupt from the line as the army realised their plan was working.

Tadgh turned to the warrior next to him, Brennus' brother Aldus, "We have them. They will either stay behind the pathetic palisade or run. The Queen's plan has worked."

"I never doubted it. She is a powerful witch and she knows things that are beyond the imagination of mere warriors like us. She will truly lead us to greatness."

The murmurings from the warriors in the font line showed that, they too, felt the same way. Tadgh felt the pride swelling his heart almost to bursting. With a Queen such as Morwenna and warriors such as these they could not only rid their land of Romans but the whole of Britannia. Tadgh almost risked a glance over his shoulder to the Queen. He knew of the liaison with Decius who was a descendant of Cunobleinus, the last king of Britain and he knew too of the child safe in Manavia. The land of the Brigante was but the first step to the land of Britannia.

One of his warriors suddenly shouted a warning as a column of Roman cavalry appeared. Where had they come from? No cavalry was known to be operating in this area. Their spies had told them that the Gallic cavalry were close to Coriosopitum so who were these? Aldus asked, "Do we halt?"

Tadgh realised that he had unconsciously slowed up. "Of course not. It is but a handful of men. What will they be able to do? What can they do against this mighty host? They must be scouts."

"They look well armed for scouts. The leader has armour and look at the standard."

With a sinking heart Tadgh could see that it was, indeed the standard of Marcus' Horse. It had been reformed! His eyes nervously scanned the horizon for more horsemen and doubt entered his mind. What if they had got around their flanks and even now were approaching the rear? It seemed like a typical Roman trick to attack the Queen while her warriors were fighting their legionaries. He could do little about that but he relaxed a little when he realised that the Queen was as astute as any and she would be able to see what he saw.

The column of riders rode to within one hundred paces and spread out in a pathetically thin line of seventeen troopers with the leader and standard bearer in front. What were they doing? Were they going for a suicidal charge? Tadgh could see that while that might be suicide a charge at the centre of the line could take out the leadership of the army. "Halt!" The whole line juddered to a halt. There was a little jostling as the ones further back pushed forward but the line was solid.

The leader rode forwards and looked to Tadgh a little familiar. Suddenly he drew out his sword and called, "I am Livius Lucullus Sallustius, Decurion Princeps of Marcus' Horse and this is the Sword of Cartimandua. I command you as loyal Brigante to lay down your weapons and surrender. Your loyalty is not to an illegitimate misguided witch but to the honour and memory of Queen Cartimandua, the last rightful Queen of the Brigante murdered by the witch's mother."

265

There was a roar of anger from the Brigante but Tadgh held up his hand to silence them. He stepped forward. "I know that the sword belongs to me as Chief of the Brigante and I would thank you to hand it over. Were he with us today I am sure your brother would take it from you himself."

Livius' face did not register any sign that he had heard Tadgh's comment but he stored the information that his brother was elsewhere. "If my brother were here he would be arrested and tried for theft and treason." He pointed to the deserters. "All of you are guilty of treason but if you lay your weapons down you will be treated fairly. I give you my word."

Tadgh could see that Livius was as persuasive as his brother and he sensed some mumblings from his left. He had to act decisively. "Roman I will fight you man to man for the weapon. If you win we leave and if I win I take the sword." His men began to bang their weapons on their shields in approval.

Livius knew he had no choice. Behind him he heard, "You can't do this sir. Remember what Marius said."

"Yes Cassius and I could end the war here at a stroke."

"You don't think the bastard would keep his word do you and besides he looks like a big bugger."

Grinning Livius said, "Do you doubt my ability now Cassius?"

"Fight me on foot Roman if you are man enough."

"No sir!" Cassius watched in horror as Livius stepped down from Star and walked towards Tadgh. The Brigante chief grinned, this would be child's play and soon the Sword of Cartimandua would be his and would guarantee their success. They were but twenty paces from each other when one of the deserters, worried that Tadgh might lose, fired an arrow at Livius. As soon as he did others launched their arrows thinking they were being attacked. Livius reacted quickly and held his shield above his head. The arrows plunged into it. Tadgh, taking advantage of his distractions leapt forward and smashed his axe into Livius' shield shattering it.

Livius yelled, "Treachery!" and swung his sword around slicing into Tadgh's calf muscle to the bone. Cassius rode up with Star and as he mounted, his left arm useless with the numbed pain, he yelled. "All Brigante are treacherous dogs with no honour." With that epithet he rode away, the column forming behind him.

Aldus did not wait for an order but screamed, "Charge! Revenge for Tadgh!"

The whole line leapt forward all thoughts of cohesion gone. They lapped around Tadgh who was busy tying a cloth around his wound. In vain he shouted for them to halt but every warrior was intent on killing Livius and claiming the sword for himself; many believing that their leader had been slain. Each warrior just wanted to get to grips with the infamous Marcus' Horse. Each warrior wanted a trooper's head as a trophy and the horde raced across the open ground in pursuit of the sword.

At the rear of her army Morwenna screamed her rage but the sound was lost amidst the roaring of the army. Her plans had been thwarted and her warriors were not fighting the way they had planned. Marcus' Horse and the Sword of Cartimandua had come to haunt her again!

Chapter 20

As the Explorates wheeled they threw their javelins; it was more in hope than expectation but the minute faltering of the pursuers fearful of the metal tipped missiles helped to slow the Brigante slightly. Rufius and Ovidius were better placed and fired three quick arrows each before wheeling and joining the line. The Brigante were so packed that each arrow found a mark and others fell over bodies of the newly fallen warriors. This enraged the Brigante even more, despising weapons which could be fired from a distance. The two last men in the column rode with their knees knowing their mounts would follow the ones in front, all the while firing arrow after arrow at the screaming Brigante warriors desperate to rip the Romans from their saddles and kill them with their bare hands. The effect of the rain of arrows was subtle, the pursuing warriors spread out to each side avoiding the killing zone. The deserters and the Brigante on the flanks pushed in to get closer to the enemy and soon all semblance of order was gone and there was just a solid block of men racing across the open ground. The five hundred wide, ten man deep line was no more, there was no more elite warrior in the middle deserters on the left and Brigante on the right; it was just a mob hurtling towards the Roman camp, in pursuit of the small column which was riding for its life.

"You alright sir?" Cassius was worried by the left arm hanging limply from Livius' side.

"Just numbed. That man had a powerful arm but I don't think it is broken. Almost time to wheel right Cassius."

"Sir. By the way sir that was their war chief Tadgh, I recognised his emblem. His brother Brennus has the same one. They could well be leaderless until he rejoins the fight."

The camp was to their front and they intended to take the Brigante down one side of the deserted camp and then wheel right to take the enemy into the killing zone. They had hoped that it

268

would funnel the Brigante and eliminate their opportunity to move right away from the missiles which would soon be amongst them.

"Now!"

In a beautifully executed manoeuvre, the column disappeared from the sight of Morwenna some half a mile back. The Brigante following also wheeled but somewhat more slowly as they had not anticipated such an action. It was almost as though they could not see the lines of legionaries calmly waiting on the low ridge but a hundred paces to their left. They were too intent upon catching the cavalry. Aldus was at the front roaring his insults at the departing Romans. Rufius and Ovidius had emptied their quivers but each held his javelin ready to turn and hurl should the opportunity arise.

Cassius, riding on the left of the column, was watching the ground for the markers which indicated the safe ground in front of the caltrops. As soon as they passed the last legionary he was desperately seeking the safe route right. At the back Ovidius and Rufius had slung their bows and were reaching into the sacks which held more caltrops to sow behind them.

The Brigante had now entered the ground chosen by the Prefect where they would be assaulted by bolts and arrows, just as Morwenna and Ernan arrived at the fort. To Morwenna's horror she saw the legionaries, not in the fort as she had assumed but to her front and lined up ready to attack. Even as she roared out an order to halt, the Prefect gave the command to fire and a volley of arrows rained down on the men who were spread out over five hundred paces. This was followed by the thud of scorpions hurling their deadly bolts to slice through lines of unsuspecting warriors. They were so tightly packed that the arrows and bolts could not fail to strike a body. Morwenna had many men but a few volleys like that would soon destroy her army. She turned to

Ernan. "Now is the time to earn your money. Take charge of the army. Take your men and destroy the Romans."

Ernan was like a hound released from the leash; his face beamed with pleasure. "Watch a real warrior fight!"

He galloped his horse towards the Romans with his men close behind. He paused only to rally the Brigante before dismounting. "Brigante," his voice rose loudly above the tumultuous noise. "Your Queen commands that we kill the Romans. Are you with me?!"

The roar told him they were and the huge Irishman took his two handed sword and raced at the head of a wedge of his oath brothers towards the auxiliaries who awaited him. The Brigante line rippled as they turned to attack the line which looked thin and vulnerable.

The Queen turned to her druids. "One of you, find Tadgh and bring him here. You, "she pointed to another, "find any who are wounded but can fight. We will have a second line here next to the camp." Her razor sharp mind had taken in that the fort could be used as a defence against a Roman attack. She was now counting on the sudden appearance of Brennus to regain the balance of power lost in the reckless charge after the Sword of Cartimandua.

The Brigante in the fore had to suffer double casualties as they were felled by both caltrops and arrows. Soon a third was added as the javelins thrown by the legionaries began to strike them. Mocius had managed to organise and control the deserters around them and they had made a testudo. This enabled them to close with the auxiliaries on the right of the Roman line. The bodies they crossed were a carpet protecting their feet from the caltrops but wearing the hobnailed caligae they suffered less anyway. Mocius was elated. This was what he was trained for. In his previous life he had been an ordinary legionary following orders now he led others and he felt powerful. To his right Ernan's wedge was also benefiting from the dead Brigante beneath his feet. Moving swiftly towards the enemy he seemed to bear a charmed life. The two columns hit the Roman line at the same time. Ernan's sword decapitated three auxiliaries at a single blow and those behind soon despatched the ones on either side. Despite the javelins thrown by the legionaries into the ranks behind the wild Irish were soon crashing their swords and war axes on helmets and shields. The power of their arms and weapons meant that although the legionaries were armoured, bones were shattered along with shields and once that happened the cohesion of the shield went.

Mocius' men were having even greater success. A second testudo had been created and was equally impervious to the javelins and arrows. The bolt throwers could no longer be depressed enough to fire and the rebels took advantage of that. The auxiliary line was no longer tight and the testudo just ran over them, the men in the third rank despatching the recumbent Tungrians as they stepped over them. Mocius knew that things would change once they reached the legionaries and he shouted, "Halt! Shield wall!" The training of years took over and soon two identical lines faced each other one Roman and one intent on ending Roman rule. It was a savage encounter much like those that had take place over a hundred years ago between the legions of Caesar and Pompey. Neither side gave any quarter nor did they seek it. Gladii sought flesh between the press of shields locked tightly together. The Ninth tried to throw javelins over the front ranks but those behind also had shields.

Ernan and his warriors were unarmoured but the power of the blows was something the Romans had not encountered before. They stabbed and slashed at the flesh they saw but if the arm came out too far it was severed and the Irishmen seemed very agile, leaping out of the way of the short stabbing swords of the beleaguered legionaries.

Livius had reached the Prefect and, as a capsarius rubbed a foul smelling but soothing ointment on his arm, he scanned the battle field. "You did well Livius and the trap worked."

"Yes Prefect but, unless the rest of your cohorts get here soon, then the testudo and the Irish will be through your lines." First Spear had seen that the right of the line was weakening and had gone to bolster it with the century kept in reserve for just such an emergency.

"The rest appear to be holding."

"What happens if the Queen brings those reserves in? "He pointed to where the Queen and four hundred warriors waited impassively. And also why hasn't she launched them. She must see that we are weak on the right. She could outflank us."

Cassius spoke up. "She might be waiting for reserves remember that Brigante said your brother wasn't here and that," he pointed at the testudo formations, "is nowhere near the whole of the deserter army. Perhaps your brother is on his way."

"In which case, we had better pray that the First and Third Cohorts make better time than we had hoped."

Almost in answer Rufius shouted above the clamour and din of metal on metal. "Sir, more Brigante from our left."

"That is what she was waiting for."

"Go and ask the centurion there to realign his men to face this new attack and could your men give some support?"

"Of course sir. Explorates to the left." Even as they turned two small figures slipped away from the auxiliary line where they had been firing arrows and joined behind Ovidius and Rufius, unseen by all.

Brennus was elated when he saw the Romans reeling. Although only armed with swords his fifty men launched themselves at the Romans who were rapidly retreating to form another line at right angles to their first. Their delay in executing the realignment meant that it was not a solid line and the Brigante hit it at a rush breaking into the line and giving the advantage to the agile, lightly armoured warriors. The centurion was still roaring his orders when Brennus took the head from his shoulder with one mighty sweep of his long sword. Soon it was individual combats which were taking place and this suited the fifty Brigante more than the seventy legionaries who began to take more casualties.

Cassius attracted Livius' attention. "That is Brennus. He is a senior chief. Brother of the one you wounded, Tadgh."

"Watch my left." Without a shield Livius was vulnerable to an attack on his shield side. Cassius stepped up as Livius roared. "This is the Sword of Cartimandua Brennus. It has crippled your treacherous brother and now it will claim your miserable life." His insults had the desired effect and Brennus and his ten chosen men hurled themselves at their new target. Although there were three other troopers with Livius, he was outnumbered. The first warrior who reached him was easily killed as he ran onto the sword held by Livius. A second man saw his opportunity and he jumped into the air ready to plunge his sword into Livius whose weapon was still embedded in the dead man's neck. Even when he was in the air an arrow plucked him and threw him onto the man behind. Brennus leapt in and crashed his huge sword towards the unarmoured arm of Livius. Fortunately the decurion had managed to extract the blade and Brennus' weapon struck the sword instead. The blow jarred Livius' right arm but he stood his ground.

They circled each other. Brennus held his sword in two hands but Livius could only use one. Brennus grinned in anticipation. "When you are dead I will give the sword as a present to my brother." Livius had no breath to trade insults and he was too busy fending off the scything attacks of Brennus. He had the longer reach and the greater strength. It was only a matter of time before he wore him down and Brennus knew it. Livius was aware of Cassius desperately defending his left side as other Brigante were trying to help their chief. He was also aware of arrows hitting other warriors. Rufius and Ovidius were doing a good job.

Brennus slashed down again and this time the blow was only deflected a little and the blade sliced into Livius' left leg."The next blow and you and your sword are mine!" Livius knew that he was right and he would have to resort to trickery. The Sword of Cartimandua could not go to a Brigante rebel. As Brennus raised his sword for the next blow, aimed at Livius' right shoulder he did the unexpected, he rolled forwards, and his legs took out Brennus who fell in a heap. Struggling to his feet first Livius plunged the sword into the unprotected back of the huge warrior lying like a stranded whale on a beach. The mighty sword cracked through ribs and ripped through his heart, the green grass was dark red with Brigante blood. Three enraged warriors behind Livius tried to get to him and avenge their chief but three arrows each found a mark and they fell dead.

The death of Brennus took the heart out of the attack on the right but Morwenna had seen her chance and launched her reserves at the vulnerable and weakened right flank. The Prefect looked in horror as the centuries on the right began to crumble and there was suddenly no line facing the four hundred fresh warriors the witch on the white horse was bringing to claim her bloody victory.

Mocius found himself fighting shoulder to shoulder with Ernan and the two grinned at each other as two more legionaries fell to their deaths. Mocius gestured to the centre. "That is the Prefect. If we get him then we win."

"The bastard is as good as dead then!" Roaring his battle cry the Irish hurled themselves forwards while Mocius rallied his men. "Reform! Head for First Spear and kill the bastard!" Every man under Mocius' command rushed to kill the most hated man in any legion, hated if you were always in trouble and these deserters had been in trouble more than most. They hacked and slashed their way through legionaries who fought valiantly to protect their First Spear.

A mile away Tribune Didius halted the two cohorts. He could see that the lines were almost overrun but his troops needed their lines dressing. As they formed into a cohort wide line he surveyed the scene. He turned to the First Cohort. They were the best eight hundred men in the legion and the First Spear fighting for his life with the Prefect was theirs. "Lads, First Spear is in trouble. I want you to double time in straight lines and take out those forces on the right with the bitch on the white horse. "The acting First Spear raised his arm and with the signifier set off at a trot. The Tribune then turned to the Third Cohort. "Third Cohort you are going to do what the First did but even better." There were grins from the front ranks. "We are going to go to the right flank and roll up the rest of these rebels. There are deserters down there and they murdered our men at Mamucium. Now is payback time. Centurion?" The senior centurion dropped his arm and with the buccina sounding set off at a trot.

On the battle field Morwenna was urging her warriors on and anticipating the victory as her Irish army closed upon the Prefect and the standards when she heard the buccina. For the first time she felt doubts creep into her mind. She glanced over her shoulder and watched as the twelve hundred legionaries raced across the ground. Even though her army still outnumbered the Romans surrounded by a tide of enemies and Brennus' reinforcements, she knew that her army, cobbled together from warriors, Irish mercenaries and deserters would not stand especially not with Decius still ensconced in Eboracum and Tadgh too weak from loss of blood to go on. She urged her men onwards. "On! We have them and Eboracum is ours for the picking. Fight for your Queen!" Inside however she was already planning her escape. She and her inner circle of druids and guards were mounted; the road south was clear and Decius might be able to join her from Eboracum bringing with him his extra men. She called over the young Irish warrior, Ardal. "Ride to Eboracum and find General Decius. Have him meet us on the road south of Eboracum." The young boy was so smitten with the witch that he did not question her command but galloped off. She turned to her druids. "Tie Tadgh onto a horse and head south, I will join you."

"But your majesty!"

Her eyes widened and her nostrils flared angrily, "Do not question your Queen! Now go." Finally, she turned to her bodyguard and as Tadgh was, reluctantly, tied on to a horse and led swiftly away, she smiled and she knew they would do anything for her. "Those who are mounted I would have you continue to protect me as I ride to raise another army. For those afoot, join Ernan your king, for there glory lies." Glancing over her shoulder she saw that the Romans were barely four hundred paces away. "I will see you in the afterlife." With that she kicked her horse on and rode away with her six remaining body guards in close company.

The last of her entourage, all forty of them, turned as a body and hurled themselves at the First Cohort now less than two hundred paces away. The acting First Spear took in the reckless charge and shook his head sadly, at the waste of brave warriors. "Halt!" With remarkable precision the whole line halted. The Irish were less than forty yards away. "First two centuries, javelins… now." The two hundred javelins plunged into the forty bodies and the Roman line carried forward over the bodies of the young men whose lives had just been discarded so carelessly.

The battle was not over but as the two cohorts plunged into unprotected backs it rapidly disintegrated as a contest. The first to flee were the recently joined Brigantes who threw away their improvised weapons and ran. The Irish and the deserters fought back to back and to the death. The prefect who had taken a sword thrust to the arm was in no mood for leniency and ordered the legion to finish them with javelins to minimise Roman losses. Ernan roared his defiance and charged the First Cohort with the last of his oath brothers. It took six javelins in each man to kill the warrior but eventually the only ones left were the Romans and the rest were dead and dying.

Cassius found the dying Mocius. "Was it worth it Mocius?"

"I died with a sword in my hand but I am glad that survived I owe my..." with that he died and Cassius wondered what he had done to merit such thanks.

First Spear had also survived but only just, around him lay the dead bodies of many of Ernan's warriors as well as the aquifer and five other legionaries. He would live but it would take a miracle for him to serve again. For the moment the acting First Spear was the Ninth's new senior officer.

Livius and Cassius found as many of their Explorates as they could. When he found Rufius he embraced him. "Thank you for the arrows Rufius but how you and Ovidius managed to shoot three arrows so quickly is beyond me."

Rufius shook his head sadly and pointed to the body covered by a red cloak. "Ovidius was killed in the first attack. It is these two to whom you owe thanks. Marcus Gaius and Macro stood nervously behind Rufius.

"We know you told us to stay near to the prefect but when you rode to stem the flank attack we had to follow. We are sorry sir."

"No Marcus Gaius, you have no need to apologise for the Allfather directed your course and I am in your debt. When we return to the farm we will talk with your parents of the future."

"Sir, the prefect wishes to speak with you."

Livius followed the legionary to the Prefect who was being fussed over by a capsarius. "Well at least I can look First Spear in the eye the next time that we discuss war, when he recovers of course. You have done well decurion but I have another task, well

277

two actually. I have received a report, unconfirmed that Eboracum has fallen to the enemy and I know that Morwenna has fled south. I need you to confirm the first and follow the Queen."

Livius looked over at his men. "I only have five men who are fit to ride sir but I will go. We will ride close to Eboracum first and ascertain the problem then I will follow Morwenna but I fear that she has got a good two hours start on us. Even if we find her then we cannot follow for long, our horses would not last."

"I know decurion. I just need to know the direction she takes. You do not need to catch her. I will send the Gallic cavalry after her. They will be at Eboracum tomorrow."

"But what if Eboracum is taken?"

"I do not think there will be many of her troops left there even if they did take it. We will follow as soon as we have cleared the field. I just need to know from you if I need to go in armed or if I can walk, or rather crawl in."

Smiling at the older man's bluff humour Livius saluted and went back to Rufius, Metellus and Cassius. The other two were new Explorates he did not know yet. He would soon have to learn their names and the replacements for the dead troopers they had lost in this campaign. "Mount up boys our war is not over."

"Sir."

"Yes Macro?"

"Can we come?"

Marcus Gaius burst in, "If you left us here we would be alone and Rufius promised mother he would take us back safely."

Cassius and Rufius both hid smiles. "Oh mount up and the first thing I will ask your father is to give you both a good beating."

Grinning they both said, "Yes sir. Thank you sir."

Metellus leaned over, his face still pale from the sword thrust. "You will not be so eager after six months in the saddle."

278

Marius and Drusus were exhausted. It had taken far longer to round up their men than they had expected and they had run out of food the previous day. Marius had suggested that they go to the river to camp and catch fish. As he had said, "We have little water and our mounts are all out. Let us call it a scouting expedition."

Drusus could find no argument to that and he had assented. As they had fished by the river they found a peace that had been absent for so long. "I could do this all day you know Drusus. Just watch the river drift by and catch supper."

"It is pleasant."

Suddenly their pleasant mood was shattered by Fabius who came racing along. He spoke urgently and quietly. "Sir, just around the bend of the river, there are deserters and a wagon. Looks like they are waiting for something."

"Typical," moaned Drusus. "Just get comfortable and…"

"Stop moaning you old woman. Leave is over, we are back in the war."

Nuada and the men were becoming nervous. They had noticed bodies floating down the river. Admittedly they were towns' people but his men had begun to talk of failure. Suppose Decius had died? What if something had happened to the Queen? Perhaps they should run?

Nuada knew that if any of that had happened they were lost but he also knew that if they fled with the gold and Centurion was still alive then he would hunt and kill them. Nuada shuddered. He feared Centurion and Tiny above all men. "We wait. We are hidden. We watch for ships none has gone either upstream or downstream so the General is still there. We wait."

To the Explorates it was child's play to get close enough to observe the deserters and, leaving Fabius on watch, they withdrew to the road. "Well it is obvious isn't it? You and Curtius find the decurion and I will wait and watch."

279

"You take Marius and remember that fishing spot. We must be due some leave soon."

Decius was becoming impatient, not with the sailors, for he could see they were working as hard as they could terrified as they were of Tiny who stood glowering over them. Decius was annoyed with that which he could not change, the weather. The wind as all could see was in the wrong direction and the narrow river meant that they had to tack back and forth. It had taken most of the morning for them to reach the juncture with the smaller river, the Fosse.

"Curse this wind."

"Perhaps Morwenna knows you have deserted her and has summoned the Mother to aid her."

Decius flashed a sharp angry look at Centurion. The thought had cross his mind but you didn't say it out loud in case the words were carried on the air and the witch heard them. "She cannot know yet. Even if she is victorious it would take time to reach Eboracum and then search for me."

"We should have destroyed the other boats, and then no-one could have followed us."

Decius shrugged, "That is hindsight but it matters not. Even if they do follow us they have to endure the same capricious wind as we."

The mate shouted over, "Sir, er captain, er General!"

"What is it?"

"Ahead is the bend in the river."

"And…"

"The wind will begin to serve us we will move quickly."

"Excellent." He slapped Centurion on the back. "There I told you the witch did not know."

'Aye', thought Centurion but you thought she had invoked the Mother.

The young Irishman caught up with Morwenna and her entourage just a mile south of Eboracum. "Your majesty. Eboracum has been destroyed."

Morwenna's mind was filled with conflicting thoughts. Her plan had half succeeded but it had not done her any good. Perhaps if she had just invested Eboracum then her gamble might have paid off but then she remembered the ordered legionaries and the wild charges of the Brigante and Irish. No the only way she could have held Eboracum was with a deserter army and Decius. "Where is the General then? Is he following?"

The druids looked up at the Queen. She would normally have seen where he was but where Decius Lucullus Sallustius was concerned her second sight was blinded by lust. The messenger looked a little shamefaced. "I found one of his men who said he had seen the General, Centurion and Tiny take a ship and head downstream."

The Queen kept her emotions under control but she now knew that the gold wagon, which had disappeared, was headed for a meeting with Decius. She actually became sad when she realised that he valued the gold more than her. She cared nothing for the gold; it had been a means to an end but for her ex-lover it was everything. She shrugged off the memory and thought of him. She would return to Manavia and her children. There she and her priests would begin again. Her revolt was not over. It would be a long journey home for they would have to endure the winter in the mountains but the Romans would be too busy repairing forts and rounding up the deserters.

"We head south and thence to Manavia. Let us ride." She urged her horse on and the band galloped down the road.

The Explorates heard the thunder of the hooves on the cobbled road and reacted swiftly, hiding in the woods off to the side. They saw the white horse of Morwenna sweep by and the bodyguards and priests surrounding her. When she had passed by they waited in case the rest of her army followed.

"Here is a dilemma. Do we follow or what?"

"It doesn't alter what we do Drusus. We still have to tell Livius about the deserters and we can now tell him about the Queen."

"Perhaps she was joining the deserters?"

"No I think that she would have been riding towards the river to join them." Marius led the patrol back to the road and watched as the crowd that was the Queen headed south. "The road is without a turning for many miles. We are not far from Livius. We can still catch them."

They headed up the road as fast as their weary horses would allow. Livius and his Explorates were heading south and they met just a mile from the place they had seen the Queen. "Are we glad to see you Livius. We have seen the Queen heading south on the road to Lindum." Marius looked apologetically at his decurion. "We didn't follow for…"

Livius held his hand up. "You have done as I would have done. The Prefect just wished to know where she had gone so that he could send the Gallic ala after her. You have done well."

He began to turn his mount around when Marius said, "There is more sir. There are some deserters with a wagon waiting at a bend in the river. We thought they were waiting for the Queen but she carried on, it can't be her."

"Decius!"

"You may be right Cassius. Drusus, you carry on to Eboracum and tell the Prefect where Morwenna has gone. Drusus, lead us to these deserters." Drusus nodded and dragged his weary horse to head north. Marius led the patrol through the scrubby undergrowth which fringed the road.

"Sir! I can see a ship coming downstream!"

282

"Arm yourselves. It may not be the general. Let us wait and see." Nuada's men lined the bank hidden by the overhanging willows and bushes.

"I can see Tiny. It is them sir."

Nuada too could see the huge figure of Tiny standing like an extra mast at the front of the ship. "Over here! General! Over here!"

Decius was elated and slapped Centurion on the shoulders. His mind had been working overtime, worrying that Nuada might have stolen his gold or that they might have been attacked and robbed themselves. Now their dream was almost realised. "We are almost there centurion!"

"I can almost smell the palm trees of Africa!"

"Helmsman, take us to the bank as close as you can."

"We'll have to put down an anchor and tie up to those trees if you want to go ashore sir. The current will take us downstream otherwise."

Irritated Decius snapped, "Just do it!" He shouted to Nuada, "Get the gold ready, form a chain of your men to the boat and mine will stack it aboard."

The mate came up his face wracked with fear and worry. "Are you bringing cargo aboard?"

"What is it to you?" Centurion's face filled the sky above the petrified mate's.

"Sir if it is a small light cargo then there is no problem but if it is large or heavy then we will have to place it correctly in the hold or the boat will capsize."

The terror in his voice told them both that he was speaking the truth. "It is gold and a lot of it."

"We need to place it as low in the hold as we can and spread it out."

"Spread it out?"

"Yes sir, one layer across the whole of the hold floor and then another," he paused, "sir we are but a small boat if there is too much gold we…"

"We will take all the gold. Even if we have to abandon the crew!"

Centurion knew that Decius' words were just a threat for they needed the crew more than their men. "General he may be right. There is no point taking too much and then sinking."

Decius could see that they were both right. "We take as much as we can. You, "he jerked a finger at the mate, "go ashore and tell us when we are getting too low."

The little man scampered ashore pleased to be away from the threatening glares of these angry soldiers.

Livius held up his hand when he heard the noise from the river. He signalled for them to dismount. Each trooper tied his horse securely to a branch; if there was noise and the horses ran they did not want to be afoot. Macro and Marcus Gaius emulated the Explorates. Livius signalled for them to spread out. Those who had bows held them ready with arrows notched. With Rufius leading they slipped through the undergrowth, the sky quickly getting lighter as they approached the wide river. They all saw the masts of the ship peering above the trees and all of them wondered what they would see when they reached the river,

Rufius held his hand up for them to halt and then he slithered away. When he returned he held both his hands up palms out twice. Every trooper knew that meant twenty deserters. Livius pointed at the men with bows and assigned them a spot. He suddenly realised that he still had Macro and Marcus Gaius with him but he could do nought about that. The ones without bows were assigned to guard the archers.

The Explorates bellied through the undergrowth until they could see the sweating line of deserters passing boxes, from one to the other and loading the ship. They were well within arrow range and, as his men all looked at him, Livius slashed down the Sword of Cartimandua, its swish making one of the line suddenly look around, startled. It was too late a warning as the arrows flew. The first ten men fell to the ground dead or dying.

The mate saw his opportunity and ran away from the river and away from the men with the bows; he assumed they were Roman but he was taking no chances. He would run away and return to the safety of another ship. He would soon get another berth out of the hell hole that was Eboracum.

Decius and Centurion watched in horror as their men died. They searched the shore for a sight of their unseen assailants. "Who is it?"

"Romans?"

"It doesn't matter. They are killing us minute by minute." Nuada scrambled across the plank onto the ship. "Did you see them Nuada?"

"I saw nothing but they are Roman arrows."

Centurion yelled to Tiny. "Get an axe and sever the lines."

"No! The gold!"

"We have plenty aboard already. Let's cut our losses and run. We cannot spend gold if we are dead," Tiny looked from one to the other uncertain what to do. There was no one alive left ashore and the few who remained on the ship were cowering below the strakes.

"But there is more than half still left on the shore."

"And more than half our men dead. We go!" He leapt to his feet and hacked the rope holding the ship to the tree.

Rufius saw his chance and an arrow struck the huge man in the top of his arm. Tiny sliced down with an axe and they were just left with one rope at the stern.

Decius could now see the wisdom of Centurion's words. Better to escape with a little than risk all with an unknown enemy. The wound to his lieutenant had unnerved him and as he ran to sever the stern rope he yelled, "Hoist the sails!"

Livius suddenly rose up from the undergrowth barely twenty paces from his brother. "Decius you traitor!"

His brother laughed as he sliced through the rope and the ship lurched forward, propelled by the river's current. "I wondered if my goody, goody little brother was on the other side. It is a shame we never fought," he noticed for the first time the magnificent blade held by Livius, "I could have killed you and taken that pretty little blade from you. It needs to be wielded by a real man."

"I will hunt you down brother and I will kill you."

"First you have to find me." Livius' men suddenly came out of the trance they appeared to be in, mesmerized by the dialogue between the brothers. Their arrows flew at Tiny and Decius; one struck Tiny but Decius appeared to bear a charmed life and the arrows clattered harmlessly into the deck. Decius spread his arms wide, "It seems the Allfather cares for me more than you brother. Think on that."

The sails suddenly unfurled and the boat leapt like a stag as the wind and the current took it towards the sea and freedom.

Epilogue

The Decurion Princeps of the Gallic ala rode wearily up to the Praetorium in Eboracum. The warm braziers could begin to thaw his bones which ached from the two week chase of the rebel Queen Morwenna. The news would not please the Prefect but then she had had such a start on them that it would have taken a winged Pegasus to overtake them. The Prefect looked better than the last time he had seen him and his wounds were healing well.

"She escaped sir. We reached the coast as she set sail with her men. They left their horses but the warriors, priests and the Queen escaped."

"Did you have any trouble finding her?"

The decurion shook his head. "We followed the corpses of the wounded and the old who were discarded as they fled and the mounts they rode into the ground," he did not add that his men had found destroyed animals the most upsetting sight they had witnessed.

"Well we know where she is going. Some of the prisoners we took told us of an island, Manavia. She has a base there."

"A job for the Classis Britannica then?"

"No. She can fester there. The warrior elite have been destroyed and now that we know of the threat of deserters the Governor has ordered a sweep of the places they inhabit to round them up. No decurion our eyes are now on the north. The Emperor has decided that we need to bolster the north. The Ninth is going to regain the land we lost and you and your ala will be helping me."

The *Dubris* pulled into the small port south of the Liger. After the crew had anchored the ship just off the beach they had their throats cut and were thrown overboard to be swept out to sea. As Decius went ashore to hire a new crew, who would know nothing of the predecessors he reflected that they probably had enough gold to start a new life but Africa might be just too far with only

287

ten of them left. He would have to start again. Centurion was healing but Decius knew that he needed his lieutenant fully fit if he was to create the kingdom which was his dream. As he waded ashore with Tiny watching his back he couldn't get the image of his brother out of his mind. It would be just like the patriot to follow Decius and fulfil his promise. Well he would make the job more difficult. He had hidden before and he would hide again.

It was the time of the burning of the bones at the farm close to Morbium and Livius, Rufius and Cassius had been invited to join the feast. Marius and Drusus had been tasked with raising and training more Explorates in anticipation of the spring campaign in the north. Ailis had accepted, after the stories she had heard from Rufius and Livius of the bravery of her boys, that they would be following in their fathers' footsteps and joining the army. She was mollified by the fact that both Livius and Rufius looked to be as fond of the boys as Gaelwyn was and she knew that they would be cared for. It did not stop her worrying about them but she realised that worrying was a mother's lot.

Gaius could not have been prouder as he heard of his boy's exploits and even Decius Gaius looked a little envious as they recounted the battles in which they had participated. "It is good to know that Marcus' Horse is not forgotten and the standard and sword rode again."

"It was not just that Gaius. The Brigante all knew, feared and respected the name. Marcus Maximunius would have been proud." He looked around. "Where is he? I thought he would have been here."

Gaelwyn shook his head sadly. "He is not a well man and I fear the Allfather is calling him. I would see him sooner rather than later if you wish to tell of the battle for he will not survive Yule."

Livius looked at the fire, its flames flickering and dancing, mesmerizing him and making him remember the deeds of Marcus' Horse and the warriors he had fought alongside, Decius, Macro, all gone. The others were equally lost in thought. Suddenly Livius looked over at Gaius, "That will make you the last of the Pannonians who rode with Ulpius, saved the Queen and held the sword."

Gaius' grey head nodded and looked at Ailis who held his hand gently. "Aye. We have passed on the standard and now new warriors will emulate our deeds." He ruffled his son's head. "You boys have high standards but from what I have been told you will gain as much honour as any."

Both boys stood proudly at attention. "That we swear, on the Sword of Cartimandua."

The End

Historical Note and Glossary of people and places in the novel

The Isle of Man was indeed invested in about 60AD by the druids and priests escaping the Roman Holocaust on Mona. As there was a whole culture and infrastructure on Mona one can only assume that this continued on the Isle of Man. This culture may well have lasted into and beyond the Irish and Viking invasions of the ninth and tenth centuries. Those new cultures would, in all likelihood have blended into the Druidic culture which prevailed. The Druids were an Iron Age culture and left little in the way of archaeology. The Romans liked to build in stone, the Iron Age in wood.

The Exploratores were very much as described although in reality they operated individually or in pairs rather than the sections I describe. As they only came to the fore at the start of the second century I have assumed that there would be a transition from the cavalry they were to the spies they became. As Marcus' Horse is a fictitious ala I felt happy to disband it and use the survivors to begin the Exploratores. There were Gallic alae, Batavian and Tungrian cohorts in Britannia throughout the period but as evidence for locations and officers is vague I have used them generically.

Eboracum did suffer burning and raids by Brigante right up to the building of Hadrian's Wall in about 120 A.D. The Ninth Legion is last heard of in Britannia in about 108 A.D., roughly when this novel is set and they were at Eboracum. The legion then disappears from history. The rumours vary from slaughter in Scotland or Dacia to disbanding for some misdeeds.

I have used the place names from the Ordnance Survey map. The fort at Ambleside is called Glanibanta although I know that locally it is called Galava. I have done this for consistency- if I am wrong at least I am consistently wrong.

Griff Hosker March 2014

Glossary of places and people
Fictional characters are in *italics*

Ailis-Gaius' wife
Alavna-Ardoch in Perthshire
Anchorat-Morwenna's acolyte
Aodh-Caledonii warrior and Morwenna's lover
Aula Luculla-Wife of the ex-governor
bairns-children
Belisama Fluvius-River Ribble
Blatobulgium-Birrens north of Carlisle
Bodotria-River Firth
breeks-Brigante trousers
Bremmetenacum-Ribchester
capsarius-medical orderly
CenturionDecius Sallustius -henchman
Centurion Cursus-First Spear Batavians
Centurion Lartius-First Spear Ninth Legion
Clota-River Clyde
Colla -Brigante chief
Coriosopitum-Corbridge
Danum-Doncaster
Decius Lucullus Sallustius-Sallustius' nephew
Derventio-Malton
Deva-Chester
Dunum Fluvius-River Tees
Eboracum-York
Ernan-Irish leader of Morwenna's mercenaries
First Spear-The senior centurion in any unit
Gaelwyn-Ex Brigante scout and uncle to Ailis
Gaius Metellus Aurelius-Ex-Decurion Marcus' Horse
Glanibanta-Ambleside
Itunocelum-Ravenglass

292

Julius Demetrius-Decurion Marcus' Horse
Livius Lucullus Sallustius-Sallustius' nephew
Luentinum-Pumsaint gold mine in west Wales
Luguvalium -Carlisle
Luigsech-Morwenna's nurse
Lulach-King of the Caledonii
Maban-Morwenna's acolyte
Macro-Former Decurion Marcus' Horse
Mamucium -Manchester
Manavia-Isle of Man
Marcus Aurelius Maximunius-Former ala Commander
Maw- a gaping hole
Mediobogdum-Hard Knott Fort
Mona-Anglesey
Morbium-Piercebridge
Morwenna-Fainch's daughter
Trajan-Emperor of Rome
Ownie-Brigante chief
Parcae-Roman Fates
Parthalan-Brigante Chief
phalerae-Roman award for bravery
Porta Decumana-The rear gate of a fort or camp
Prefect Fulvius-Prefect Ninth Legion
Rufius-Explorate
Sergeant Cato-Horse trainer Marcus' Horse
Seteia Fluvius-River Mersey
Tadgh-General of Brigante rebels
Taus-River Solway
Tava-River Tay
Tiny-Decius Sallustius' bodyguard
Titus Didius Blaesus-Tribune of the Ninth
Tribune Didius-Tribune Ninth Legion

293

uncia-Roman inch
Vedra-River Wear
vicus (plural-vici)-the settlement outside a fort

Northern Britannia

Other books
by
Griff Hosker

If you enjoyed reading this book, then why not read another one by the author?
For more information on all of the books then please visit the author's web site www.griffhosker.com where there is a link to contact him.

Ancient History
The Sword of Cartimandua Series
(Germania and Britannia 50A.D. – 130 A.D.)
Ulpius Felix- Roman Warrior (prequel)
Book 1 The Sword of Cartimandua
Book 2 The Horse Warriors
Book 3 Invasion Caledonia
Book 4 Roman Retreat
Book 5 Revolt of the Red Witch
Book 6 Druid's Gold
Book 7 Trajan's Hunters
Book 8 The Last Frontier
Book 9 Hero of Rome
Book 10 Roman Hawk
Book 11 Roman Treachery
Book 12 Roman Wall
Book 13 Roman Courage

The Aelfraed Series
(Britain and Byzantium 1050 - 1085 A.D.)
Book 1 Housecarl
Book 2 Outlaw

Book 3 Varangian

The Wolf Warrior series
(Britain in the late 6th Century)
Book 1 Saxon Dawn
Book 2 Saxon Revenge
Book 3 Saxon England
Book 4 Saxon Blood
Book 5 Saxon Slayer
Book 6 Saxon Slaughter
Book 7 Saxon Bane
Book 8 Saxon Fall: Rise of the Warlord
Book 9 Saxon Throne
Book 10 Saxon Sword

The Dragon Heart Series
Book 1 Viking Slave
Book 2 Viking Warrior
Book 3 Viking Jarl
Book 4 Viking Kingdom
Book 5 Viking Wolf
Book 6 Viking War
Book 7 Viking Sword
Book 8 Viking Wrath
Book 9 Viking Raid
Book 10 Viking Legend
Book 11 Viking Vengeance
Book 12 Viking Dragon
Book 13 Viking Treasure
Book 14 Viking Enemy
Book 15 Viking Witch
Bool 16 Viking Blood
Book 17 Viking Weregeld
Book 18 Viking Storm

Book 19 Viking Warband
Book 20 Viking Shadow
Book 21 Viking Legacy

New World Series
870-1050
Blood on the Blade

The Norman Genesis Series
Hrolf the Viking
Horseman
The Battle for a Home
Revenge of the Franks
The Land of the Northmen
Ragnvald Hrolfsson
Brothers in Blood
Lord of Rouen
Drekar in the Seine
Duke of Normandy

The Anarchy Series England
1120-1180
English Knight
Knight of the Empress
Northern Knight
Baron of the North
Earl
King Henry's Champion
The King is Dead
Warlord of the North
Enemy at the Gate
Fallen Crown
Warlord's War

Modern History
The Napoleonic Horseman Series
Book 1 Chasseur a Cheval
Book 2 Napoleon's Guard
Book 3 British Light Dragoon
Book 4 Soldier Spy
Book 5 1808: The Road to Corunna
Waterloo

The Lucky Jack American Civil War series
Rebel Raiders
Confederate Rangers
The Road to Gettysburg

The British Ace Series
1914
1915 Fokker Scourge
1916 Angels over the Somme
1917 Eagles Fall
1918 We will remember them
From Arctic Snow to Desert Sand
Wings over Persia

Combined Operations series
1940-1945
Commando
Raider
Behind Enemy Lines
Dieppe
Toehold in Europe
Sword Beach
Breakout
The Battle for Antwerp

300

King Tiger
Beyond the Rhine
Korea

Other Books
Carnage at Cannes (a thriller)
Great Granny's Ghost (Aimed at 9-14-year-old young people)
Adventure at 63-Backpacking to Istanbul

Printed in Great Britain
by Amazon